ALREADY GUILTY

A C.T. FERGUSON PRIVATE INVESTIGATOR MYSTERY (#4)

TOM FOWLER

Editing by Chase Nottingham.

Cover design by 100 Covers

 Created with Vellum

For Lisa and Isabel.

CHAPTER 1

Whoever blushes is already guilty; true innocence is ashamed of nothing.

—Jean-Jacques Rousseau

You can't go out in Federal Hill on most nights without tripping over a gaggle of hipsters at every turn. Any time after dark whatever the occasion, they're unavoidable. Baltimore doesn't seem like a city that would have a hipster population issue, but there's evidence of it in every "upscale" corner bar, restaurant, or pub. It's doubly hard to avoid the goateed brigade if you're celebrating something in the middle of March.

Such was my fate this night.

My cousin Rich had just turned thirty-six. In accordance with our tradition—all two consecutive years of it, but tradition must begin somewhere—I took him out for dinner and drinks. Rich brought his girlfriend of two months, Jeanne Corsetti. I brought Gloria Reading, whom I'd known for almost a year and a half and who was the closest thing to a girlfriend I'd had in a while. We'd spent more and more time together without making anything official. One of these evenings, we'd have to sit down and have a real conversation. Only not tonight.

Rich, for his part, dressed even worse than the hipsters. Some people overdo it on St. Patrick's Day. My cousin is one of them. He could boast twelve and a half percent of his corpuscles laid claim to Irish ancestry and dressed like a leprechaun desperate for a part in a Lucky Charms commercial. I stifled a snicker every time I looked at him. He wore a green sportcoat over a white shirt, a green bowtie, green corduroy slacks, green socks, and green tennis shoes. Everything managed to be the same shade or very close to it. The outfit should have been repellent to anyone whose taste extended beyond their mouths. Jeanne looked at Rich's getup often and smiled. I did, too, though I suspected not for the same reason.

"You're dressed conservatively," Rich said over the crowd. We occupied a table toward the back of the pub, but the throng at the bar created a din permeating the whole place.

"Compared to you, the Dropkick Murphys' fan club is dressed conservatively," I said.

Gloria squeezed my forearm. I think she laughed, but Jeanne's louder peel drowned it out. "I think he looks damn good," she said, grabbing Rich's face and planting a kiss on him.

Not to be outdone, Gloria did the same to me. If this were going to be a competition, I liked our chances. I hoped a lascivious wink captured my sentiment.

Our waiter dropped off our second round of beers and a gigantic basket of onion rings. Rich and Jeanne ordered emerald-dyed brews. Gloria opted for a Killian's Red, and I ordered the only acceptable Irish beer: Guinness. Why was everyone else at the table a Philistine? Rich took a lime-colored swig and speared a crusted ring with his fork. I eyed the appetizer but decided to let everything cool. Lunching frequently with my food-loving friend Joey Trovato has taught me to pick my spots where first courses are concerned.

"What do you do?" Gloria asked Jeanne. I realized then I'd never mentioned it, and it didn't come up on the ride over.

"I'm a cop," she said.

"A detective?"

"Not yet." She looked at Rich and smiled. "I wear a uniform. One of these days I'll take the detectives' exam. By then, he might be a lieutenant," she said, jerking her head toward Rich.

"What do you mean, might be?" he said.

Jeanne punched him playfully in the shoulder. "Not everyone can be on the fast track like you." She turned to Gloria. "What do you do?"

"I . . . uh . . . play tennis," Gloria said.

"Professionally?"

"No, just local tournaments."

"Oh." She frowned. "What else do you do?"

"In fairness, Gloria's playing well in those tournaments," I said. "And she looks damn good in a tennis outfit."

Gloria smiled and blushed. I saw something in her eyes when she looked at me, like she was grateful for me coming to her defense. She squeezed my hand, then turned back to Jeanne. "I don't work full-time," she said. "I just . . . pursue things I enjoy."

I thought Jeanne had a follow-up remark ready to go, but Rich cleared his throat, and she didn't say anything. I capitalized on this lull in the conversation to snag an onion ring.

"You're a private detective, right?" Jeanne said to me.

I nodded around my bite of food, then answered her once I swallowed it. "We prefer to be called private investigators, but yes."

"Rich told me you don't have a law enforcement background."

"He flatters me," I said.

For the second time, Jeanne started to say something and stopped. The waiter rescued her by coming to take our order. Rich and Jeanne both requested corned beef and cabbage. I resisted the urge to vomit in my mouth. Despite being twice as Irish as Rich, I detested corned beef in general, and considered the pairing of it with boiled cabbage to be a violation of the Geneva Convention. Gloria ordered a salmon dish. I honored my Irish ancestors by getting bangers and mash.

"Rich tells me you work together pretty often," Jeanne said once the waiter fought through the hipster mob to make it back to the safety of the kitchen.

"He needs me to set him straight," Rich said. He tried to suppress a smile and failed. Good thing.

"Actually, Rich needs me to win his awards and commendations," I said. "If he does make lieutenant in a few years, part of it will be me carrying him there."

Rich rolled his eyes and quelled his response with a long pull of green beer. "C.T. thinks solving cases is something done as a hobby with as little time in the field as possible."

"So far, I've been right," I pointed out.

Jeanne looked between us, then at Gloria. "Are they always like this?"

"Only when they talk shop," Gloria said. "Or sports. Or anything where they might be able to compete."

"We've been doing it most of our lives," I said.

"And I've won most of them," said Rich.

"Being almost seven years older matters a lot when you're younger," I said.

"Yeah, yeah." Rich smiled. A drop of shamrock spittle ran off his lip and down his chin. "That sounds like an excuse."

"All right, let's run a race tomorrow morning. Four miles around Federal Hill Park. I'll even run backwards the first lap."

"And here they go again," Gloria said.

"Rich knows I'll beat him," I said.

"Ah, the smell of testosterone." Jeanne took in a deep breath. If it were in the air, she couldn't smell it past the food, booze, and sweat.

"Must come in the green beer."

The waiter scuttled any further witty repartee by returning with our meals. We asked for a few condiments and another round of brews, which he returned with a minute later. Rich and Jeanne practically drooled over the bilge set on their plates. Gloria's fish smelled wonderful, a product of the fruity salsa atop it. My bangers and mash looked like typical Irish sausages and potatoes. They probably tasted typical, too, but the fact my plate held no corned beef and cabbage allowed me to overlook the lack of excellence.

After all, the cook was probably a hipster, too.

* * *

We were well into our fourth drinks. I hired an Uber for the evening so none of us drove anywhere. Jeanne looked at Rich, then at me. "So you've been a detective about a year and a half now, right?" she said to him.

Rich needed to think about it. One of his beers was an Irish Car Bomb, and it had to be fogging him over. "Sixteen months," he said with only minor slurring of his words.

Jeanne regarded me again. "And you've been in business about the same amount of time?"

I nodded. "Almost to the day."

"Interesting," she said and downed the rest of her beer in one gulp.

"What's interesting about it?" said Rich.

"How closely your careers overlap."

"And how closely my cases overlap with Rich's commendations and handshakes from the brass," I added.

"You always have to throw in your contribution," Rich said.

"If I didn't, who would? *You're* not going to mention it."

"Because it isn't true!"

I gave a bemused shrug and turned to Jeanne. Her brown eyes were a shade or two lighter than Rich's but much softer. "What your boyfriend fails to grasp is I handed him quite a few arrests," I said. "Arrests he wouldn't have been able to make if I hadn't been working a case."

"We would've caught them eventually." Rich added a syllable or two to the last word.

"But you caught them when you did because I did the heavy lifting."

"Help me out here, Gloria," Rich said. "Do something with him."

"I plan to," Gloria said, "but it'll be later, when we're alone."

"Until then, I am incorrigible," I said.

"You pretty much are all the time," Rich said.

The waiter dropped off our check. I reviewed it, handed him my card, and he walked away. "Who's up for dessert after this?".

"Dessert after beer?" said Gloria.

"It's a holiday. Why not?"

"We're in," Jeanne said.

"Good. There's a really good bakery about a block from here."

Rich looked at his watch. "Open at nine o'clock?"

"I know the owner. She'll let us in."

"Will there be cake?" Jeanne said.

"The best you've eaten in a long time."

"We're definitely in," she said.

* * *

We walked a block down to Cake and Able. Like many businesses in Federal Hill, it was small. The window decorated with pictures of cakes and various confections was dark as we approached. A sign on the door listed the shop hours and mentioned a special event tonight. I knocked. Lights in the front half of the shop flickered on. Francine Simmons, the owner, emerged from the kitchen. Her apron and jeans were splattered with flour. She smiled at us as she opened the door.

The display cases still held some less perishable items. Most of them were empty, though, to be restocked with fresh cookies and pastries the next morning. A book filled with pictures of various cakes lay on the counter. The bakery and counter consumed most of the square footage; four tables, each with as many chairs around it, made up the whole of the seating.

A few minutes later, Francine brought out the cake. There was barely enough room for plates, cups, forks, and elbows. Francine displayed her creation, beaming as we oohed and ahhed at its subtle green icing. She set it on a table behind us, then fetched a cake cutter, a candle, and a lighter. I took care of lighting the candle. We serenaded Rich with a semi-sober version of "Happy Birthday." No one slurred their words too badly. At the end, Rich closed his eyes for a few seconds and blew out the candle.

Francine cut the cake into pieces meant for defensive linemen and set them before us. "Red velvet?" Rich said with a smile.

"Like I don't know your favorite," I said.

"I'm impressed. You really do pay attention."

"Must be all that time as a PI," Jeanne said.

"My observational skills are first-rate," I said.

Rich took a large bite. The icing smeared on his lips as he shoved the cake into his mouth. I couldn't watch him eat it at that point; too many lunches with Joey flashed before my eyes. "Holy shit, this is good," Rich said a few seconds later. He dove in and scooped up another bite with his fork.

"Did you really know his favorite cake?" Gloria whispered to me.

"Of course not," I said. "I asked my mother. She knows these things about everyone."

Gloria looked at me and smiled. We enjoyed our dessert in silence. Francine checked on us, blushed when we complimented her baking skills, then disappeared into her kitchen. We'd mostly finished our cake when Rich's phone rang. He looked at the number, frowned, and got down off the chair to take the call. Jeanne knitted her brow, too, but didn't go after him. I couldn't hear any of the conversation, although Rich hung his head at one point. When the call ended, he shoved his phone back into his pocket hard enough to rip it free from his jeans. "I have to go," he said.

"What's going on?" Jeanne and I said simultaneously.

"We've lost one of our own," Rich said to Jeanne.

"Oh, no." She closed her eyes and shook her head. "Who was it?"

"Ben Harrison."

"I didn't know him."

"I did." Rich looked at me. "Is the car nearby?"

"I'll check." Rich and Jeanne engaged in quiet conversation as I checked with the driver. "A couple blocks away. He said he's hurrying."

"He'd better." Rich looked at Jeanne. "You go home. I'm going to my house, getting my weapon, and going after the son of a bitch who killed Harrison."

"Do they know who it is?"

"A guy was seen running away. Uniforms are pretty sure they know where he is."

"I want to go with you."

"No." Rich shook his head. "I'm only going because I know . . . knew Ben. I want to get the prick who did this."

"I'm sure you will," I said.

"This driver will take me home?"

"And wherever you need to go from there."

"I can get to the scene myself," said Rich.

"You've had too much to drink," I said. "Use the Uber. Gloria and I can walk back. I'll get another car for Jeanne."

"I can drive my—"

"Not up for discussion," I said. "I know you want to get this guy. Your chances are better if you don't drive. You can catch a ride home with someone later."

Rich stared at me for a few seconds, then nodded. "All right." He gave Jeanne a quick kiss. "I'll call you." Outside, a black sedan double-parked and honked.

"Go get him," I said.

"We will," said Rich.

* * *

Jeanne left in a Lyft she summoned herself; Gloria and I ended up going back to the pub and ordering another beer each. We attempted to walk to my house from there, but when it became obvious that straight lines eluded us, I summoned a different Uber. A few minutes later, a white Kia Optima pulled to the curb. Never in one until then, I liked the leather seats. They were hard to climb out of after the short drive.

After we went upstairs and to bed, Gloria lay with her head infringing on my pillow. A few locks of her chestnut hair splayed across my neck and chest. "Has Rich ever dealt with a cop killer before?" she said.

"Not to my knowledge," I said.

"He'd probably tell you something like that."

"Probably. Why?"

She frowned. "I've just never seen him so . . . focused before. I mean, he's normally focused on some level, but tonight was something else. He. . . ."

"Went from four drinks to sober in the span of a phone call?" I said.

"Exactly," Gloria said, a smile briefly crossing her lips. "He drank four beers, though. I hope he doesn't do something stupid."

"Like shoot someone who killed a cop?"

"Yes, like that." Gloria nodded, causing some of her hair to tickle my chin.

"I don't think Rich will fly off the handle."

"Are you sure?"

I took a few seconds to think about it. "Rich served in Afghanistan," I said. "He's been a cop for about seven years. He knows the rules. He understands due process. I'm sure he's pissed at what happened, but it won't compel him to shoot someone in cold blood."

"That's good," Gloria said.

"If they find the guy who did it, though, he's certainly going to get his ass kicked."

"It sounds like he should."

"I don't think we have much to worry about there."

Gloria threw an arm across me and snuggled her head against my chest. "Have you ever dealt with a cop killer before?"

"No," I said. "Even with the unrest and violence of the last couple years, not many police get killed in Baltimore."

"I imagine that would be a difficult case to work," said Gloria.

I said, "Here's hoping I never have to find out."

* * *

About an hour later, Gloria and I lay in bed, having thrown off the effects of the alcohol to entertain ourselves. My cell phone rang. I looked at the caller ID; it was Rich. "Hello?" I said.

"We got him," said Rich.

"I never harbored a doubt."

"Son of a bitch says he didn't do it, of course. He can keep saying it. We got him." I heard some raucous voices in the background.

"Are you at a police station?" I said.

"Central Booking," Rich said. More voices went up in the background. I didn't care for dealing with the popular madness of crowds at this hour.

"I'm glad you got him, Rich, but we were about to go to sleep."

"Sure," he said. "I'll talk to you tomorrow."

"Good night." I put my phone back on the nightstand.

"They got him?" Gloria said.

"They got him."

CHAPTER 2

The next day, Rich called midmorning and said he wanted to meet somewhere. I suggested Hull Street Blues, and he agreed. We settled on one o'clock to try and skirt any lunch rush the place might have on a Tuesday. I arrived promptly at one-oh-seven to find the crowds successfully beaten back. Rich sat at a table in the dining room. Only three others were occupied.

Hull Street Blues occupied a building as old as the rest of Federal Hill, which is to say very old. It shows its age in a few spots—the bathrooms in particular are shopworn—but overall looks none the worse for wear. Floors are hardwood and the dining room boasts vaulted wood ceilings with old beams still visible, plus ample pictures on the walls, most trumpeting Baltimore's nautical history. Rich sat under one such picture. The old sea captain in the painting wore a similarly inscrutable expression to my cousin as I joined him.

As he often did when I arrived, Rich made a point to look at his watch. "Not bad for you," he said.

"I'd complain about traffic but it's a short drive," I said.

"I wouldn't believe it anyway."

A cute waitress came up, smiled at both of us, took our drink orders, and sashayed back to the bar area. Rich canted his head to follow her departure all the way out the door. "I'm sure Jeanne would appreciate you keeping your powers of observation sharp," I said.

"She's a cop," Rich said, "so she'd understand."

The waitress returned a minute later. I ordered us a crab dip appetizer. Rich opted for a burger while I chose the portabella sandwich. The waitress made sure to smile at both of us again, but especially Rich before she walked away . This time, I took note of her hip movements as she vanished behind the wall. "Would Gloria appreciate you honing your observational skills?" Rich said with a wry smile on his face.

"You never know who might be carrying a concealed weapon," I said. "Besides, the waitress seems to like you better."

"A girl of fine taste," Rich said.

"Make sure to order some dessert, stud."

The crab dip arrived steaming and accompanied by a tray full of bread. Even in a city known for serving crustaceans, it's a very hit-and-miss dish. Some restaurants taint it by adding all manners of cheeses. Most use cream cheese and a few spices. So long as the crab-to-cream-cheese ratio is high, I offer no objections. Hull Street mixed in some vegetables with theirs. It disconcerted me the first time I ate it, but I've come to appreciate it. Rich frowned at a sliver of green pepper in the portion on his bread but ate it anyway.

"I can't believe you've waited so long to tell me about last night," I said after we'd each dunked a few chunks of bread in the dip.

Rich leaned back in his chair, wiped his mouth with his napkin, and let a smile spread over his face. "We found the bastard quickly," he said. "It wasn't hard."

"I'm glad you caught him," I said. "But why did you get a call if it was your night off . . . and your birthday, no less?"

Rich grabbed another piece of bread and soaked it in the still-steaming crab dip. He let it cool while he answered. "I knew the cop who got killed," he said. "He was my first training officer."

"Oh, I didn't know you were close. I'm sorry." Rich nodded as he ate his appetizer, then washed it down with a sip of beer. "How did it happen?" I went on.

"He ran after he did it," Rich said. "We were able to talk to some people nearby, follow his footprints when it was muddy, and get a bead on where he was going. It didn't take long to find him."

I noshed on some more dip while Rich talked. "How many people did you have?"

"About twenty. He wasn't getting away."

"Good," I said with a bob of my head.

"The son of a bitch said he didn't do it, of course. Get this— he admitted he was there when it happened, but he *obviously* had nothing to do with it." Rich shook his head and snorted.

I frowned. "What an odd admission."

"What do you mean?" said Rich.

"Why would he admit to being there but deny that he did it? A full denial makes more sense."

"Who knows . . . who cares? He's the guy."

"There is a chance that he's telling the truth, you know," I said.

Rich glared at me. "Don't start," he said through clenched teeth.

I gave Rich a few seconds to cool off by eating some crab dip. "Why not lie about being there?" I said.

"It doesn't matter," he said. "Everyone says they didn't do it."

"Statistically, some of them have to be telling the truth."

"You don't want to get involved in this one, C.T."

"I'm not trying to. I'm fine to stay far away from a cop killer case. I'm just . . . acknowledging the possibility the guy you like might be telling the truth."

"None of us thought so last night." Rich said.

I was going to point out the obviousness of the conclusion, but the waitress returned with our food. She refreshed our drinks, took care to double-check we didn't need anything else, and gave us another premium view of her backside going away. Rich and I both watched her again. Neither of us needed to comment on the ability of a pretty girl with a great ass to defuse the budding tension at the table.

We both focused on our food for a while. When we slowed, I picked up the conversation again. "I guess this guy is going to get arraigned pretty quickly?" I said.

Rich nodded. "Should be happening today," he said. "Cop killers move through the system quickly."

"As I would expect."

"The justice system takes care of its own."

I raised my glass of tea. Rich raised his new mug of beer. "To justice being done," I said.

"To the bastard frying for killing a cop," Rich said.

I extended my glass in a toast.

* * *

When I got home, I read the *Sun* article about the "alleged" cop killer's arrest. Jack Bennett sported a shiner to soon turn into a nice black eye, a couple of cuts on his face, and wild hair making him look like he'd been rolling on the carpet and touching doorknobs for an hour. His expression was one of someone not ready to be photographed and bewildered by the presence of a camera. I saw nothing hard or sinister in his eyes, only a lot of confusion.

I recently finished a case and didn't feel too eager to jump back into another one. It also took me a couple weeks to get over a concussion earned in a car accident. I got a couple of calls asking me to look into possibly cheating spouses and rejected them all. Those jobs are best left to the ambulance chasers of my profession. My first case dealt with an accusation of infidelity, turned into a lot more, and I vowed never to work such a matter again. Who sleeps with whom is really none of my business.

Gloria left for a tennis lesson and an evening with her parents. She mentioned I still needed to meet them. Her parents and mine moved in similar social circles, but she and I never met until I came back from Hong Kong and got arm-twisted into working as a detective. Since then, I'd not met her parents, and she hadn't met mine. Meeting the folks lent a status to what began as a relationship of fun. Perhaps Gloria was coming around on the idea of making it more official. I pondered it myself but didn't broach the subject.

After Gloria left, I went to the dojo for a training session. An hour and a half later, having gotten some good practice in and worked up a nice sweat, I drove home, showered, and began investigating dinner options. My ringing cell phone interrupted my ruminations. The number looked familiar but didn't have a name associated with it. "Hello?" I said.

"C.T.?" a female voice said in a cool, professional tone.

"Yes, who's this?"

"Liz Fleming from the Public Defender's Office. Remember me?"

"I do." Last year, Liz took on a case without any investigators to support her. I filled in ably as always, and the client was exonerated. I thought Liz and I possessed some good chemistry, but we hadn't seen each other since then. "What can I do for you?"

"I just caught a bastard of a case."

"This one doesn't involve an idiot blogger, does it?"

She chuckled. I liked the light sound of it. "No, thank goodness. Same as last time, though, we're understaffed on the investigative side. I want to be sure I can defend this one. Can you meet me at my office? Maybe we can talk about it."

"I'm sure the city would make allowances for its own Public Defender's Office being shorthanded."

"You've gotten more optimistic since we last spoke," she said.

"Not really," I said.

"Then will you help me? Or at least hear me out?"

What could it hurt? "Sure, I'll be there," I said. "Give me twenty minutes."

TWENTY-FOUR MINUTES LATER, I emerged from the staircase and walked down the hall toward Liz Fleming's office. I knocked on her door. "Come in," she said, "it's not locked."

I opened the door to find Liz's feet on the desk, showing off long, lean legs. Her skirt stopped a couple inches above her knee and had retreated farther up her thighs in her current posture. She wore a white blouse buttoned a little too high for my liking. Her dark brown hair was done up in a professional bun starting to frizz and fray after a day in the office. Liz smiled as I walked in. Her eyes scanned me as mine did her. "I was beginning to wonder when you'd show up," she said.

"I'm no more prompt than the last time we worked together," I said.

"I'll remember that if I ever need to subpoena you." Liz took her feet off the desk and leaned forward in her seat. "Thanks for coming. I'm hoping you can help me out with a case. Are you busy?"

"You know me," I said, "I don't like to keep my work calendar too crowded."

"Between cases?" she said.

"Yes."

"Terrific. I hope you'll change that status for me," she said with a smile.

"Maybe." I sat in one of her red fabric guest chairs. It felt not unlike sitting on a slab of concrete. Liz's desk looked like a haven for file folders and stray papers, doubtless a result of her caseload. A year passed, but nothing in the office changed. "Tell me about the case," I said.

"I caught a murderer," she said. "Things look pretty grim for this poor soul, though. The cops think his alibi is shaky, and I have to admit I agree."

I crossed my legs to try and achieve a modicum of comfort. It didn't help. "What else can you tell me?"

"He needs a competent defense and can't afford one," Liz said. "You and I might be his only hope."

"Should I change my name to Obi-Wan?" I said.

"Do I have to be Mara Jade?"

I raised eyebrows. "You've read some *Star Wars* books. I'm impressed."

"Had to read something besides dusty old tomes in law school," she said with a grin. "Is my college reading helping me secure your services?"

"It's certainly not hurting. You really haven't told me a lot, though, Liz. I don't have much to go on here."

She nodded. "I know. I don't know much more than you at the moment. Maybe we could talk to this man, get his story in his own words. Would that help you decide?"

"It would."

"Want to take a ride to Central Booking?" she said.

"You know just what to say to a guy," I said.

* * *

CENTRAL BOOKING, as usual, was a morass of humanity disguised as a police intake facility. People came and went, some on their own and others strongly encouraged by the officers guiding them toward their destinations. Liz approached a sergeant behind the large desk. I lingered a few feet back. The ambient—and unpleasant—noise prevented me from hearing much of what they said, but I saw him nod a couple times, then get up from his chair. Liz waved me along, and I fell in step behind her. "We're going to meet him in a room," she said.

"And here I expected to talk across a glass wall," I said.

"So did I."

The desk sergeant led us to a small, nondescript cubicle. A round table sat in the center with four chairs spaced haphazardly around it. The room had no other features or accoutrements. Liz sat in a chair facing the door, and I took a seat beside her on the left. Her skirt rode up her legs again. "Wait here," the officer said before disappearing.

"Why did you expect we'd be talking to this guy across a glass wall?" I said.

Liz shrugged. "He's an accused killer. They don't get treated the same way as accused tax evaders."

"With good reason."

"We're all equal under the law," Liz said without any trace of humor.

I laughed. "You need to take those jokes on the road."

Liz shook her head but didn't say anything else. Last year, she might have debated me. I wondered if the job beat the idealism out of her and replaced it with cynicism. I hoped not.

A moment later, the door opened. Two officers glowered as they walked into the room. I saw why a second later, as a third prodded Jack Bennett to walk through the door. I glared at Liz. She offered a wan smile and a shrug. "Seriously?" I said.

"If I told you who it was, would you have met me?" said Liz.

"No." I stood. "You should have known."

Liz put her arm on my wrist. "C.T., please. I . . . I know I wasn't fully up front with you, but I had to play this one a little close." She looked at Bennett. "This man is accused of killing a police officer. It's a red ball. I need all the help I can get. Please."

Bennett looked at me, then stared down again. The three officers glared at me. I didn't know any of them, nor they me, but I knew they didn't want me to help defend an accused cop killer with a shitty alibi.

I leaned down close to Liz's face. "I have to be able to work with the police, Liz," I said in a whisper. "It's important to my job. If I help you on this, I become a pariah. Hell, if there's something worse than pariah, they'd reserve it for me."

"I know what I'm asking," she said. Her eyes softened. "Please. Just hear him out. If you think he's full of it, you can leave."

I looked at Liz, then at Bennett. He still studied the floor. Someone in his position didn't make eye contact in self-defense. I'd posited for Rich their suspect might be telling the truth in his flimsy alibi. If I walked away now, everything I said to Rich would paint me as a hypocrite. Bennett may not have been the kind of person my parents envisioned me helping when they arm-twisted me into this career, but he was a man with little recourse beyond me. "Fine," I said, "I'll hear him out."

Liz smiled. "Thank you." She looked at the cordon of brothers in blue. "Can you give us a few minutes with him?"

"We're not leaving you alone with him," one of them said. "I'll stay in the room." The other two left and locked the door. The cop who remained leaned against the wall near the only exit. He glared at Bennett and didn't have more charitable glances for Liz or me. "You got five minutes."

"You can go, too," Liz said.

"I'm staying."

"You've heard of attorney-client privilege, right?"

The cop jabbed a finger in my direction. "He's no lawyer!"

"He works for me. You work for the system trying to put Mister Bennett away. You need to leave."

It took a minute of glowering and muttering, but he did. "Don't take too long," Officer Friendly said on his way out.

"Have a seat, Mr. Bennett," Liz said. Bennett ambled to the table and slumped into a chair like he was weary with the world.

I sympathized.

CHAPTER 3

Bennett's loose, floppy posture in the chair suggested he didn't have a spine. He fixated on the tabletop or his fingernails or his shoes or anything but Liz and me. Liz looked at me and sighed. I shrugged. "He's your client," I said.

Liz cleared her throat. "Mr. Bennett," she said.

"Jack," said Bennett. "Call me Jack. I never done nothing to be called mister."

"All right, Jack," Liz said. "Why don't you tell us what happened?"

"I knew Ben. Let me say it right away."

"You mean Ben Harrison, the deceased officer?"

"Yes," he said.

"How did you know him?" said Liz.

"He . . . he arrested me before."

"He arrested you once?"

"Twice."

"And now you go and hang out at his house?" I said.

"Sort of." Bennett fidgeted some more. "Ben liked to fix cars. His place has a garage, and he used it to work on people's cars. Always gave them a good deal. Ben couldn't take advantage of nobody."

"Did you help him?" said Liz.

"No, I'm not a good mechanic. I can change my oil and all, but not much else. Ben would take engines out and work on them . . . stuff that's way beyond me."

Liz said, "How often would you say that you were at his house?"

"I was at his garage," Bennett said. "I knew his family, but I rarely went inside their home."

"Why?"

"I don't know. They were always nice to me and all. I guess I just never wanted to impose."

"Why did you spend time with a man who arrested you twice?" I said. "I'm wondering why he would want you around."

"It's how he was," Bennett said.

"What'd you get arrested for?"

"Assault, both times. Look, Ben knew I wasn't a bad guy. He kept up with me after I got out after the second charge. He made sure I stayed on the straight and narrow . . . even put in a good word to get me a job."

The door opened. The cop who lingered a mere five minutes before entered again, looking at his watch. "Your time's almost up."

"We'll take as much time as we need," said Liz.

"Listen, Miss Fleming—"

"No, *you* listen. I know what this man is accused of, and I know how you feel about it. But he's entitled to a legal defense exactly like anyone else. I'll take as much time as I need to talk to him, and I'll have my boss call everyone you report to if you want to make an issue out of it."

The uniform looked at Liz for a moment before offering her a fake smile. "Take all the time as you need, Miss Fleming," he said.

"Thank you. Now, Jack, you say Ben Harrison helped you from time to time after your second assault conviction."

"He did," Bennett said. "I wouldn't have my job without him. Oh, man . . . what am I gonna do about my job? They'll fire me for sure."

"Right now, I think you have bigger things on your plate," I said. "You said Harrison would fix cars out of his garage. How many jobs did he have lined up?"

"It depends."

I rolled my eyes. "How many did he have lined up last night when you were there?"

"Oh. Let's see . . . when I got there, Ben and his wife both parked their cars on the street. He had two cars side-by-side in the garage and two more in the driveway."

"So four cars?" Liz said. Bennett offered a tentative nod. I hoped it was nerves and not a failure of preschool math. "What happened last night, Jack?"

"I was with Ben, just talking to him. We were shooting the shit about the Orioles and what they might do this year." Bennett shook his head. "Ben wasn't very optimistic."

"Then what?" said Liz.

"I guess I'd been there about an hour when this guy walks up," he said. "He has a hoodie on, so I can't see his face. Ben has the hood up on a car, so he doesn't see the guy. I'm standing off on the side of the garage. This guy just pulls out a gun and shoots. The first shot gets Ben to step out from behind the hood. Then he shoots him twice." Bennett closed his eyes and took a deep breath.

"He didn't see you?"

"I don't know. He never looks my way. I don't know how he didn't see me there. I was quiet when Ben gets shot . . . don't want to attract attention to myself."

"Then what?" Liz said.

"Then the guy tosses his gun down, gets in one of the cars in the driveway, and drives off in it."

"And what did you do?"

"Like I said, he never saw me. I pick up the gun and shoot at him when he speeds off."

"He drove off in a car?" I said.

"Yeah, a silver one."

"Why not just drive off in it?"

"He did."

I struggled not to roll my eyes again. "I mean, why go through all the trouble of shooting Ben Harrison when he could have simply driven away in the car?" I said.

"Oh. I don't know, man."

"This mystery shooter had the keys to the car?"

"Yeah," Bennett said. "He didn't pick any up in the garage, and he got away too quick to hot-wire it."

"Then I really have to wonder why he'd shoot a man—a cop, no less—over a car he could have just driven off in."

Jack Bennett—I was thinking of him as Jack now, dammit—shook his head. "I don't know. It all happened so fast."

Liz made some notes in her folio. She filled up most of a page. "After this man shot Harrison and drove off, what happened then?" she said.

"I got the hell out of there."

"You didn't wait to see if Harrison was OK?"

"He took two slugs in the center of his chest. No one's OK after two solid hits. I knew . . . I knew he was dead. I wanted to get out of there in case the crazy son of a bitch came back for me. I shot at his car, after all."

"So he left and you ran," said Liz.

"Yeah," Bennett said, "I ran for a while. Every time a silver sedan went by me, I got spooked. After a while, I got tired and decided to walk home from there. I took as many side streets as I could."

"Do you live alone?"

"Yeah, I do."

"Did you tell anyone what happened?" Liz said.

"Who was I gonna tell?" Bennett said.

"The police?"

"I didn't want to call them."

"Why not?" I said.

"Look at it. A cop gets shot in his garage. I'm there. I fired the gun. He busted me twice. What's everyone gonna assume?"

"You killed him," Liz said.

"Right."

"And you didn't?"

"No, I told you. It was the guy in the hoodie. He drove off."

"Did you get a license number off the car?" I said.

"Man, I was scared for my life," Bennett said. "I was worried the asshole was gonna come back with another gun and shoot me down like a dog."

"And you didn't get a good look at this man?"

"He had a hoodie on."

"I presume the lights were on in the garage, though," I said. "Most people don't do car repairs in the dark."

"Yeah, the lights were on," Bennett said.

"And you still didn't get a good look at him?"

"What do you want to know?"

"Was he short? Tall? White? Black? Hispanic? Martian?"

"Not too big, I don't think. I didn't see much of his face. I guess he was white . . . maybe Hispanic."

I looked at Liz and shook my head. She shrugged, flipped to a new page in her folio, and wrote a few more notes. Most women I've known have good penmanship. Liz may as well have been writing in Klingon for all the legibility her words possessed. I hoped she could read them. "Jack, you understand this is tough to believe," she said.

"I know," he said, "I know. But it's the truth." He looked at both of us in turn. "I swear it's the truth. I'd never do nothing to hurt Ben Harrison. He's been way too good to me over these past few years."

Liz looked back through her notes. I guess she could read them after all. "You're not giving us a lot to go on here, Jack," she said. I kept my objections to the term "us" to myself for now. "It's my job to defend you, and I'll do that job as best I can, but there isn't much here. Is there anything else you want to tell us, anything else you can remember that might be important?"

"I don't know," Jack said. He threw his head back and looked up at the ceiling. "I can't believe this happened. Ben is dead, and everyone thinks I did it." He wiped sweat from his face. "I'm sure we ain't got much of a case but promise me you won't plead me into doing time. I'm innocent. I want to see the whole thing through."

"Accused cop killers generally don't get plea deals," Liz said.

"You'll stick it out, though? Everyone thinks I did it. No one believes me. I need someone who does."

Liz looked at Jack for a few seconds before she nodded. "I promise," she said.

* * *

WE SCORED DRINKS from a nearby Starbucks right before they closed for the evening. I drank a vanilla latte, and Liz sipped a skinny caramel macchiato. She didn't need to skinny up the drink. One of these years, I would have to start watching my sugar intake. Until then, I planned to continue indulging the sweetness and the calories. One thinks about these things when one is turning thirty in a few months.

Liz and I sat in my Audi and drank our coffees. "I don't know what the hell I'm going to do," she said, shaking her head. "He didn't really give me much to work with there."

"Thanks for backing off of the 'us,'" I said.

She gave me a wry smile. "I can't expect you to come along on this one. Hell, I'd run away if I could. My boss dumped it on me, though, so it's my baby."

"And it looks like a guaranteed win for the prosecution."

"It does. The police haven't been popular for a while; you know that. They're starting to make some gains, though. Small gains, but they're winning a few people over. The state's attorney is going to say that a crime like this has enraged the city again and galvanized them in the quest for vengeance." She said those last parts in a very affected proper voice.

"I've never heard her talk in such a refined way," I said.

"She doesn't. Her top prosecutor does whenever there's a reporter nearby. He sounds like he's trying to be a barrister."

Or get a promotion, I thought as I took a sip of my latte. "Liz, how are you going to work this case? You don't have any good leads to follow up on, your suspect got arrested by the victim twice, his story is flimsy, and a cop killing isn't popular anywhere. I know this is a red ball, but it's shitty."

"My office gets a lot of shitty cases," she said. "Comes with the territory. Not all of us can pick and choose the cases we work."

"More's the pity."

"You know, I don't live too far from here." Liz smiled at me. "I have more interesting things to drink."

If she made the offer the first time we worked together, I would have jumped at it. Now I pictured Gloria sitting at my table, lounging on my couch, and sleeping in my bed.

Maturity sucks sometimes. "I don't think it's a good idea, Liz," I said.

"You're seeing someone?" I didn't really know the answer, so I gave her a small nod. "I guess I should have asked you before."

"You would've gotten a different answer."

We were silent for a moment. It started to weigh on me. Then Liz said, "The car thing bothers me."

"What?" I said.

"The silver car in the driveway."

It constituted an awkward subject change, but I went along with it. "It bothers me, too."

"I think it bothers me for a different reason," Liz said

"I don't like it because killing Harrison is pointless if the shooter can easily get in and drive away," I said. "What's he going to do, run after a carjacker?"

"That's a fair point," she said. "It bugs me because the police haven't investigated yet. I don't even know that they've acknowledged it."

"They think they have their man."

"I'm not so convinced."

"After talking to him, I'm not so convinced, either," I said.

Liz smiled. "Does this mean you're going to help me?"

Pariah status awaited me if I said yes. When I agreed to work for my parents' foundation, I signed on to take cases *pro bono*. Jack Bennett was the kind of person they would want to help. He didn't have anywhere else to turn, and the system would grind him under its considerable heel. Liz could only do so much; she wasn't getting any help from her office. Saying no meant turning my back on all of them. "Against my better judgment . . . I will."

Despite the cramped quarters in the car, she gave me a quick hug. "Thanks so much."

"I have enough doubts as to Jack's guilt." I took a deep breath. "Working this case is going to be tough for me, though. I can't imagine it'll make me popular with the BPD."

"You're already pretty unpopular with them," Liz pointed out.

"True," I said, "but now they'll really have a reason to dislike me. I'll be trying to convince everyone an accused cop killer is innocent. This isn't going to be easy."

"No, it's not," she said. "I'll help you when I can."

"You'd better," I said.

CHAPTER 4

THE NEXT MORNING, I GRABBED SOME BREAKFAST FROM Panera and went to my office. For about my first year in business, I worked out of my house. As I took more cases, I got threatened more often, and having an office in my house became a dangerous proposition. For the last three months, I've maintained an office in the CareFirst Tower in Canton. The building offers security, and they didn't care how I set up my computers. If only they knew.

I ate my morning meal at my desk while I poked around on the Baltimore Police Department's network. During my first case, Rich left his computer unattended long enough for me to snag his IP and physical addresses. Since then, the BPD's network accepted my computer as one of its own. Occasionally, they try new e-measures to stop enterprising hackers such as yours truly, but those never deter me for more than a few minutes. It probably makes some bean counter in City Hall happy to know they tried.

The BPD posted the current case file online. I perused it as I polished off my breakfast sandwich and nursed my latte. Sure enough, the report mentioned nothing about a silver car. Jack must have told them, but because the rest of his alibi sounded like bullshit, the police probably dismissed the silver car as just a yarn. I couldn't blame them. The rest of their chronicle of Jack's side of things seemed pretty much like what he told me.

I read the responding officers' notes of the crime scene. One bullet indeed blasted through the hood of a gray Ford sedan. Two more bullets took Ben Harrison in the chest. The ME's initial comment said either could have been fatal and Harrison died quickly. Robbery did not appear to be a motive as many expensive tools—not to mention several cars—were undisturbed at the scene.

I pulled up all crime scene photos next. Ben Harrison kept the cleanest garage I'd ever seen. Other than the large pool of his blood, the floor looked completely spotless—not a stray drop of oil, not the usual collection of dust, nothing. Tools hung in neat rows on pegboards, and each section was labeled. Loose parts like screws and wingnuts sat in clearly marked jars.

The extreme neatness of the garage removed an easy way to prove Jack's alibi: the mystery shooter wouldn't have left a shoeprint in any dust, grime, or grease. The police report mentioned no shoeprints found in the blood. Other than details of the crime scene, the report mentioned a suspect seen fleeing on foot. The suspect was apprehended after "falling down" a few times and injuring himself. Detectives questioned him, and he maintained his innocence. The report commented on the flimsiness of Jack's alibi. It also mentioned gunshot residue on his hand.

Other than the GSR angle, I was able to check out other aspects of the story. I set off to do it.

* * *

THE HARRISON FAMILY lived at the end of a street barely over the county line. Their house looked like many others in the community save for the size of the garage.Most residences featured two-car units; the Harrisons' just looked wider and deeper. It boasted a long driveway leading up to it. The house itself was nice in the plain, soulless sort of way most modern homes are. A brick front, white siding, blue shutters, maroon door, and nothing that would excite or offend anyone's sensibilities. Welcome to 21st-Century suburbia, population: boring.

I couldn't access the garage, however; the police had closed it and put their gaudy crime scene tape all around it. Cars still sat in the driveway. I guess those people could only wait for their keys to be processed and released. No vehicles were parked on the street in front. Seeing the interior would have helped, but breaking into a crime scene, especially in daylight hours, did not strike me as a sensible plan. Instead, I followed the path the police said they took in pursuing Jack Bennett.

He said he ran for a while, and the muddy ground the night of the shooting would have helped the pursuit. The report also mentioned witnesses who saw a man look panicked and running. Eventually, the police caught Jack at his house. It was a little more than a mile away. I recreated his route as best I could. Most of it would have left him exposed to any witness walking or driving by. Only near his own place would he have been safe. Bennett lived amid a nest of side streets. His residence looked old enough for his grandparents to have bought it after World War II. Crime scene tape covered the front door.

I'd learned all I could right now under the daylight and the watchful eyes of neighbors in both places. I walked back to the Harrisons' neighborhood, got in my car, and drove to my office. Jack Bennett had been arrested twice. I wanted to talk to as many people as I could who were involved with him at the time.

* * *

Tracking down Jack's older brother proved easy. He managed a chain restaurant in Glen Burnie. I would have rather eaten raw sewage than taken a meal there, but I walked in anyway. After the hostess showed me to my table, I asked a waiter to see the manager. Edward Bennett walked out of the kitchen area a moment later. He was larger than his brother, and he walked with his chin up and eyes forward. "Can I help you?" he said when he got to my table.

"I hope so," I said. I showed him my ID. "I'm investigating a case involving your brother Jack, and I'm hoping you can tell me about him."

Edward snorted. "Jack," he said. "What the hell did he do now?"

"He's accused of murder, but I don't think he did it." Edward's mouth fell open at the news. "Judging by your reaction, I'd say you agree."

"Yeah, I do." He looked at his watch. "I'm taking a break in ten minutes. I'll come talk to you then. In the meantime, order whatever you want. It's on the house."

I managed to thank him even though the menu didn't interest me. My breakfast was a few hours in the rearview by now, and my stomach gave a grumble, so I decided to suck it up and order something the place probably couldn't screw up—a grilled chicken Caesar salad, light on the dressing, washed down with iced tea. The food arrived a minute before Edward Bennett did. I'd taken a couple bites of the salad and found it adequate. The greens weren't vibrant, but they also weren't brown. Score one in the win column.

"How's the food?" he said, forcing a smile.

"Edible," I said, "which is more than I expected. Have a seat."

He sat and looked around. The restaurant wasn't crowded, and most of the guests were in one large party too busy making noise to bother with anything we said. "What happened to Jack?" he said.

"He got arrested for murder recently."

"Who do they say he killed?"

"A cop," I said.

Edward winced. "I'm sure he's had a rough go of it, then."

"Probably." I kept eating my salad as we conversed.

"You don't think he did it," he said.

I shook my head. "His public defender doesn't think so, either. The problem is he has a shaky alibi, a history of assault, and got arrested by this cop before."

"Jesus." Edward closed his eyes and pinched the top of his nose. "He really landed in the soup on this one."

"You grew up with him. He's obviously capable of assault, but do you think he could kill someone, especially someone he claimed to like?"

"He was friends with the cop?"

"Says he was," I said.

"Wait a minute . . . was it Ben . . . something?"

The main details were public record, so I didn't see the need to hold back. "Harrison, yes."

"I know Jack liked Ben," Edward said. "He talked about him a lot. Said he was fair and willing to help my brother get back on the right path."

"Jack said Ben got him his job," I said.

"I don't doubt it. I tried to get him something here, but my district manager squashed it." He scowled and shook his head. "Prick."

The loud group nearby quieted long enough to harass the poor waitress about separate checks for everyone—after the fact, of course. I suspected Edward Bennett would soon be needed elsewhere.

"You don't think your brother would kill Ben Harrison?" I said.

"God, no," said Edward. "Flimsy alibi or not, he didn't do it."

"Jack's alibi involves another person. Do you know anyone who had it in for him, maybe would try to kill Harrison and make it look like your brother did it?"

Edward shook his head. "If he has enemies, I don't know who they are. He didn't really talk about it a lot."

"No one he met in prison who'd try to get even for something on the outside?" I said.

"Jack always said he kept his head down in prison and kept to himself. I don't think he made any enemies there."

I finished my salad and wiped my mouth with the moderately soft cloth napkin. The board of directors probably chose them to save two cents per unit. "If you think of anything we might use to help your brother, let me know." I took a business card out of my wallet and slid it across the table to him.

"Hey, I've read about you in the paper," Edward said when he looked over my card.

"The price of success," I said.

* * *

THE SYSTEM PRESUMES people who get popped twice for assault have anger issues. Sure enough, some judge made this exact presumption about Jack Bennett. After his second arrest, Jack spent some time in jail, then visited a court-appointed psychologist as a condition of his parole. I hadn't been in a shrink's office since my last session with the cretin my parents insisted I see after my sister's untimely death. I doubted psychology made many strides in the last thirteen years.

Dr. Janishefski's office said he could fit me in, though they couldn't promise he'd be able to tell me a lot. Doctor-patient confidentiality and all. I hoped for the best as I sat in the drab waiting room. The walls were painted a sedate light blue. Even the furniture was a non-threatening tan color. Magazines looked carefully culled to remove red colors and anything to induce aggression, including current events and politics. Can't have slugfests in the antechamber, I suppose. Instead, everyone gets to read rags about knitting or something equally boring.

I spent a few minutes playing games on my phone, interrupted when a tall, thin man entered the waiting room from another door. "Mr. Ferguson?" he said.

"The one and only," I said.

"Please follow me."

He led me down a hallway, then another until we entered an office. He stayed at the door to close it behind us. The room was about the size of my bedroom. A bookshelf crammed with stuffy psychological tomes dominated one wall. A large desk sat just off-center in the room, a comfortable chair on either side of it. I wondered if the doctor positioned it to troll his OCD clients. A point for him if he did. Other than a small end table and floor lamp, the floor space was open from door to desk. Maybe the *feng shui* reduced aggression too.

I sat on the patient's side of the desk; the other man took the opposite. "I'm Dr. Janishefski," he said, not offering his hand. He was slender to the point even his full beard didn't fill out his face. Janishefski wore a cheap tan suit with a white shirt and a light blue tie, a non-threatening wardrobe. I noticed his diplomas on the wall behind him. The years on them made him about twenty years my senior. Either his hair refused to betray his age, or the color came from a bottle. "My secretary told me you're here about Jack Bennett."

"Correct," I said. I showed him my ID. "I'm working with the Public Defender's Office on his case."

"His case? What does it involve?"

"He's accused of murder."

Janishefski's eyes widened, and his face dropped into a frown. "I find that difficult to believe."

"It's true," I said. "He's currently awaiting arraignment."

The doctor shook his head. "That's not a course of action I would have predicted," he said.

"Can you tell me about Jack Bennett?"

"Well, a lot of it is privileged," Janishefski said, steepling his fingers under his bearded chin. I imagined he made the gesture often when a patient said something deserving mild disapproval. Any moment now, he would ask me how this all made me feel. "What Jack and I talked about is subject to doctor-patient confidentiality."

"He's accused of murdering a police officer. I don't think he did it, and I think you feel the same way. Something you tell me might be able to assist in his defense. He's not going to get a lot of help from the system on this one."

Janishefski sighed and leaned back in his chair. "I can tell you I don't believe he's capable of murder."

"But he was capable of assault . . . twice . . . which is what got him sent to you."

"Assault is a much different crime, governed by a much different impulse. It is often a spontaneous thing borne of the situation at hand. Murder is frequently premeditated."

"What makes Jack incapable of murder?" I said.

"He doesn't have the drive to plan something like that out," the doctor said. "He's impulsive, and it's why he committed assault twice. What he isn't going to do is plan something elaborate against someone . . . who is he accused of murdering?"

"An officer named Ben Harrison."

"Then I definitely don't think he did it."

"Did Jack talk about Harrison often?" I said.

"His name came up several times," Janishefski said after a studious pause.

"In a positive light?"

"Jack felt Ben Harrison made a very good impression on him and his life. Harrison was a positive force."

"Despite arresting him twice?" I said.

"It's uncommon for something like that to turn into something causing constructive change, but it can happen."

"So it's your professional opinion Jack isn't capable of murder," I said, "and especially not the murder of Ben Harrison."

"Yes," Janishefski said. "If it comes to it, I will testify to those opinions on Jack's behalf. I've been an expert witness at over a dozen criminal cases."

I expected Janishefski's degrees to sparkle on the wall as he made the pronouncement. The wattage remained subdued. I hid my disappointment. "Good to know, Doctor." I put a business card on his table. "I hope it doesn't come to it, but it's good to know."

"Good luck, Mr. Ferguson." The doctor didn't offer his hand this time, either. Neither did I.

I simply left.

* * *

LATER IN THE DAY, Liz Fleming called me. "Jack Bennett has been denied bail," she said.

"Had to be expected," I said. "The prosecution is sure the police have a good case and at first blush, they do."

"I know . . . I know." I heard frustration creep in at the worn edges of Liz's normally upbeat voice. "I tried to get him some kind of bail but it wasn't happening."

"Where's he going now?"

"The state's attorney painted him as a flight risk because he fled the scene of the crime, so he's probably looking at maximum security."

I shook my head. "He'll be in jail with real killers," I said.

"Yep," Liz said. "I tried to argue that, too, but the judge went with the state down the line."

"Cops, prosecutors, judges . . . they're all part of the system. They see it as sticking up for their own."

"And here I thought I'd be doing the legal analysis," Liz said with a chuckle.

"I won't charge you extra for it," I said.

"Good. I can't afford any more than your going rate."

"I've gotten used to it," I said.

* * *

OF ALL THE people who dealt with Jack Bennett, the one I wished I could speak to was Ben Harrison. I could talk to Harrison's shift commander, but doing so would tell the BPD I worked a cop killer case from the "wrong" side and torpedo any gains in my relationship with them. Dr. Janishefski was on board if I needed a witness. What I wanted to find were those who could keep the case from going to court. I clung to the hope I could uncover a cavalcade of such people in Jack Bennett's recent past.

I hadn't yet done a thorough background investigation of Jack Bennett, so I started one. I used his police file and went from there. Jack's family would likely paint a picture of him colored with sunshine and roses, but I needed to start somewhere. I ended up with a decent pool of family and friends who might be able to help me construct enough about Jack Bennett to save him from the needle.

His parents had been dead for several years, so I decided to start with his barely-younger brother. Victor Bennett claimed to be very busy but relented and agreed to meet me over coffee in

Fells Point. When I walked into the Daily Grind, one man stood out as a non-hipster. He wore a dark blue suit looking good for being off the rack, shoes not quite going with it, and a punchy red tie picked to complement everything. A drink sat on the table, so I ordered a vanilla latte before I joined him.

"You're the detective," he said.

"C.T. Ferguson." I showed him my ID.

"Victor Bennett." He offered a handshake, and I took him up on it.

"I'm glad you found some time to meet me," I said.

He inclined his head. "I'm a stockbroker," he said. "It's a busy day like any other, but there's enough coverage for me to get away."

"Is this the part where you recommend a diverse portfolio?"

"I do, but I don't think it's the reason we're here."

"No," I said, "we're here to talk about your brother. Do you know what's happened to him?"

"Did he get arrested for hitting someone again?" Victor Bennett rolled his eyes. "Jack has always needed to work on his impulse control."

"He's accused of murdering a cop."

My last line cracked the pompous stockbroker veneer. Victor's eyes widened, and his jaw went slack. When he recovered, his voice lacked an affectation he'd injected before. "Jack . . . murder someone?" he said.

"It's the accusation. I don't think he did it, but acquitting an accused cop killer is an uphill battle."

He shook his head. "No way he did it. Assault, yes. He's always been something of a slave to his impulses. But murder? Jack . . . how do I say this?" He frowned in thought. "Accidental manslaughter I might believe, but Jack would never take the time to plan out a murder. He doesn't have the patience for it."

The stockbroker echoed the shrink. I didn't know which to

devalue more. "Did he ever mention a cop named Ben Harrison?"

"Sure," said Victor. "He said Harrison arrested him, but they ended up forging a friendship. I thought it was kind of odd, but Jack said he was a great guy. Harrison even helped him get his job."

"You ever meet him?" I said.

"No," he said, "just heard Jack talk about him a lot."

"Do you know of anyone who would want to make it seem like your brother killed Ben Harrison?"

"You mean, does my brother have any enemies?"

I shrugged. "Or maybe Harrison does, and someone guessed your brother would make a good fall guy." It was a good theory. I'd have to remember it.

"I don't know if Jack has enemies," Victor said. "If he does, he never mentioned them to me."

"No one from his time in jail?"

"He didn't talk much about it."

I gave Victor Bennett one of my cards. "If you can think of anything to help your brother's case, give me a call," I said.

He took the card and put it into his wallet. "I will," he said.

I downed the rest of my vanilla latte and left the coffee shop. Finding someone who could actually help me prove Jack Bennett's innocence would be nice.

* * *

Liz called me on my way back to my house. Having absorbed as much malaise as I could for one day, I let it go to voicemail. As I drove to Federal Hill, I realized I could have gone to my office instead. The idea of having a separate place of business still felt foreign to me. It made what I do so official, and I preferred the feeling of playing things fast and loose. The office added legitimacy I didn't want and wasn't convinced I deserved. But it did mean that miscreants wouldn't be able to stake out my house as easily as before.

I got home to find Gloria relaxing on my couch. She'd kept a key for a while, ever since she wanted to stay with me during a particularly troubling case. I'd never bothered asking for it back, and she didn't offer. Over time, I've gotten more used to her coming and going. I certainly wouldn't lodge a complaint about the T-shirt and tiny shorts she wore as she lay on the sofa.

"You have that working-a-case look about you," she said.

"Is it a subtle furrow of the brow?" I said.

"No . . . just a focus that you don't normally have. It's always how I can tell. The harder the case gets, the more focused your look becomes."

"How about when I stare at you looking sexy on my couch?" I said.

Gloria smiled and sat up. "About the same, but I think we need to test it and make sure."

"An experiment. I think you're right."

"What about your case?" she said.

"It'll keep," I said. "This is for science."

CHAPTER 5

The next morning, I went downstairs and fired up my computer while Gloria remained asleep. I didn't have much luck looking into Jack Bennett. I would keep looking, but I also needed to poke around the life of Ben Harrison. If I couldn't find someone who hated Jack, I felt sure I'd discover someone who hated a veteran cop. Harrison made a lot of arrests. Some of those people were bound to be assholes, and a percentage of those assholes were bound to hold grudges.

I got onto the BPD's network and looked for the case file. It was gone. I hunted in other folders but couldn't find it anywhere. Ditto the crime scene photos. Maybe the BPD considered the case closed and took everything down. It didn't jibe with the way they normally did things, though, especially for cases like this one. Why did they remove the data? I developed a strong theory I would need to test.

My Keurig turned itself on every morning. I rewarded its consistency by dropping a pod of coffee into it and brewing a cup for myself. Next, I took out the waffle iron, whisked together some batter, and made waffles. While the first one bubbled, I sliced strawberries and put them on the table along with a bottle of real maple syrup. I added raw sugar and some creamer to my coffee, then brewed another cup for Gloria. The caffeinated aromas wafting upstairs soon became too much to bear, and I heard her light footfalls on the stairs.

I put the first waffle on the table and cooked a second. Gloria sat in the chair at the waffle without asking who it was meant for and buttered it. She used enough to give a cardiologist a heart attack, then added sufficient syrup to make a diabetic flee the room. I winced as I extracted the second waffle from the iron. I sat at the table, used perfectly reasonable amounts of butter and syrup, and ate.

"What's your case?" Gloria said.

"One I really don't want," I said.

"You don't seem to want a lot of them."

"Doubly true this time."

"What could be so bad?" she said.

I told her.

"Wow," Gloria said. She raised a forkful of waffle to her mouth but stopped halfway, then gave up and put it back on her plate. "A cop killer, C.T.? Why?"

"I talked to him," I said. "I don't think he did it."

"And the police do."

"In their defense, they have a pretty good case."

"Could they get him convicted based on what they have now?"

I shrugged. "I'm not qualified to answer. Indicted, sure. You can get a ham sandwich indicted for being eaten. Their evidence is pretty circumstantial, but enough circumstantial evidence could get it done."

"I can't imagine this will win you any friends with the BPD," Gloria said.

"It might cost me the few I have," I said.

Gloria frowned. She still hadn't eaten any more of her waffle.

"I don't like this, C.T. You're going against the people who could help you most."

"I know." I shook my head. "I'm sure I'll run into some resistance."

"Like what?"

"I don't know. I always work outside the BPD in a manner of speaking, but I've never really worked in opposition to them before. I have no idea what to expect, but I'm certain they won't be happy if they find out I think they have the wrong man."

"Do you think they'll discover you're working the case?" she said.

"I hope not," I said, "but they did pull the case file and crime scene photos from the network."

"They may know."

"It's possible. I'm going to hope they don't and see if I can get some old-fashioned cooperation."

Gloria finally ate her bite of waffle. "I hope you find it."

"Me, too," I said, not optimistically.

AFTER BREAKFAST AND A SHOWER, I drove to Rich's precinct. He wasn't there when I went to his desk. I looked around for someone I knew who liked me. My usual disregard for the law and proper procedure curried few fans in the BPD. After a moment of surveying the situation, I spotted Officer Jennings walking into the squadroom from the opposite side. I made my way to him, noticing the occasional hairy eyeball glared in my direction. "Jennings, old pal," I said as I got near.

He stopped and looked at me. "What do you want?"

"A smile would have been nice, but I'll live. I was hoping to get a case file."

"Of course you were. Let me guess which one."

"The Harrison file. I figure you guys want all hands on deck for this one." I offered my best winning smile. With women, the effects were usually lowering of inhibitions and rapid disrobing. With Jennings, I only hoped for a bit of cooperation.

"We already caught the guy who did it," he said. "Why do we need you?"

"It's circumstantial evidence. It might be enough to get a conviction, but why not have someone else working to gather evidence?"

Jennings shook his head. "I can't help you."

"Should I bring some donuts next time?" I said.

He spat out a mirthless chuckle. "Yeah, those'll help your cause," he said and walked away. I got the impression following him would have accomplished little, so I didn't. I also got the impression I would be met with a similar uncharitable attitude if I asked others for the case file. The BPD rank and file would never number among my biggest fans, but this was more stand-offish than I'd become accustomed to. I left and would see if Rich might help me out later.

As I left, an officer I didn't recognize went out of his way to bump shoulders with me. He stopped and glared at me but didn't say anything. Neither did I. After a few seconds of this boring standoff, he turned and walked into the precinct house. I turned and left for my car.

I hoped word hadn't gotten out.

* * *

Rich called me after I got home.

"You motherfucker," he said. So much for my hopes.

"Damn," I said, "I fuck some kid's mother once, and I'm labeled for life."

"You know what I'm talking about."

"Actually, I'm pretty sure I've never slept with a woman who had a kid."

"This isn't a joke, C.T.," he said. "You're working with the Public Defender's Office, trying to get the cop killer off."

"I'm looking into things and making sure the right man goes on trial," I countered.

"We have the right man!" In my mind's eye, I envisioned Rich's face turning red. It's not like I hadn't seen it before.

"What if you don't?"

"He was there, Harrison arrested him twice, his hands tested positive for GSR, and he fled the scene. Do the math, will you?"

"Rich, it's all circumstantial," I said.

"A jury will see the facts," he said.

"Did anyone look into the car someone drove away from the scene? You know, the one maybe with the actual killer inside?"

"Why would we? It's a lie told by a cop killer."

"Nice groupthink conclusion."

"He's going to say whatever he can to try and wriggle off the hook."

"What if, in the process of saying whatever he can, he spoke the truth?"

Rich sighed. It sounded like a snake hissing right into my ear. "Did you know he was high?" he said. I didn't have a clever rejoinder for this new data point. In fact, I didn't have anything to say at all. "You didn't know, did you?" Rich continued. "We ran a tox screen after we booked him. It didn't make it into the police report before we pulled it offline."

"Just because he was on something doesn't mean he hallucinated a shooter and a silver getaway car," I said.

"It goes to his credibility. Speaking of which, you're losing whatever credibility you have with us if you work this case. We take care of our own."

"You think I don't want to see a cop killer go down?"

"Based on your helping the public defender, I'm not sure."

"I talked to him, Rich," I said. "I don't think he did it."

"You're in a definite minority in your opinion," said Rich. "And it's not a good place to be for a case like this."

"Do I detect a threat?"

Rich sighed again. "Just a warning. People already know you're working this case. Some of them might try to . . . discourage you."

"To serve, protect, and harass when someone disagrees with us?" I said.

"If you're going to be stubborn, C.T., at least be careful. Unlike some people, I actually don't want to see anything bad happen to you."

"Thanks, I think."

Rich hung up. I looked at my cell phone for a few seconds before I spiked it onto my desk.

CHAPTER 6

My parents called and invited me to lunch. I met them at The Waterfront Hotel in Fells Point. The Waterfront had been in Baltimore since there was a Baltimore. Ages ago, it had been a hotel; more recently, it became a restaurant and bar. My father must have picked this place. He and I shared similar tastes in restaurants; my mother would only enter after some nose-wrinkling and a vigorous round of sniffing. A hostess directed me to a table on the second floor.

The wooden stairs creaked under my feet. Like many places in Baltimore, the Waterfront was tall rather than wide and flat because it was part of what may have been rowhouses ages ago. I walked past the bathrooms, made a right, and entered one of the dining rooms. The hardwood floors groaned a bit each time I took a step. My parents occupied a table by the window. I slid into a chair across from them. We enjoyed a great view of the cobble-stoned streets of historic Fells Point. It's a neighborhood that feels like historic Baltimore, yet it manages to seem quaint and modern enough to appeal to hipsters. Somewhere on the menu, avocado toast called to them like a siren song.

My father smiled as he gazed out the window. In contrast, my mother looked as if she'd discovered a turd in her favorite purse.

She gave me a small smile when I looked at her. "Hi Mom . . . hi Dad," I said.

"Hi son," said my father. He didn't look his almost-sixty years, though the graying hair gave him away. I favored him in appearance, and we shared the same very dark brown hair. In thirty years, if mine looked like his did today, I would be happy. By contrast, my mother's hair color got reapplied every couple weeks. It was very close to the shade of blonde I remembered from my youth but not exact.

"Are you OK, Mom?"

"Ah, she'll be fine. You know your mother: it takes her a while to process her surroundings whenever she's not in a four-star restaurant."

"Are you boys having fun talking about me?" my mother said.

"If we say yes, can we keep it up?" I said.

"No, Coningsby, you may not. Robert, I don't know what you're carrying on about. We eat at all manners of places. This is very . . . quaint."

"The food is really good," I said. "I've been here a few times."

A waiter came and took our drink orders. My mother and I both ordered iced teas; my father ordered a beer which caused my mother to give us one of her patented delicate sniffs. We didn't pay it any mind.

"Are you working a case?" my mother said.

"I am," I said, "and it's a red ball from the start."

"Is that bad?"

"In this case, definitely."

"Why? Tell us about it."

I did.

"Coningsby, why would you try to acquit a person who killed a policeman?" my mother said, looking at me like I was the very rapscallion who tainted her purse with the offending turd.

"Because I think he's innocent, Mom. Isn't it the point of my free detective service? I help people who wouldn't have any other recourse."

"And he doesn't?" she said.

"He's represented by the public defender," I said. "His case lawyer is pretty good, but let's just say the deck is stacked against them. The entire legal system wants him to go down for this, whether he did it or not."

"And you don't think he did it?" said my father.

I shook my head. "I don't."

"Then you should do what you think is right," he said.

The waiter returned with our drinks and took our food orders. I opted for fish tacos, my father selected a burger, and my mother an entrée salad. When the waiter left, I said, "The BPD knows I'm working the case. I've already seen their attitude change toward me. Rich called me and warned me how I won't be popular for a while."

"Do you think they'll do anything to you?" my father said.

"I don't know. I've been threatened and menaced before but always by criminals. It'll be jarring if the police are the ones trying to shake me down."

"Will Richard help you?" said my mother.

"I don't think so," I said. "He doesn't want to see me hurt, but the BPD is convinced they have the right man. And I have to admit they have a pretty good case."

"Then maybe you should consider they do have the right man, son," my father said.

"They don't, Dad. I believe him. His lawyer believes him. We're going to be swimming upstream on this one, but we'll be doing what's right."

A moment later, the waiter came out with our food. After checking to see if we needed our drinks freshened, he moved on to another table. We focused on our lunches for a few minutes. My mother's expression softened since I joined them, and she smiled when she ate her salad. My fish tacos and garlic fries were so good I needed to remind myself to eat at a reasonable pace lest I devour them and get accused of gluttony by my mother. She wouldn't care about the deadly sin aspect; she just wouldn't want to be seen in public with an accused glutton. "You be careful, Coningsby," my mother said when she had consumed about half her salad. "You're not going to have any help to fall back on with this one."

I nodded around a bite. "I know," I said. "I'm going to have to build a good case and then take it to the BPD. I can't count on them to fill in any of the blanks this time."

"Good luck, son," my father said.

"I get the feeling I'm going to need it," I said.

AFTER LUNCH, I went to my office. To my mild surprise, the BPD's network still accepted my computer. Either they didn't bother with trying to keep me out, or they couldn't detect my presence. Regardless, I went hunting for the case file on the network again and came up empty. I spent time and looked in every nook and cranny I could access. It simply wasn't there. Any crime scene photos formerly online were similarly removed.

I could pay a visit to the ME's office. I had an in with one of the doctors there after catching him releasing a woman's body to her killer. Since then, I've used the threat of blackmail to get him to give me information and opinions. On this case, however, I didn't think even my usual ammunition would get me very far. The BPD was rallying its troops and circling their collective wagons, which would include the ME's office. I was just a rogue outside the protective perimeter, meant to be used as target practice for the arrows.

I pondered my next move. Investigating Jack Bennett hadn't

gotten me very far, so I kept my attention on Ben Harrison. Their fit of pique with the case file aside, my computer still accessed the BPD's network. I poked around until I found HR. Sure enough, Harrison's file remained online. Someone removing case data proved careless, and I copied the file locally so the BPD getting their shit together wouldn't lock me out of something else. Sometimes, stealing data is about being brilliant. More often—as much as I dislike admitting this—it's about capitalizing on nonchalance.

Harrison had been a decorated officer. He refused a move to detective because he felt being a uniform made him closer to the people he swore to protect and serve. Commendations and awards littered his personnel file. Harrison got promoted about as far as a uniform could go. He worked regular training details, and his file mentioned the many fine detectives who trained with Harrison when they were coming up—including the similarly-decorated Richard Ferguson. One of Harrison's reviews described him as a "cop's cop," and everything I saw in the lengthy file supported this.

Now my task was to discover who wanted him dead and why. Harrison sent a long list of people to jail for offenses trivial and major. Any of them could have wanted revenge, but I would need a fleet of assistants to chase down all those leads. Even considering only the major offenders still left an impressive list of names. Jack Bennett would be banished to prison long before I investigated them all. I needed something more immediate and sought inspiration in Harrison's file.

Inspiration is a fickle mistress. Several minutes and even more abandoned ideas later, I closed the file as a lost cause. I still needed to figure out why someone wanted Harrison dead, and I saw only one easy means of investigation.

I needed to break into his house.

* * *

GETTING into residences undetected is a delicate enterprise. Any idiot can do it—and many have—but doing so without getting caught or alerting anyone takes skill. I learned all of this and got valuable practice in Hong Kong. My hacker friends broke in to steal; I did it to acquire a new and interesting skill. In the end, we both got what we wanted.

I drove the Caprice and parked it a couple blocks away. Google Earth laid out the terrain for me earlier. It made reconnaissance so much easier. The Harrisons' single family house marked its territory on each side by a privacy fence and about forty feet. A grass alley ran behind the homes with another block of houses pressed from the same cookie cutters on the other side. I planned to access the alley from where it terminated on a nearby quiet street.

After locking the car, I slipped on a pair of thin black gloves. I walked two blocks to where the alley ended between two identical back yards. It must be unfortunate when someone else cuts out the same cookie you did. Lights were off in the homes; it was after eleven. The moon hid behind a thick cloud cover most of the time, and the area was way too metropolitan to have a lot of starlight. Darkness may have been Simon and Garfunkel's old friend, but it was a solid acquaintance of mine.

I walked down the alley, made a ninety-degree right at the corner, and continued to the fourth house. At seven feet tall, the Harrisons' privacy fence rose close to a foot over me. Even in the dark, I noticed the consistent board spacing and uniform bolt work. Whoever hung their sign on it earned the placard. I found a gate around the middle of the fence. It was locked. I fished my small LED flashlight out of my jeans pocket and shined it on the lock long enough to see how it worked.

My special keyring would come in handy here. My Hong Kong friends gave me an assortment hoop with all the tools I would need to pick a lock. Recently, I picked up a snap gun to make the lockpicking process faster. Tonight, I stuck with the old school methods. The Harrison house was a crime scene, and snap guns are more likely to damage a lock. Soon, I pushed the gate open barely wide enough to squeeze through and closed it but didn't lock it behind me.

I padded across the backyard in a crouch. The fence was taller than I was, but neighbors on higher ground may still spot me. I passed a crabapple tree and a maple and stepped onto the back patio. Yellow crime scene tape covered the door in a giant forbidding X. If I got in there, the police would know someone went into the house. I wanted to avoid giving them the knowledge. I needed to find a window.

On the left side of the house, I found one at the bottom left unlocked. I slid the pane back slowly and shined my light inside. It looked like a six-foot drop to the basement floor with nothing in my way. I slipped into the opening feet-first, jumped down, and closed the window behind me.

A shelf teeming with boxes on the long adjacent wall stared at me from my left. I landed beside the washer, dryer, and sink. A workbench dominated the right-hand wall, along with more cartons neatly stacked. I looked back at the shelf. Whoever placed the boxes there had done so with military precision. Every one was in exactly the right space with its contents labeled on the outside. I walked over to the workbench. It looked sparse and empty compared to others I'd seen. No abandoned projects lay splayed out on it, and only a smattering of tools hung on the pegboard behind it.

Seeing nothing of interest down here, I made my way up the carpeted stairs. They ended at a closed wooden door. I listened at the door for a few seconds, didn't hear anything, and opened it. I peeked around, and even in the darkness, I could see I looked at a kitchen. With the beam from my flashlight, I gaped at a room making my gut burn with envy. An island bisected the floor and held a cooktop. A two-door oven stood next to the sink. Atop the island, a kids' book sat opened and another lay strewn on the floor. The bistro table held a mostly-empty glass of water and a plate covered in what looked like cake crumbs. Life had been interrupted here, right after one ended outside in the garage.

Past the kitchen and around the corner, I found the garage. Inside was Ben Harrison's real workbench. Car parts he'd worked on sat atop it, and the surface proved to be the only thing messy. The pegboard behind the workbench burst at its particle board seams with tools, yet all were hung neatly and showed clear labels above them. Another shelf held jars of screws, nuts, bolts, and random car parts, each marked with enough detail to inform a novice exactly what was inside. Standing in this garage made me feel like I could rebuild an engine.

Two cars, works in progress, sat in the garage. One showed a bullet hole in the hood, exactly like Jack Bennett said. I looked down and saw a few bloodstains unlikely to come out of the stone. The opposite wall held a series of power tools and toolboxes atop a long desk. Beneath were two manual jacks. A small monitor occupied the far end of the desk. I looked for a computer to go with it but found only loose wires and a now-unused power strip. Ben Harrison kept his car repair work on file electronically. This had been a very organized man. He owned at least one of every tool imaginable in this garage; no way he would trust all his records solely to a computer. People like Ben Harrison didn't abide single points of failure.

I hunted for hard copy records. Under the workbench, I found a few plastic file boxes. A quick peek inside showed notes talking about clients and car repairs. I guess the cops were happy to have the computerized records. All the better to hide them from me and my electronic snooping. I condensed the folders by cramming them into two boxes and took the pair with me out of the garage.

I walked back into the kitchen, opened the window, and gently tossed my haul out. Both landed without bursting open and spilling paper all over the backyard. I climbed out after them and closed the window. When padding back across the lawn, I heard sirens in the distance. Keeping in my crouch, I ran to the gate, threw it open, gave it a hard shove to shut it, and took off down the alley. The cops would approach from the front of the house. Still, I needed to avoid any enterprising uniforms who decided to scope out the back exit. I took the left turn at a full run, hit the street, and kept going. Only when I got closer to the Caprice did I slow to a jog. I unlocked the door, set the stolen boxes on the passenger's seat, and drove away with a shriek of the rear tires.

CHAPTER 7

I went home with my purloined file boxes. My parking pad already held my Audi and Gloria's rocket-shaped Mercedes coupe, so I parked the Caprice on the street about a block from my house. From there, I ducked down the alley running behind the row of homes. Darkness broken by the occasional back porch light and bordered by chain-link-topped stone fences surrounded me. I opened my gate and went into my house via the back door.

My arrest in Hong Kong compelled me to take certain precautions in the event something similar happened—or threatened to—again. My second bedroom upstairs served as a library, its walls lined with bookshelves and a comfortable reading chair near the center of the room. One bookshelf slides aside to reveal a hidden closet. I set the files down, pulled my two copies of Machiavelli's *The Prince* forward, and watched the bookcase slide to the right. Inside the closet, I kept my backup server, a spare laptop, two burner phones, a go bag, and a reserve of cash. I squeezed Ben Harrison's hard copies into the space, secured the bookcase, and left the room.

The only other people who knew about the hidden chamber were Gloria and my fellow paranoid who designed and built it. Before I even changed a lightbulb in the house, I ordered that secret closet set up. You're not paranoid if they're really after you, or if there's a good chance they might be someday.

I walked down the hall. Gloria was already asleep, nestled under the covers on her side of the bed. The thought of it as her side actually made me smile. I did my best not to wake her as I got undressed. She stirred when I climbed into bed but went right back out. I watched her sleep for a moment before turning over and closing my eyes.

* * *

MY VIBRATING cell phone forced my eyes open. I looked at the time: 7:10. Someone needed a good reason to be calling at this hour. Caller ID told me it was Rich. I had a feeling I knew what he wanted.

"Hello?" I mumbled.

"Ben Harrison's house was broken into last night," said Rich.

"Very unfortunate."

"You wouldn't know anything about it, would you?"

"Why would I?" I said.

"Because it's just like you," Rich said.

"To break into a dead cop's house?"

"So you don't know anything about it?"

"Rich, it's a high-profile case," I said. "Anyone can read *The Sun* and see Harrison is dead and his family is in hiding. The house is a prime candidate to be robbed."

Rich sighed into the phone. I pictured steam leaking from his ears as pondering my point tempered his anger. Considering the time at which I took the shot in the dark, I allowed myself a second to be impressed by my own reasoning. "I guess you have a fair point," he said.

"You guess?" I said.

"OK, it is. It doesn't mean you didn't have something to do with it."

"Did you find my fingerprints anywhere at the scene?"

"No."

"Did anyone report a handsome man in a stylish Audi speeding away?"

"No," he was forced to admit.

"There you go," I said. "The defense rests."

"We're still looking into it. You'd better hope you didn't do it."

"Rich, it's early. If you're going to make me the bogeyman for everything going wrong in your case—and I'm sure it'll be a lot— at least have the decency to do it at a more respectable hour."

"Oh, go to hell," Rich said and hung up.

I put the phone back on the nightstand. To my surprise, I fell back asleep.

* * *

NORMALLY, I would look at Ben Harrison's files at my office or at least my workstation at my former home office. With the police putting me under a microscope, I needed to take precautions. I set one of the two boxes beside the reading chair in the spare bedroom. If the BPD decided to drop by, I could stash the files in my secret closet. I carried a small, little-used end table up from the living room and placed it beside the chair to hold my coffee and notepad. So far, I needed the former more than the latter.

Ben Harrison's files showed he supplemented his income nicely with regular car repair work. He did at least two jobs in a typical week and raked in over two hundred doing it. Maybe he didn't declare it as income and an IRS auditor shot him. It would be easier than whatever trail I would have to follow. Harrison bought enough on his Auto Zone card to sit on the board of directors. This didn't tell me anything useful.

After some financial paperwork, I dove into a thrilling set of invoices and write-ups of individual repair jobs. Nothing stood out at me here. Harrison performed work like oil changes, tire rotations, brake jobs, and spark plug replacement—with the occasional complicated engine job sprinkled in for a challenge. Like a good cop would, he took notes on his clients. Some were his fellow officers. Several were neighbors.

An idea formed. The police would be watching Harrison's house a lot more closely after my recent break-in. Getting inside or even onto the property would be impossible without inviting arrest. Nothing prevented me from talking to the neighbors, however. The case against Jack Bennett was considered a lead-pipe cinch so few witness statements had been collected. I wondered if someone saw or heard something to contradict the official version of events.

There was one way to find out.

* * *

I PARKED a block away from Ben Harrison's house and walked. Why announce my arrival to the BPD? Sure enough, a patrol car sat in front of the house. The cruiser was empty and the police tape gone from the front door. Let them waste their time looking around inside. The only things I took were things the BPD didn't seem to care about. I planned to see at least two neighbors today.

The first on my list, Charlie Kane, lived two doors up. His place looked almost the same as Harrison's except for different shutter colors and one large garage door instead of two smaller ones. Rowhouses like mine may have looked similar to their neighbors, but each possessed character these newer homes couldn't match. I knocked on the door. Footsteps approached from the inside, and the door opened a moment later. A tall, medium-built black man looked at me through the glass.

"I talked to the cops already," he said.

I winced. "I'm not a cop."

"You here about what happened to Ben?"

"I am." I showed Kane my ID. "I'm working with the Public Defender's Office."

"Why?"

"We're not convinced the right man has been arrested."

"I never saw the guy," Kane said. "Can't help you there."

"Actually," I said, "I'm looking for more information on Ben Harrison."

"Why?" Kane frowned behind the screen door. I needed to tread carefully, or he would close the other door on me, too.

"There's not much out there on the guy in jail. I'm hoping to find someone or something I can use, and the only other source is Ben Harrison."

Kane pondered my words for a moment before opening the storm door and inviting me inside. His living room sat right inside the door. Beige carpet ran the entirety of the first floor. Magazines, books, and pens lay strewn about on the coffee table along with a well-used coffee cup. The floral-print curtains, by contrast, were neat and dust-free. The dining room table featured a bouquet of fake flowers in an attractive vase sitting at its center. Either Kane lived with a woman at one point, or he hired a maid service.

Kane sat on the sofa and gestured to a pair of matching tan recliners. I took a seat in the one on the right, and it immediately reclined and threw the leg extension up. Kane chuckled at my surprise. "You picked the touchy one," he said in the understatement of the day.

"I noticed," I said. I pushed the leg extension back into place and the recliner returned me to a more upright posture. I hoped it was the end of the touchiness.

"What do you want to know about Ben?" he said.

"Anything is useful at this point. I have his BPD file but don't know much about him outside of it."

"You got the man's file?"

"Like I said, I'm working with the Public Defender's Office." Appeals to authority, while logical fallacies, often quelled questions like those.

Kane nodded, mollified. "Ben is . . . was a good man. I don't know who would have it in for him."

"He was a cop. Anyone he arrested could have something against him."

"I guess." Kane looked toward the dining room and kitchen as if listening to a voice I couldn't hear. "I'm being rude," he said. "You want a soda or anything?"

"No, thanks," I said. "I don't want to take up too much of your time. How long have you lived near the Harrisons?"

"About ten or twelve years now."

"No problems with violence before?"

"No, they're good people, good neighbors."

"The night Ben Harrison got shot, did you see or hear anything?"

"I didn't see nothing."

This was a typical response of potential witnesses in Baltimore, but I believed Kane. He didn't strike me as a nosy neighbor. "Did you hear anything?" I said.

"Loud bangs," Kane said. "I guess they were gunshots."

"You remember how many?"

Kane shook his head. "No. A few. The guy next to me has been doing some home repairs, so I probably chalked it up to being a hammer at first."

I could buy the conclusion. "Ben ever work on your car?"

"Yeah," Kane said with a smile. "He was good. Always charged a lot less than a dealership or shop, you know. They'd want four hundred for a brake job. Ben called them thieves. He'd do it for a hundred plus parts."

"You notice anyone hanging around the garage of late? Maybe an unhappy customer?"

"You think someone shot him over a bad brake job?" said Kane.

I shrugged. "People have been shot for less."

Kane sighed. "Ain't it the truth? I haven't seen many people. Ben always kept a car or two I didn't know in the driveway. Part of having his repair business going, I guess."

"Had you seen a silver car there recently?"

"Why? Did someone in a silver car shoot him?"

I offered my best noncommittal shrug. "Just something we want to look into."

"I guess you gotta play it close to the vest, huh?" He paused. When I didn't say anything to fill the gap, he continued. "I don't remember a silver car in the last few days, but I haven't paid a lot of attention. Could have been. Lotta silver cars out there."

Whatever skeletons Ben Harrison may have stashed in a closet somewhere, Kane didn't have the key. He didn't even know where the closet was. "OK, I think I've taken up enough of your time," I said. "Thanks for your help." I stood and so did Kane. We shook hands, and he showed me to the door. I went outside and looked at the Harrison house. A uniform watched me from the bay window at the front. I fought the temptation to wave as I walked a few addresses up to the other person I came to see: Anna Baker. I knocked on her door. Her house was the smallest model on the street. It looked like the builder left the Harrison's model in the dryer too long. For a person living alone, it would be plenty. I got by with less room, and I didn't live alone half the time. Thinking of Gloria brought an involuntary smile to my face as Anna Baker answered the door.

Her gray eyes regarded me skeptically. I showed her my ID. "I'm looking into what happened to Ben Harrison," I said, "and I'm hoping you can help me."

"He got shot," she said. Great. I went from Major Understatement to Captain Obvious.

"Yes, ma'am. We want to make sure the right man pays for it."

She nodded. "All right. Come in."

I followed her inside, and we sat in the living room. My spot was on a shopworn loveseat, and Anna Baker sat in a new recliner. Tacky plastic protectors covered the Pergo flooring beneath the sofa and chairs. All the furniture I could see was a mix of new and weathered, like Anna Baker kept some older furniture sentiment forbade her from replacing. Her graying hair and encroaching wrinkles on her face put her well into her fifties. The running pants, Under Armour shirt, and athletic shoes she wore challenged the number, as if she flipped Father Time the bird. "Can I get you anything?" she said.

"No, thank you," I said. "I don't want to take up too much of your time."

"It's no trouble," she said with a smile.

I gave her a small one in return. "I'm working with the Public Defender's Office. You may have heard a suspect got arrested in the Harrison shooting. We want to make sure he's the right man."

"You have doubts, then?"

"Some. Right now, I'm looking into Ben Harrison and trying to figure out if someone else would have wanted to shoot him."

"I can't think of anyone," Anna Baker said with a frown. "Ben was a good man."

"And a good cop," I said, "from everything I've read."

"Yes."

"Good cops arrest a lot of people. Some of them hold grudges."

"I didn't see anyone like that hanging around, if that's what you mean." She paused. "Well, there was one fellow who spent some time with Ben while he worked on cars. I asked about him once. Ben told me he was a former criminal who simply needed some help keeping his life on track."

That sounded like Jack Bennett. I wondered if Anna Baker knew Jack currently sat in jail for Ben Harrison's murder. If she didn't, I couldn't see how mentioning it helped my cause. "Was it something Ben did a lot?" I said.

"If he did, I didn't hear about it," Anna said. "I think he was proud of how he helped that young man."

"How long have you lived here, Miss Baker?"

"Call me Anna, please." She gave me another smile. "Six years. I decided to downsize after my husband passed away."

"I'm sorry."

"Thank you. It's been a while now. I've gotten used to this place."

"Did Ben work on your car?" I said.

"Yes, he did." She smiled again, but this time, it looked wistful. "Ben was good with his hands. Anything mechanical, he had a knack for fixing."

"So he did good work."

"Oh, yes."

"Anyone you noticed who might have disagreed?"

"I never knew anyone who was unhappy with Ben's work," she said.

I could have asked Anna Baker more questions about Ben Harrison's work with his hands, but it would have been indelicate —not to mention unrelated to my case. If I found a connection later, I could always come back. "It seems everyone liked Ben," I said. "I haven't found anyone yet who's had a bad word to say about him."

"I doubt you will," she said.

"Did you notice any shady characters dropping a car off recently?"

"No. I don't think Ben would have done work for someone like that."

"Always a cop."

"I imagine it's hard to turn that off at the end of your shift."

"I'm sure it is," I said. Thank you. I don't need to take up any more of your time."

"It was my pleasure," she said. "I'll walk you to the door."

Anna Baker escorted me, and as I stepped off her porch, a BPD uniform walked briskly up the sidewalk. "What do you think you're doing?" he said.

"Leaving a lady's house," I said.

"Are you harassing people?" He strode up to me and glared. I didn't flinch.

"I'm not the one giving someone a hard time for doing nothing."

"Ma'am, did he bother you?" he said past me. I read his name tag: Fletcher.

"Of course not, Officer," Anna Baker said. I turned and saw her standing in her doorway, the storm door open. "We had a pleasant conversation."

Fletcher turned back to me and gave me The Stare again. "Is your hard look supposed to intimidate me?" I said.

"Leave these people alone," he said. "I don't know what you're doing here, but I'm sure it's nothing good."

"If you don't know what I'm doing, you can't come to a conclusion," I said.

"Listen, smartass, I'll come to whatever conclusion I want."

Fletcher gave me a good shove to the chest. I saw it coming but didn't stop it. It drove me back a step.

"Officer!" Anna Baker said from behind me.

"Better watch out," I said. "I'm more popular than you here."

Fletcher's hand rested on his nightstick. "You think I care?" he said. "You're messing with our case."

"I gave you the shove," I said. I took two steps forward and stood close enough to Fletcher to know what he ate for breakfast. "It's all I'm going to give you. You pull your nightstick, and we're going to have a problem. And I'll have a witness."

Fletcher looked between me and Anna Baker. "Stay out of this neighborhood," he said before storming off.

Anna Baker came down the walkway and stood beside me. "What was that all about?" she said.

"The police have a suspect," I said. "They don't like the fact not everyone thinks he did it."

"There are certainly better ways they could express that."

I nodded. "Yes, there are," I said.

When Fletcher stomped off, I walked back toward my car. I reached it without being further harassed. As I drove home, I checked frequently for red and blue lights in my rearview mirror.

CHAPTER 8

AFTER MY CONVERSATIONS WITH BEN HARRISON'S neighbors, I didn't have much more than when I started. They told me things I already knew. I could have inferred something between Ben and Anna Baker, but it was a longshot based on phrasing and interpretation. None of it seemed relevant to the case, nor did it get me any closer to who shot Harrison. I needed someone closer to him.

I needed his widow.

His children were youngish—twelve and fourteen—and may not have known enough about their father's life to help me. I wanted to find Julie Harrison. Everything I read after the shooting said she had taken the kids and gone to an undisclosed location. It was a reasonable precaution. As I thought about it, I realized it also meant she didn't know who killed her husband. If she did, she would have told his friends with the BPD and accepted their protection (which they were probably providing off the books anyway). Fleeing for her and her children's safety meant she didn't think Jack shot Ben and was hiding because the real killer wasn't in jail. This conclusion was, of course, lost on the police.

Going into hiding normally meant staying with relatives who

would lie for you. I started a background check on Julie Harrison, then stopped. Staying with family meant she could be found. If I could find her, a resourceful killer could, as well. Being married to a cop for two decades meant Julie would be smart in situations like this. I let the background check continue but made a phone call. I needed a consultant.

* * *

Joey Trovato would be late for a lot of things but never a meal. If there would be food, especially Italian food, and someone else was picking up the tab, Joey would be the first one there. He sat in a booth against the wall on the left as I walked in, and he already had an appetizer and soda in front of him. I slid into the booth opposite him. "Just one appetizer?" I said, nodding toward his mozzarella sticks. "Are you ill?"

"They're still cooking my other one," Joey said around the food in his mouth. It was one of his more endearing traits.

"Of course they are."

As if on cue, our waiter set down a tower of a dozen or so onion rings. Two containers of ranch dressing flanked the tower. The topmost onion ring threatened to tumble from the tower. If the ranch didn't catch it, I knew Joey would. "Anything for you, sir?" said the waiter.

"Unsweetened iced tea," I said.

"No appetizer?"

"I wouldn't want to interrupt the gluttony with even more food."

He looked at me like I wore a scaly face, then walked toward the kitchen.

"Help yourself," Joey said when the waiter left. "*Mi comida es su comida.*"

"Mighty generous of you," I said, grabbing a smaller circle of crunchiness.

"When have I ever failed to be generous with your money?" Joey said.

"Never." I let the onion cool on a small plate.

"They have good rings here." Joey grabbed one and dunked it in the ranch dressing as if trying to scrape the bottom of the container. He popped the whole thing into his mouth, oblivious to things like heat or manners which might worry ordinary mortals.

"I'm sure they do," I said, looking away from the spectacle. Joey could have his own show on a cable food channel if it wouldn't have to be rated M for graphic eating.

The waiter returned with my tea. He took our orders. Joey requested spinach ravioli with a side of garlic bread. I opted for veal parmesan and a Caesar salad. Joey rested his elbows atop the booth and surveyed the restaurant. "I might have to stop eating like this," he said.

"Gluttons Anonymous canceled your photo shoot?" I said.

"You're hilarious. No, I've lost three pounds the past two weeks." Those three pounds represented maybe one percent of Joey's body weight. He was a black Sicilian who'd always been heavy, but the girth hid a surprising amount of athleticism. If Joey wanted to be in better shape, he could do it.

"Good. Have you changed your diet?"

"Not really," he said.

"Started exercising?"

"I take more walks now it's starting to get warm."

"Don't let the warm weather fool you. Next week is as likely to be thirty and snowing as it is fifty and sunny."

"No shit." Joey took another onion ring from the pile. I seized the opportunity to pilfer a mozzarella stick from the basket. Joey frowned at me, mostly to keep up appearances, then dunked and devoured the onion "I assume you asked me here for my professional opinion?" he said around his snack.

"Certainly not for your table manners," I said. Joey, like me, worked in a job designed to help people, though he couldn't advertise in the Yellow Pages. His business was setting people up with new identities. In a field of tightening regulations and changing technology, Joey always managed to be ahead of the curve and under the radar of the legal system.

"You could learn a thing or two from me," he said.

"But is it something I'd want to learn?" I said.

Joey grinned and shrugged. "Probably not. What's up?"

I slid a picture of Julie Harrison across the table. Joey managed to avoid picking it up and marring it with his greasy fingers. "Not bad for an older broad," he said. "Who is she?"

"Someone whose husband recently got killed," I said.

"Awful," Joey said, frowning.

"I think she fled her home in case the killer came back for the family. Just wondering if she came to see you."

Joey shook his head. "Haven't seen her."

"No shit?"

"Look, I know I kind of fucked you over on the one a few months ago," he said. "My bad. I'm telling you the truth. I've never seen her." He looked at the picture again. "Kinda wish I did, though. How old is she?"

"Old enough to avoid a horndog like you."

"Like you're any better."

I drew a breath to say something but stopped. Joey smirked. "OK, you have me there," I said. "My interest in her, however, is strictly professional. I have other women to chase after for my more prurient interests."

"Women or just one?"

The waiter arrived with a crowded tray, saving me from answering. He set it on the next table and delivered our food. After freshening our drinks, he disappeared back into the kitchen.

After a few minutes of quietly devouring his lunch, Joey said, "You think she's gone into hiding?"

"Yes," I said. "I'm sure she's left their house with her kids. I just don't know where she's gone."

"Who was her husband?"

"A cop."

Joey grimaced. "What the hell are you doing sniffing around the case?" he said. Don't they have someone in custody?"

"I'm working with the Public Defender's Office," I said. "We're not convinced the right man is in custody."

"Wow. You're already not very popular with the police. This one is going to make you a fucking pariah."

"A distinct possibility." I didn't need to tell him the process had already begun. "Still, I want to make sure the man who's in jail is the right one. If not, I want to find him."

Joey took another monstrous bite of his ravioli and washed it down with a swig of soda. "How's finding the widow going to help you?" he said.

"I haven't had much luck looking into the suspect," I said. "Might as well see if the victim had any skeletons in his closet. Also, there's the fact the widow is in hiding while the primary suspect is safely behind bars."

"You're definitely going to be *persona non grata* for this one." Joey shook his head. "The public defender must be a looker."

I grinned. "You know me too well."

"Be careful, C.T. The cops are going to protect their own. You're not going to get any help."

"I've already found out."

"Good luck. Let me know if you need anything."

"I will. Thanks."

Joey ate a little more. "I'd hate to miss out on these free meals if something happened to you," he said.

"It's what I like about you Joey," I said, "you're all heart." I looked at him. "And stomach."

"You're hilarious," said Joey.

* * *

By the time I got back home, my background check had long finished. Julie Harrison, nee Dickinson, lived the kind of life expected of a cop's wife. She'd been a cheerleader in high school, graduated with a liberal arts degree, married Ben a year after graduation, and worked as an office manager for the intervening twenty years. She was active in police wives' charities and sounded like a model citizen. If anyone wanted to kill her, it would only be for the sake of completeness after killing her husband.

Julie had family in the area, but I ruled them out. She wouldn't go there, and they wouldn't tell me anything if I talked to them. I was left with her friends. Background checks don't provide a helpful list of personal references, but some additional digging can always turn something up. If worse came to worst, I could see if anyone at Julie's office knew anything.

Additional research told me most of Julie's friends were other cops' wives. It made sense. It also meant they wouldn't talk to me, either. Julie's Facebook friends, like most people's, were a mish-mash from all walks of life. She enjoyed almost four hundred friends, and I didn't have a way to prioritize them. The results left me with talking to her office-mates and hoping for the best.

I grabbed my keys.

* * *

THE ALTDORF CORPORATION provided a plethora of home and industrial contracting services. Julie served as their office manager for seven years. I talked to the frumpy secretary and snagged some face time with the boss. His office door opened, and he waved me in to sit on his hard plastic guest chair. His seat, by comparison, was a garish red leather number. The office looked lived-in with papers and folders semi-organized throughout. A large Apple monitor took up much of the desk's usable space.

"Sean Mahoney," he said, extending his hand. I shook it. He was a middle-aged Irishman whose red hair gave up and welcomed the gray. "What can I do for you? Something about Julie?"

"Yes," I said. I showed him my ID. "I presume you've heard what happened to her husband."

"Yeah, saw it on the news. Terrible."

"You haven't heard from her?"

"Nope," he said. "Didn't figure to, really. Something so tragic happens, work is the last thing on your mind. She needs time with her family."

"I'm sure she does."

"Are you trying to find her?"

"I'm concerned about her safety," I said.

"Who hired you?"

"I'm afraid I can't say."

"How do you know it wasn't the guy who killed her husband?" Mahoney said.

"Because I'm not stupid, nor am I an asshole."

Mahoney nodded. "Fair enough. I figure a lot of people are concerned about her safety right now."

"Besides her family, do you know of anyone outside these walls?"

"Not really," Mahoney said. "Julie didn't talk a whole lot about her personal life. I know she did a lot with police wives. Maybe you could talk to them."

Yeah, those conversations would go well. "They're on my list," I deadpanned. "Does she have an office cell phone?"

"We gave her a BlackBerry a few years ago, yeah."

If I never found who really killed Ben Harrison, I could lay claim to solving another mystery: the last company in Baltimore to use Blackberries. "Can you give me the number?"

Mahoney looked at me. "I'm not sure I should," he said. "If Julie's not talking to anyone right now, I'm sure she has a good reason. I mean, Christ, her husband just got gunned down. She might be scared."

"She might also be in danger," I said.

"You think whoever killed her husband is going to come for her?"

"I think it's irresponsible to ignore it as a possibility."

"You could be right. It might be." Mahoney frowned for a moment and then shook his head. "Sorry, I can't give you her BlackBerry number. Julie needs her space right now and I think she should get it."

I nodded. "All right," I said. "Anything you can tell me to help me find her?"

"I don't know where she would go."

"You think anyone here would?"

"Probably not. Like I said, Julie didn't talk a lot about her personal life."

I wasn't going to get any more out of Sean Mahoney. He retreated into a shell when I asked for the BlackBerry number. "OK," I said, "thanks for your time."

He shook my hand again. "Good luck," Mahoney said. "Julie's a great lady. I hope she's OK."

"I hope she is, too," I said, trying one last time to guilt him into giving me the number.

"Have a good day," he said.

So much for guilt.

CHAPTER 9

I didn't need Sean Mahoney to give me Julie Harrison's BlackBerry number. It would be easier, but I could find it on my own. Even when I did, I needed Julie to answer the phone and talk to a stranger selling the idea her husband was murdered by a still-unknown person. I might as well wish for the Easter Bunny to hop through my window and leave me a basket of chocolate.

Once I found Altdorf's website, I snagged the IP of their web server. Breaking into it only took a few minutes. They ran Microsoft's Internet Information Services with minimal protections. From there, I learned about the rest of the servers on their small network. None of them carried public-facing IP addresses, so I pivoted from the web box to where I needed to go. Firewalls are good at keeping people out, but once someone like me gets into a network, moving around is rarely a challenge. Within ten minutes, I located records containing accounts paid, including BlackBerry devices. Finding out which was issued to Julie Harrison took another minute. Armed with the data I came for, I erased my electronic footprints and broke my connection.

What would I say to Mrs. Harrison? She was a cop's wife; she'd be as up-to-date on the case as anyone. As far as she knew, the man who shot her husband was in custody. Why go into hiding, then? She must have feared a different killer. I hoped I could use it to reason with her. I called her BlackBerry number. Someone picked up on the third ring. "Hello?" a woman's voice said.

"Mrs. Harrison," I said, making sure not to intone it as a question.

"Do I know you?"

"I'm a private investigator. I'm sorry for your loss. Someone who's afraid for your safety hired me."

"How did you get this number?" she said. Accusation oozed out of the phone.

"I'm resourceful," I said.

"I'm safe right now. People are looking out for me. My husband's killer is in jail."

"If you were convinced of it, you wouldn't be off the grid with people looking out for you."

Her sigh was a hiss in my ear. "What do you want?"

"I want the right person to be in jail," I said. "I want you to be safe."

"I don't know how I can help you."

"Someone had a reason to kill your husband. Do you know who, or what the reason may have been?" I hated asking questions like this of a grieving widow, but I needed to.

"My husband's friends have the right man in jail," she said.

"Are you sure?" I said.

Her response came in the form of a click in my ear.

* * *

ABOUT A HALF-HOUR LATER, Rich called me. "Decided to help me after all?" I said.

"You called his widow?" Rich shouted. I held the phone away

from my ear. "What did I tell you? Leave this alone."

"She's in hiding, Rich."

"So?"

"So why would she hide herself and her kids away if she were convinced you put the right man behind bars?"

"She's a cop's wife," he said. "She trusts us. We have the right man."

"It's not a unanimous opinion," I said.

"You don't get a vote! This isn't a democracy. The Bennett asshole is a good suspect, and we got him."

"If only it were so simple."

"It is."

"I'm going to keep looking," I said.

Rich let out a long, slow breath. "Leave this alone, C.T.," he said. "You're messing around where you don't belong."

"What if you have the wrong man?" I said.

"We don't."

"You won't even consider the possibility."

"I'm considering arresting you for harassing a grieving widow," said Rich.

"Oh, come on," I said. "If no one is worried about her, why are people looking out for her?"

"Because she's a cop's widow! You're never going to understand this."

"I understand you may not have the right man in custody."

"Last warning," he said. "Leave it alone. You're not winning any friends with this one."

"What did Jules Winnfield say about the path of the righteous man?" I said.

Rich hung up on me. I guess it was going around. Or maybe he simply wasn't a fan of *Pulp Fiction*.

* * *

I took a break from digging into Jack Bennett's and Ben Harrison's lives to get some badly-needed groceries. Whenever I worked a case, my grocery buying lapsed, and I ended up with a refrigerator to shame a poor college student. I crammed the trunk of the Audi full with bags from Harris Teeter and was headed home when blue and red lights appeared in my rearview mirror. I reined in my speeding when this case grew ugly. The flashing lights drew closer and the cop flashed his high beams at me. I coasted to the side of Key Highway, put my window down, and turned off the ignition.

I watched in my mirror as the car door opened behind me. A tall officer began his slow walk to my vehicle. I noticed him checking out the rear of the Audi. Suspicion gnawed at me, and I picked up my cell phone from the passenger's seat and tucked it under my leg. The officer stopped at my window. He flicked his flashlight on and shined it in my face. I squinted and turned away. I couldn't even get a good look at his nametag. All I could tell of him was his height and medium brown complexion.

"Did you know your taillight is out?" he said.

"It's not," I said.

"I think it is. Maybe I should look again." He started toward the back of the Audi. I grabbed my phone from under my leg and fired up the camera. The cop reached the back of my car and bent down to look at the taillight. He put his hand on it, then took his nightstick from his belt. I snapped a picture of him reflected in the mirror. He brought the baton back and took a good swing at the taillight. I snapped a series of pictures in rapid succession, then winced at the sound of my taillight shattering under the force of his blow. I tucked my phone away again as he walked back up to my window.

"Your taillight is out," he said. He shined the flashlight in my face again.

"I wonder how it happened," I said.

"I'm going to have to give you a ticket. And you'll need to get it fixed soon."

"Of course."

He took out a ticket book, and to do it made him lower the oppressive flashlight. I saw his nametag now: Rodgers. Rodgers gave me a fake smile as he wrote on his book, flipped the page to write another, then wrote a third. "Here's a ticket for your taillight," he said. "There's also a work order to get it fixed and another citation for speeding."

"I wasn't speeding," I said.

Rodgers glared at me. "I clocked you going forty-five."

"Then your clock is broken."

"Tell it to the judge," he said through clenched teeth. "And while you're at it, leave the Bennett case alone. It can get a lot uglier than this."

"It's already pretty ugly," I said.

"You want to step out of the car?"

"I don't think you want me to."

"No?" Rodgers patted his nightstick.

"No." I fixed him with the best thousand-yard stare I had. "You don't."

He glared back at me for a few seconds, then smirked. "Just get on your way," he said, "and leave the Harrisons alone."

I fired up the Audi and pulled away before Rodgers got back to his car. My house was a few short minutes away. I made it home without any further incidents.

* * *

THE NEXT MORNING, I left Gloria in bed, postponed breakfast, and drove the Caprice to BPD headquarters. I parked a couple blocks away and walked into the building. Inside, I took the elevator to the upper floors. When I got off the elevator, I marched straight down the hallway to Captain Leon Sharpe's office. His secretary fixed me with a neutral expression as I approached her desk.

"Good morning, Karen," I said.

"Good morning," she said, frost dripping from her lips.

"*Et tu*, Karen?"

"I don't know what you're talking about."

I saw Sharpe through his large window. "I'm here to see the captain."

"He's not in."

"I just saw him in there," I said.

"He doesn't want to see you," she said.

"I'll take my chances." I walked past her desk, pushed Sharpe's door open, and walked into his office. He looked up at me, then back down to the mound of paperwork on his desk. It left me staring at his bald black head. "Good morning, Leon."

Sharpe kept his attention on his documents. Even seated, he possessed size and presence. "Oh, good morning, C.T.," I said in my best Leon Sharpe voice. "It's good to see the assholes who work under me haven't scared you off the Harrison case. We need someone as smart and handsome as you to figure out the truth."

"Handsome has nothing to do with truth," Sharpe said.

"It does when you look this good," I said.

"What do you want?" I tossed my two tickets and work order onto the top of Sharpe's pile. "We don't fix tickets," he said.

"I'm not paying those," I said.

"You should tell it to a judge."

"I'm not paying them because one of your cops smashed my taillight with his nightstick, then wrote me a ticket for it."

Sharpe frowned as he looked at the tickets I'd dropped onto his desk. "Do you have any proof of your allegation?"

I tossed three high-quality prints of Officer Rodgers vandalizing my Audi onto the pile. "Taken with my phone last night," I said.

Sharpe looked at the pictures. "Which car was this?"

"The Audi," I said.

"If you can afford an Audi, you can afford a taillight for it," Sharpe said, putting my papers toward the back of his desk.

"So it's OK for the police to harass people and vandalize their property so long as the victims are rich enough to pay for it?"

"Not what I meant."

"Sure sounds an awful lot like what you meant," I said.

"You must have misheard me." Sharpe shook his head.

"I guess Freddie Gray and the federal smackdown weren't enough. Now a captain in the BPD is endorsing the harassment of people who have money if they support positions the department doesn't like."

Sharpe looked up at me with narrowed eyes. "You're pushing it now," he said.

"Because I'm wrong about what happened a couple years ago?" I said.

"Past administrations!"

"Of which you were a part."

"I'm done listening to you, C.T.," Sharpe said. "You're out of line here."

"Was I out of line the second I started thinking Jack Bennett didn't kill Ben Harrison?" Sharpe ignored me, focusing on his work. "Or did I only get out of line when I didn't knuckle under to your people's harassment?"

"Karen," Sharpe said, activating the intercom on his desk, "send an officer to show Mr. Ferguson to the exit."

"I got here by myself," I said. "No need for an escort to the street." I walked up to Sharpe's desk and stared at him. "I expected better of you, Leon." He lowered his eyes.

I stormed from his office.

CHAPTER 10

No sooner did I get home from my *TÊTE-À-TÊTE* with Leon Sharpe than my mother called. The morning kept getting better. Maybe I would discover Gloria ignited the kitchen while trying to make herself toast. I answered the phone as I let myself in the front door. "Hi, Mom." I noticed my kitchen had not become a charred wasteland. One for the win column.

"Coningsby, I hoped you'd be awake," she said in her frequent I-expect-you-clean-your-room tone.

"I've been awake for a while, Mom," I said.

"That's very good, dear."

"I supposed you called for more than an update on my sleeping patterns?"

"Of course," she said. "I wanted to remind you of our charity dinner tonight because I know you've forgotten."

I cursed under my breath. "Forget?" I said. "Not me. I'm all over it."

"Where is the dinner, then?"

Now she stumped me. "The Walters?"

"No, dear," she said, "we rented Tio Pepe for the evening."

It sounded much less snobby than the Walters. "Oh, right. Yes, I'll be there."

"I presume you mean you and Gloria will be there. You did buy two tickets."

"Yes," I said, thankful my mother remembered all these things for me.

"Good. You can introduce your father and me to Richard's girlfriend, too."

"Rich is coming?"

"With his girlfriend, yes," my mother said.

"Then maybe he can introduce you to her."

"Coningsby, are you and Richard having problems?"

"No more than usual," I said.

She paused. I pictured her expression: pursed lips and a curious frown. I saw it plenty of times over the years. "Well, I certainly hope you two will be on your best behavior tonight."

"We'll be fine." I hoped.

"I know you will. We'll see you at seven. Try not to be late for a change."

"No promises," I said. "Bye, Mom."

"Goodbye, dear."

As I hung up, I heard Gloria coming down the stairs. I watched her long, shapely legs, barely covered by her shorts, as she walked up to me and planted a big, minty kiss on my lips. "I didn't even hear you leave," she said.

"I tried to be quiet," I said.

"What did your mother want?"

"She was reminding me about the charity dinner tonight."

"You'd forgotten?" Gloria said with a frown.

"Of course not."

"I hope not. I have to pick up my gown around lunchtime."

"I'm sure you'll look amazing in it."

She gave me another kiss. "That's the plan."

"And I'm sure the gown will look even better crumpled up on my bedroom floor," I said.

Gloria grinned and poked me in the ribs. "No crumpling. You can ravish me all you want when we get home, but don't mess up the gown."

I smiled. "Deal." Gloria walked into the kitchen. I watched her progress with some interest. Then I realized she said "get home" instead of "get back" a moment ago. I'd been thinking about her side of the bed and similar musings. Maybe our relationship was changing.

We just needed to be ready for it.

* * *

I MADE bison burgers and spinach salads for lunch. When nearly half my lunch was finished, Liz Fleming called. "Your timing could be better," I said.

"About to have a nooner?" she said in a randy voice.

"Maybe, but I'm in the middle of lunch right now."

"Jack Bennett is being moved to maximum security before his trial."

"Didn't we think it was likely?" I said.

"Unfortunately," she said.

"Is it normal in cases like this?"

"Not really. It happens sometimes. Because Bennett has priors, I think he's getting railroaded by a judge who likes the police."

"Don't most judges like the police?"

"There are a few who don't."

"So what does Bennett's pending move mean for the case?" I said.

"It means it'll be harder to talk to him when he's in Supermax," said Liz.

"And you think he has valuable insights to add?"

"You never know until you ask."

"I'm pretty sure I know right now," I said, "but if you want me to go with you for the asking, I will."

"Can you meet me down here in twenty minutes?" she said.

"I will."

I hung up and went back to my lunch. Bison burgers are far too good to put on hold for prisoners who have nothing useful to say. If we were crunched for time, I would have taken the burger with me. "You have to head out?" Gloria said.

"In a few minutes," I said. "I hope it won't take too long."

"Did you remember to dry-clean your tux?"

I gave her a shifty look. "Let's go with yes."

Gloria grinned and shook her head. "Your mother will notice," she said.

"I have more than one tux."

"She'll still notice."

She would, and she would comment on it like the lady of the manor upbraiding the peasant for having dirty shoes. "Can you take one to the cleaners and ask them to rush it?" I said.

"They charge a lot extra for that," Gloria said.

I wolfed down the last of my burger. "Good thing we both have money, then."

* * *

TWENTY-FOUR MINUTES AFTER OUR CONVERSATION, I met Liz Fleming at Central Booking. She wore a white blouse under a sharp blue blazer paired with a matching blue skirt capable of captivating inmates and private investigators alike. I took a careful inventory of every inch of her legs as she talked to a burly guard who jangled a keyring in his hand. Liz turned and smiled when she saw me. "You're almost on time," she said.

I declined to take the bait. The guard led us into the room, then closed and locked the door behind us. No one made any decrees about how many minutes we would get this time. Liz showed them the pointlessness of arbitrary limitations on our last visit. Jack Bennett sat slumped in a chair like a kid in detention waiting for the teacher to show up. He looked at us briefly when we entered, then went back to an intense study of the floor tiles.

Liz sat opposite Jack at the table and I took the chair to her right. If he noticed her short skirt and luscious legs, he didn't give any indication. "I guess you've heard what's happening by now, Jack," said Liz. He simply nodded. "You know Supermax is a rough place. It's where real hardened criminals go."

"Then why am I going there?" Jack said, voice small like a child dreading going to the dentist.

"You're an accused cop killer with priors."

"Can you keep me out of there?"

"I've filed a pretrial motion with the judge," Liz said. "We'll see what happens with it, but I wouldn't get your hopes up. The judge likes cops."

Jack shook his head. "I didn't kill any cop."

"Knowing it and proving it are two different things," I said, "and we're having a problem with the latter."

"Can I help?"

"It would be a nice change."

"We need to know it all, Jack," said Liz. "Everything that happened. Everything you think happened. Some nugget somewhere might be useful."

Jack looked at us and sighed. "I don't know what else I can tell you. It went down just like I said it did."

"A stranger came up and shot Ben Harrison," I said. "Then he dropped the gun, got in a silver car, and drove off. You picked up the gun, fired at the car, saw Ben was dead, and fled. I miss anything?"

"Yeah, it's exactly the way it happened," he said. "You have any luck finding the shooter?"

I laughed. "We don't know the first thing about him," I said. "You didn't give much of a description. The one man who might be able to describe him is dead."

"We don't have much to work with here, Jack," Liz added.

"I know . . . I know." Jack lowered his eyes again. When he looked back up, they were wet. "I didn't do it," he said. "You gotta believe me."

"What I have to do is be able to get to reasonable doubt in court," Liz said.

"I've done some looking into you and Ben Harrison," I said. "So far, I haven't found a suspect or a motive."

"Someone has to know the guy," Jack said. "Did you talk to the neighbors?"

"A couple of them."

"I think one is a gang member, or maybe he was as a kid. He lives two or three houses to the right of Ben. Maybe he was involved."

"I'll see what I can find," I said, leaving his straw-grasping alone.

"Anything else you can give us?" Liz said.

A few tears slid down Jack's cheeks. The grave reality of his situation finally hit him, and all it took was a shovel to the head. "You gotta help me," he said. "I don't want to die in prison."

"You're not going to, Jack." Liz's voice lacked its usual power when she spoke. It sounded a little more soothing but a lot more uncertain. I wouldn't have believed it. I don't know if Jack did, but it seemed to mollify him.

"I know you got my back," he said.

"We both do," said Liz. I stayed quiet.

"I don't know anything else I can tell you, though."

"Nothing?" I said. "Nothing you remember about the shooter? Anything he said, a certain way he moved?"

"I don't think he said anything. He just walked in, shot Ben, and left."

"How did he walk?" I said. "Did he have a limp? A prosthetic leg?"

"No, nothing like it I can remember." Jack frowned in thought. "He walked faster on the way out."

"He'd just shot a cop."

"Not like he was scared. It's like he was more sure of the way out than the way in." Jack shrugged. "It's hard to describe."

I added it to my mental notes. If I ever found a suspect, how he walked into and out of strange garages would be a significant test. "Maybe it's something I can use," I said, summoning a few scraps of optimism.

"Really?" A small smile cracked Jack's face.

"All we have is hope," Liz said.

* * *

JACK BENNETT HAD GIVEN me one potential nugget of information, but I needed more and took advantage of a few hours to kill after I got home. My investigation into Ben Harrison bore little fruit thus far. I needed to unearth more on him. The BPD would have been a great resource if they weren't lining up to push me off a cliff for working this case. Julie Harrison didn't offer much. I could try her family. Earlier, I dismissed them because they probably wouldn't tell me anything. I took my chances now.

Her brother wouldn't talk to me and accentuated his point by suggesting I attempt a biologically impossible action. I tried her sister Ingrid next. To my surprise, she didn't hang up on me right away. "I'm concerned about your sister," I said after we exchanged introductions.

"So am I," she said, "but she has the best protectors in the world right now."

"The thing is I'm not convinced the man in custody is the

man who killed your brother-in-law."

"The police think he is."

"He's a convenient suspect," I said. "It doesn't make him the right one."

"What if he didn't do it?" she said.

"Ingrid, it means the killer is still out there. I was able to talk to Julie. I'm talking to you now. Anyone who really has it in for her will be able to find her."

"What are you saying?"

"I'm saying if the right man is in jail, Julie doesn't need to be hiding. If the wrong man is in jail, being in hiding may not be enough."

"You're worrying me, Mr. Ferguson," she said, and I heard the shakiness in her voice.

"I'm trying to," I said. "I couldn't seem to get through to your sister. Maybe you can."

"I'll talk to her. Are you working with the police on this?"

"The Public Defenders' Office. Let's say I'm not winning friends and influencing people within the BPD."

"OK, if the wrong man is in jail, I hope you find the right one. Anything to keep my sister and her kids safe. Ben was her world." Ingrid's voice cracked. "She's being strong for the kids, but I know it's tough on her."

"How did you get along with Ben?" I said.

"Fine," Ingrid said. "I didn't see him all that often, but when I did, we got along well. He was a good man, very devoted to his family."

"It's what everyone says about him."

"I guess it must be true, then."

"It doesn't help me figure out why someone wanted to kill him."

"I can't help you there, Mr. Ferguson," she said.

"Join the club," I said.

CHAPTER 11

After hanging up with Ingrid Dickinson, I reviewed what I knew. I didn't know much, so the process didn't take long. Questions still outnumbered facts. I didn't have a case file, though I did have a lot of Ben Harrison's personal ones. Then I remembered his personnel file, swiped from the BPD network before they could pull it down. I scanned it for career details and possible enemies. Now I reviewed it for family members and people who might be willing to talk to me and uncovered a brother named Ronald.

My unexpected good fortune continued as he agreed to meet me at the Fells Point Square in a half-hour. When I got there thirty-two minutes later, I saw the area mostly empty. It was almost 3:45. Fells Point would fill up with happy hour revelers soon. A few people meandered about the square, cutting across it to bars on the other side. One man sat on a bench near the lemonade and pretzel stand, and I approached him. "Ronald Harrison?" I said.

"I could go for a lemonade and a pretzel," he said.

As I got closer to the stand, the smell of fresh dough reminded me that lunch was a few long hours ago. A pretzel called to me, but I ignored it. I returned to the bench a couple minutes later, armed with a lemonade for each of us and a hot pretzel for Ronald. He looked at the specks of salt covering the pretzel, frowned, and took it anyway. "You're the private investigator," he said.

"I am," I said. "Thanks for meeting me."

Ronald broke off a piece of his snack. A cool breeze whipped from the harbor at Thames Street. I zipped my windbreaker a little higher. Coffee would have been a better choice than lemonade. "You think the man who killed my brother is still out there?"

"I think the possibility needs to be considered."

"It should." Ronald ate some of the pretzel and nodded. "Ben's friends are keeping me updated. They tell me the killer is in custody. He's going to some top security jail today, in fact." I nodded with him. "Doesn't that mean he's likely the killer?" he said.

"He's not a bad suspect, but the evidence against him is circumstantial. I think his story of what happened is credible."

"What's his story?"

I relayed what Jack Bennett told Liz and me. Ronald listened, eating bits of his pretzel and drinking tiny amounts of lemonade as I talked. Each sip would have left room to spare in a thimble. "The police have basically dismissed his story," I said in conclusion. "They have their version and they're not straying from it."

"I doubt they will," he said. "Ben was a good cop. His friends think they have the killer in custody already."

"I was hoping you could tell me something about Ben."

He ate another small piece of the pretzel and drank enough lemonade to quench a tadpole's thirst. "What would you like to know?"

"Any information to lead me to who killed him or why someone would want him dead."

"He was a damn good cop," Ronald said.

"It's exactly what I hear," I said. "The problem is he arrested a lot of people. Even if only a quarter of them are the revenge-seeking type, finding a killer from the pool will take forever. Jack Bennett will be convicted by then."

"So you want dirt on my brother?" Ronald finished a bite and looked at me through narrowed gray eyes.

"Not dirt," I said. "Not even dust. I just want to know if anyone hated him for the very reason he was such a good cop."

Ronald studied me as he took micro-sips of his lemonade. The cool wind shifted and swirled around the square. More people milled about as happy hours kicked off. The aroma of freshly-baked pies wafted from Brick Oven Pizzeria. If I listened hard enough, I could almost hear burgers sizzle at The Abbey. My parents' charity dinner and its free swanky food felt days away. "I think you believe in what you're doing," he said after a moment. I bit down on a snotty reply and he continued. "I wish I could give you something solid."

"At this point, I'll take something amorphous."

He gave a faint chuckle before continuing. "Ben was convinced people were running drugs in his community," Ronald said. "He said he was looking into it in his spare time."

"Do you know what he found?" I said.

"He never said. I only know he would stick with it. If there were drug dealers in the area and they learned Ben was onto them, they might have tried to do something about it."

Ben Harrison's death didn't strike me as an organized hit. A professional killer wouldn't ignore Jack Bennett at the scene. Still, Ronald gave me something. "It's an avenue I can go down," I said.

"Good luck," he said.

Such fortune would be a nice change.

* * *

I GOT HOME and changed for a four-mile run. Traffic grew heavier, and I was glad of only a short trek to and from Federal Hill Park. I got home, stretched, then showered. By the time I emerged and toweled off, Gloria returned with my tuxedo and was putting her gown on. I didn't try to conceal my leering.

"You like watching me get dressed?" she said with a smile.

"I admit I prefer watching you get undressed," I said, "but this isn't bad."

"OK, but you'll have to wait until after this charity dinner." She gave me a lascivious wink.

I looked at my watch. "If only there were more time before the dinner."

"If only. I need some bathroom time for my hair, if you're finished."

I cleared out and let Gloria have free reign. My second bathroom would have burst at the strain of trying to hold her salon-sized load of hair products. Never did I see so many bottles, jars, and random containers as when Gloria and I played dress-up and went somewhere. Her house featured bathrooms big enough to play Wiffle Ball in. I didn't have such luxuries. Until she hauled her personal salon back home, I would be stepping around bottles and almost knocking them over every time I moved.

I put on a white dress shirt and added my favorite pair of cuff-links. The dry cleaner did a nice rush job on my tuxedo. It still felt warm to the touch and the creases in the pants were immaculate. About fifteen minutes later, I was dressed, deodorized, cologned, and ready to walk out the door. Gloria, of course, was still in the latrine. This would mark a rare occasion where tardiness wouldn't be my fault.

"Are you about ready?" I said.

Gloria answered a moment later by opening the door and walking out. I stopped and stared at her. She wore a flowing medium purple gown hemmed at mid-calf, with a neckline which would make her a popular high school teacher and a string of polished pearls around her neck. Black shoes with about a three-inch heel covered her feet, and the heels showed her strong and shapely calves—honed by frequent tennis practice—when she walked. Gloria held a silver clutch in her right hand, which matched the bracelet around her wrist. She kept her chestnut hair wavy and it spilled past her shoulders. It took me a few seconds of looking at her before I could say anything. "Absolutely stunning," I finally managed.

"Really?" Gloria said. She smiled as color came to her cheeks.

"Really. I think I'll have to fight off every other guy there to leave with you."

Gloria walked up to me and kissed me. "You look very nice, too."

"Thank you."

"Sorry I'm making us late."

I grinned. "I'm sorry we don't have a better reason to be late."

TÍO PEPE LOOKS like a small dive from the outside. It would be easy to glance at it, sneer, and keep walking. Once you strolled down the steps and into the dining room, however, the impression would do a quick 180. The vaulted Spanish-inspired ceilings, elegant chandeliers, and soft white tablecloths bespoke top-drawer ambiance and excellence in dining. Sounds of sizzling meat and smells wafting from the kitchen provided another reminder of how hungry I felt.

We made it only a few minutes late. My parents stood near the front door to greet arrivals. They rented the whole restaurant and at least a hundred people filled the place already. My father looked at his watch as Gloria and I sauntered down the steps. My mother regarded us as we approached. She wore a cream-colored gown, a ruby necklace, and long white gloves lending the look of a Victorian matron. My father donned a classic tuxedo with an obvious clip-on bowtie. Either my mother hadn't noticed, or she'd already fainted at the thought. I hated bowties, so I opted for a regular tie with a double Windsor knot. "Coningsby, you're actually close to prompt," said my mother. "Hello, Gloria, dear."

"Good evening, ma'am," Gloria said as she and mother did a quick near-embrace. Neither wanted to muss their gown. I watched amused as they almost hugged, realized how doing so might cause an unsightly wrinkle, held their awkward distance, then pulled back.

"Looks like a lot of people were early," I said.

"They just wanted to get their bids in on the art," my father said. I noticed easels strategically placed throughout the restaurant. Each held a painting on it and a placard below it.

"I just want to eat," I said.

"You two are at our table," my mother said. "Sit down whenever you like."

We walked slowly through the restaurant, arm in arm. Gloria smiled and exchanged polite hellos with people she knew from socialite circles. I recognized a few of my parents' friends, shook some hands, exchanged some pleasantries, then looked for our designated table. Rich and Jeanne were already there. He frowned when he saw me. My reaction was about the same.

"This might be an interesting evening," I said near Gloria's ear as we approached.

"Be nice," she said, keeping up a smile for everyone as we walked.

"I'll do my best. I might need some sangria, though."

At the circular table, my assigned seat was beside Rich's. I thought about taking Gloria's and making her sit in mine, but Rich and I bickering across her wouldn't be pleasant for anyone involved—least of all Gloria. I sucked it up, slid out Gloria's chair, pushed it in for her after she sat, then took my seat to Gloria's right and Rich's left. Jeanne and Rich shared a mushroom toast appetizer and a pitcher of sangria set between them.

"Hi, Rich . . . Jeanne," I said, adding a smile I hoped didn't look forced.

"Hello," they said as one, neither wearing an amicable expression of any sort.

"You remember Gloria." I leaned back and extended my hand toward her.

Rich only nodded. Jeanne said, "Hello, Gloria. It's nice to see you again."

I stifled a smirk. "You too," Gloria said.

Waiters dressed in off-the-rack tuxedos and over-starched white shirts patrolled the seating area. One in his forties came to us, filled our water glasses, and went over the specials. My parents made sure to offer a decent menu, which sat on cards in the center of the tables. It looked like a third of the regular Tio Pepe's menu. The selections didn't justify the $250 per plate we prepaid, but I'm sure their foundation would enjoy the considerable proceeds. As a contract employee of said foundation, I wondered if any would trickle down to me. Gloria and I decided to split shrimp in garlic sauce. The waiter complimented us on our appetizer choice and zoomed away.

I looked at Rich and Jeanne's pitcher of sangria. "Pour me a glass?"

Jeanne moved the pitcher of sangria closer to herself and away from me. Rich's neutral expression never changed. "I guess not," I said.

Neither of them said anything. I leaned closer to Gloria. "I'm trying," I said, keeping my voice low.

"It's a long night," she said. "Maybe alcohol will loosen them up."

"Here's hoping."

The waiter soon returned with our appetizer. We ordered a pitcher of sangria for ourselves. Gloria opted for veal medallions in red wine mushroom sauce, and I chose prime rib with garden vegetables. Shortly after he walked away, the waiter came back to drop off the pitcher and two red wine glasses. I poured a glass each for Gloria and me. Rich and Jeanne also filled their glasses. "A toast?" I said.

Rich picked up his glass. "To the spirit of charity," he said.

"Hear, hear," we all said in unison. Tio Pepe's sangria deserved its reputation. Bits of fruit floated in the red wine. Biting into a grape or slice of orange marinating for hours in red wine was a true joy of sangria. A middle-aged couple, friends of my parents I hadn't seen since before my Hong Kong excursion, sat at our table. We spent a few minutes catching up—they loved hearing my Hong Kong stories, during which Rich cleared his throat in a few strategic places—until our food came out. I didn't bother taking it up with Rich; I was determined to be nice tonight.

My parents joined us a few minutes later. Their allotment of greeting and glad-handing left little time for their dinners. Between sporadic bites, they each managed to eat about half their meals before they were required to go to the front and talk some more. My parents—my mother in particular—were great patrons of the arts and could say something about each piece being auctioned. One captured the soul of the artist. Another was a paean to simpler times. A certain artist cited Picasso as an inspiration, and so on. To my untrained eye, all the paintings looked like art projects hanging in the wall at a high school. The administration might not be proud, but they hung it anyway because a student made it. My mother sniffed delicately during a few of the introductions, and I could tell she didn't care for those pieces.

"It's great that your parents are putting this on," Gloria said as she finished her dinner. "Isn't the charity a women's shelter?"

I nodded. "House of Ruth," I said. "My mother has been a supporter for years."

"Is this the first *soirée* like this they've put on?"

"They've done them in the past but not on the scale of this one. Rich and I attend every year."

Rich took my invitation into the conversation and offered a small smile. "Glad to do my part for a good cause," he said. It sounded like something a politician would say if pressured to make a comment and his best speechwriter were incommunicado. At least he said something.

"And you two are getting along tonight," Gloria said. She smiled and I groaned. Rich and I didn't need a reminder of the wedge between us. We'd always been a distant sort of close, and the events of the Harrison case hadn't helped. "It's good to see. I like it when you're getting along."

Against my better judgment, I took the bait. "Me, too," I said.

Rich looked at both of us and sighed. "I'd sit across the room if they'd let me," he said.

I looked at the pitcher he and Jeanne had killed off and wondered if it was their first. "Is it you or the sangria talking?" I said.

"All me."

"The good news is no one's stopping you from changing seats. Some people have left. Go if you want to go."

Gloria put her hand on my arm. Jeanne and Rich both glared at me. "I wouldn't want to upset your mother," said Rich.

"Sure, you'll just upset Gloria and me instead," I said.

"You have it coming."

I took a deep breath and fought to retain my calm. Breathe in. Breathe out. "We agree to disagree."

"No, you have it coming," Jeanne said.

"Hiding behind your girlfriend now?" I said, fixing Rich with a faux grin.

"I don't need to hide behind anyone," he said.

"This is a nice event," I said. "Let's not ruin it with our bickering."

"I agree," Gloria said.

Rich leaned closer to me. I could see red trails in his eyes. His breath smelled of wine and fruit. "You've been told a few times to leave the Harrison case alone," he said. I stayed quiet and let him ramble. "You keep going anyway. You never could take advice. You always think you're right . . . always think you know more than everyone else."

"I usually do," I said.

"There you go again."

"You're not even willing to admit the possibility you have the wrong man in jail. Maybe you have the right guy. Good job if it's actually the case. But maybe you don't."

"We do." The high ceilings enabled Rich's voice to carry. Nearby diners looked at our table. My parents didn't notice anything yet, but I couldn't count on the oversight to continue for long.

"I'm not convinced," I said. "And no cold shoulders, drunken threats, or taillight breakings are going to dissuade me."

"You should be careful," said Rich. "Some people really don't like you right now. They might try to break more than your taillight."

"Wouldn't you find their jackbooted tactics grand?"

He shrugged. "You've been warned."

"Go to hell, Rich, and take your warnings with you."

"We could settle this right now," he said." Rich gave me a glare practiced on the miscreants of Baltimore. Not being a miscreant, I didn't cower.

"Listen to yourself," I said. "This is a charity event."

"It's time you listened," Rich said, emphasizing his point by jabbing me in the chest. I swatted his hand away after the second. He glared at me.

"I'm guessing this pitcher is your second?"

"What if it is?" He ended the last word with a hiss.

"Then it means you're drunk. At my parents' function."

Rich jabbed me in the shoulder. "Wouldn't need to drink if you'd leave well enough alone." He went to poke me again. I grabbed his finger.

"The more you move, the better the odds you break it," I said.

"Now who's ruining the evening?" Rich said.

"Still you."

"We could go outside," he said.

"Fine," I said, "if it means you'll stop acting like an ass in here."

I checked to make sure my parents were engaged with guests, then ducked through the kitchen toward the back door. Rich followed. I answered any questioning glances by gesturing we were going to smoke. I pushed the rear door open and stepped into the alley behind Tio Pepe. A blue Dumpster sat against the wall to the left past the restaurant. A broken wood pallet, a couple trash bags, and general detritus lay scattered near the huge bin. Rich shoved me in the back. I staggered forward, got my feet under me, and swung around.

"Take some deep breaths, Rich," I said. "We're away from everyone else now. There's no need to keep carrying on."

"What if there is?" He balled his hands into fists.

I turned, presenting my side to him, and assumed a defensive stance. "Who went to Garrett County with you? You didn't take another cop. You took me. We got justice for your friend."

"So what?"

"This is my parents' charity event. Your aunt and uncle. They've been damn good to you over the years. What would they say if they saw the way you're carrying on now?"

Rich stared at me. His glower softened, and he nodded slowly. "Good," I said, moving closer to him. "Now let's go back inside and try to be civil to each other for another hour or so."

Instead of saying anything, Rich shoved me with one hand. I returned the favor. Then he grabbed my wrist. It wasn't an expert move, but Rich possessed a grip like a vise. I struggled for a painful moment before freeing myself.

When he tried again, I seized his arm in return. He fought against me. "Can we rejoin everyone now?" I said.

"Let go of me," Rich growled. He struggled against my grip some more, then I released him. He took a step to the rear, crossed his feet, and fell right on his ass. Before he could do anything else, my father burst through the back door, followed by my mother, then Gloria.

"What the hell are you doing?" my father said, looking at both of us.

"Richard!" my mother said.

"You think I started it?" Rich said.

"You did," I said.

"This is a charity dinner," my father said through clenched teeth. "I don't give a damn what you two are fighting about, but you're going to put it behind you, go inside, and smile to everyone who comes near you. Do you understand?"

"Yes, Dad." I held my hand out to help Rich to his feet. He slapped it away and stood on his own. I fought the urge to kick him back down.

"Richard, I know C.T. is working on something you don't like," my father said. "Forget about it, if just for tonight. And for God's sake, grow up, both of you. You're not teenagers."

"Fighting in an alley. Really!" my mother said. She looked around and a fierce bout of sniffing ensued. "You boys shake hands and put this behind you," my mother said. "I don't want any unpleasantness inside."

I held out my hand. Rich looked at me. "Cops like Ben Harrison are my brothers," he said. "You're just my cousin." He spun on his heel, stormed between my parents, and went back inside.

I let my hand fall back to my side.

CHAPTER 12

Back at home, Gloria and I both changed out of our fancy clothes and into our sleepwear. As Gloria knelt on the bed and leaned over me to examine the bruises on my wrist, I enjoyed the fantastic view down the front of her nightgown.

"He must've grabbed you pretty hard," she said.

"It'll be fine," I said. "I've dealt with a lot worse."

"It doesn't look bad."

"Take your time checking it out."

Gloria looked at me, saw where my eyes were focused, and grinned. "You're incorrigible." She let go of my arm and kissed me.

"All part of my charm."

"I'm sorry about Rich." Gloria lay beside me and rested her head on my shoulder. Some of her hair spilled over my chest and midsection. "He's not normally like that."

"No, he's not," I said. "I think it was a combination of the tension between us from this case and too much sangria."

"Where does this leave you two?"

I shook my head. "I'm not sure. We've had our differences before, but they've never . . . exploded like this. This is uncharted territory."

"And you just helped him with that case in Garrett County."

"He seems to have a short memory on this one. Rich somehow doesn't see we're on the same side. We both want the truth. He thinks it's already been found and won't accept any other opinion."

"I'm sure you'll patch this rift."

"I guess we'll see," I said. My voice didn't sound optimistic.

"Do you need some cheering up?" Gloria said. She traced kisses over my neck.

"Now that you mention it," I said.

She pushed herself onto all fours and slinked her way atop me. "Let's see what we can do about that," she breathed.

* * *

THE DRUG ANGLE gnawed at me the next morning. Gloria and I enjoyed a pleasant enough breakfast, after which she left to run a few errands and take a tennis lesson. True to Baltimore form, the high for today was supposed to be 20 degrees above yesterday's, and then it would dive back down again in two more days.

Ben Harrison was a veteran cop and a good one by all accounts. If he thought someone operated a drug business in the neighborhood, he must have harbored adequate reasons for thinking so. Maybe gathering evidence and running his own investigation got him killed. It was a theory, and even better, it bore plausibility. I needed to know if there was, in fact, a drug operation in the area for Ben Harrison to be investigating.

Detective Paul King worked in the BPD's vice unit. He and I collaborated a few times before. I hoped he would take my call. "What the fuck do you want?" he said as he picked up.

"I wondered if you'd answer," I said.

"Mystery solved. Anything else?"

"I know I'm unpopular right now, but I'm after the truth. I

think there's a good chance Jack Bennett didn't kill Ben Harrison."

"You have any proof?" he said.

"Working on it."

King sighed. "And I guess you have a theory you want to run by me."

"I do," I said.

He fell silent. Helping me must have gone against everything he learned during his years on the force. Finally, he said, "All right, go ahead."

"Harrison's brother said Ben became wise to some drug activity in the neighborhood, and he might have been looking into it."

"That's your theory?"

"Drug dealers tend to disapprove of police investigations."

"No shit." I heard King exhale into the receiver. "His brother didn't think Ben would have simply reported it?"

"Maybe he didn't have enough to go on yet," I said. "It's a possibility at this point, but I think you have to admit it has some legs."

"If someone in Ben's neighborhood was dealing," King said. "Today's my day off."

"It might help the case," I said.

King fell silent again. I knew I was putting him in a dreadful position, but I didn't see much alternative. Investigating a possible drug angle from scratch by myself would take way too long. "Look," he said, "I can't be seen in public with you. You're a pariah."

"If you want to meet me somewhere, we can go into the county."

"A little farther out. You know where Chiaparelli's is?"

"In Little Italy," I said.

"Not that one," King groused. "There's another one in Havre de Grace, up in Harford County."

"I'll find it. Same menu?"

"Same food, half the crowd. I don't know how they stay open."

"I'll meet you there. What time?"

"Give me until two," King said.

"You got it."

King hung up. I did the same. At least he was working with me. If all his digging turned up nothing for drug activity, however, I would have to take a couple steps back. Considering my confrontation with Rich last night, I wanted this case over as soon as possible. Popularity was never my goal, but I also never wanted to be a pariah and I definitely never wanted to get into an alley shoving match with my cousin.

I hoped Paul King could bring a mountain of evidence to lunch.

* * *

I PARKED on a dinky side street after circling the nearby roads to make sure no one followed me and walked about a block to Chiaparelli's. The dark wood motif screamed this once was another restaurant, maybe multiple other restaurants. It possessed none of the atmosphere of the "real" Chiaparelli's in Little Italy and also little of the crowd. I spied King sitting at an isolated table against the far wall.

"This doesn't feel like an Italian restaurant," I said as I took the chair opposite him.

"Used to be a steakhouse," said King. "Pretty fucking good steaks, too."

The wallpaper sported patches of faux brick painted in as part of its design. It was on the cheeky side but didn't do anything for the ambiance. I hoped the food—and information from King—would redeem my trip. The menu resembled the one to which I'd grown accustomed. A pretty waitress dropped off an order of fried calamari and asked me what I would like. I requested an unsweetened tea and eggplant parmesan. King ordered veal parmesan. I noticed King watched the waitress walk away. Getting to a restaurant early and picking the good seat had its advantages.

"Have some calamari," King said. "You're paying for it."

"I hope it's good, then." I took a medium-sized piece, dipped it in the warm marinara sauce, and ate it. The batter's distinctive spice reminded me of calamari I'd enjoyed at the Little Italy restaurant.

King grabbed a chunk and ate it sans marinara. "It's good," he said.

"I may have to fight you for it."

"You don't need any more enemies in the BPD right now."

I winced. We paused while the waitress returned with our drinks. King gave her a big smile she ignored. "I guess she's not into shaggy-haired guys with questionable shaving habits," I said.

"Her loss," said King.

"I'm sure she's going back into the kitchen to weep right now."

King chuckled and popped another piece of squid into his mouth. "It's a shame I'm supposed to hate you. I actually kind of like you."

"What an unqualified endorsement."

"Don't get me wrong," he said. "You're an asshole but just the kind of asshole I can work with."

"As long as you won't be tarred and feathered for it," I said.

"The reason we're way out here."

I nodded to a file folder King placed on an empty seat. "I presume you found something?"

"Not a lot, really." He set the folder atop the table. "A few rumors here and there, nothing we could substantiate."

"Did anyone look into the rumors?"

"Some."

"Some?" I said.

"Look," King said, "we got bigger fish to fry. If some guy wants to grow a pot plant or two and light up with his old lady on the weekend, I don't give a shit. We're after the big ones, the ones who are distributing, the ones shooting people."

"So it's possible someone could have a drug business going in Ben Harrison's neighborhood."

"If they do, it's small. Not something we'd take the SWAT team and tear apart."

"Would Harrison have concerned himself with it?" I grabbed the file, opened it, and flipped through pages. King's summary was right: there wasn't a lot to be found.

"I don't know," said King. "Ben wasn't a real hard ass. He was a cop, but I don't think he cared if someone smoked weed in their own home."

"His brother mentioned it to me," I said. "I presume Ben mentioned it to him."

The waitress emerged from the kitchen, carrying our dueling parmesan dishes on a large round tray. She set them before us, asked if we would like fresh-grated parmesan—I accepted; King, like a philistine, declined—then walked away again. The conversation paused as we cut up and ate some of our lunches. After getting our drinks freshened, King put his fork down and pointed toward the file. "I don't know what Ben told his brother," he said. "Maybe his brother heard wrong. Maybe he's searching for a deeper meaning with Ben dead."

"Or maybe someone's running drugs," I said.

"Right now, we ain't got the resources to look into it. If a neighbor is, they're small-time. When they show up on our radar, we'll go after them."

"I'm on my own with the drug angle, then."

"Yep."

I nodded. "Seems appropriate with this case," I said.

"I guess it is," King said. "Look, if you find something, I can get you some help. I ain't holding out on you because everyone hates you right now."

"Comforting to know . . . I think."

King finished his last few bites of lunch. "I gotta run. If you find something we can use, let me know. I'll call it an anonymous tip."

"No, I want them to know it's coming from me."

He shrugged. "Whatever," he said. "Thanks for lunch."

"Yeah," I said.

King got up, waved at the waitress, and left. I studied the last few bites of my eggplant parmesan, looked at the file folder, and wondered what the hell I got myself into by agreeing to work with Liz Fleming.

* * *

ON MY WAY BACK HOME, I made a stop. With the BPD hampering me by keeping the case file off the network, I could only interview people and hope they wouldn't stonewall me. I drove past the medical examiner's office, parked in a public garage three blocks away, and walked back. I didn't encounter anyone who hated me on the way.

Once inside, I went into the lab area to find Dr. Hunt, my inside man in the office. He didn't always like the arrangement, but I knew serious dirt about him, the kind to get him fired and force him to change careers. For a while, at least, he indulged me.

I found Dr. Hunt involved in paperwork. A cadaver lay on

the table. The fantastic ventilation system in the ME's office beat back the smells of death and chemicals. Dr. Hunt sat on a stool at a long desk when I walked in. He never smiled at me, but he didn't frown this time as he looked up from filling out forms. I would take it as warmth right now.

"No coffee?" he said.

"Impromptu trip," I said. "I didn't come prepared."

"You would have made a bad Boy Scout."

"There are a slew of reasons why I would have made a bad Boy Scout."

Hunt cracked a small smile. "You probably would've operated under a loose interpretation of scout's honor," he said.

"Yes," I said, "but I would have earned my don't-release-a-woman's-body-to-the-man-who-killed-her badge."

The reminder made Hunt roll his eyes. By now, I was used to it. "What do you need?" he said, returning to his paperwork.

"I'm looking into the Ben Harrison shooting."

"I thought the police closed it."

"They may have," I said. "The Public Defender's Office isn't convinced, though, and I'm working with them."

Hunt regarded me for a moment. "I'm sure it hasn't been a pleasant experience," he said.

"No, not really, and it's one I plan never to repeat."

"What do you want from me?"

"Are you familiar with the Harrison case?"

"I examined his body myself," I said.

I hoped I'd caught a break. "Anything stand out?" I said. "Anything unusual? Something the police overlooked?"

"No, nothing," he said.

So much for the break. "Can you tell me what your exam showed?"

"Not much you probably don't already know, I'm sure. He

got shot twice in the chest at close range . . . I'd say eight feet. Either shot could have killed him."

"So the gunman knew what he was doing?"

"Hard to miss so close," Hunt said. "But I don't think this guy was an amateur. Both bullets went into his heart."

I got the feeling Jack Bennett would struggle to hit a target from five feet with a shotgun. "Anything else?" I said.

"Yes. I guess this is interesting. I discovered shavings, like from a thin sheet of metal, in his hair and on his clothes."

"Consistent with the accused's story." Hunt shrugged at me. "He says the shooter fired a shot through the hood of the car Bennett was working on," I said.

"It would account for the metal shavings," Hunt said with an inscrutable frown.

A thought popped into my head. "You wouldn't be able to get me a copy of the police report, would you?" I gave Hunt a winning smile. It wasn't the high-wattage one I reserved for pretty girls, but it usually got the job done.

Hunt pursed his lips. "Everything we access and print is monitored," he said.

"I'm sure I can get you around those controls."

"I'm not comfortable with it," Hunt said, frowning. "I'm willing to help you out, maybe more than I probably should, but I have to draw some lines."

"And you're drawing one here," I said.

"I am. And threatening to tell someone what I did isn't going to make me erase it."

I needed Hunt to go along with my request, but I really couldn't blame him for refusing. He didn't need to become a pariah, too. "All right, Doctor," I said. "I didn't sign your guest-book because I don't want to leave a trail where I go. I'd appreciate it if you wouldn't tell anyone I was here."

"I don't see why I'd want to," he said.

* * *

I LEFT the ME's office not knowing any more than when I went in. If I wanted to see the case file, I would have to resort to more extraordinary means. I pondered the possibilities as I walked. I didn't make half a block—and accomplished little in the way of pondering—when I spied a member of the BPD hurrying in my direction. This was normal around the ME's office but still something I wanted to avoid. I clung to the hope he hadn't seen me when he scowled and stood right in my way.

"Here you are," he said.

I checked to my rear to make sure he really meant to deliver such a lame line to me. No other intended recipients queued up. "Here I am," I said. "Wherever you go, there you are." I looked at his nametag: Summers.

"What are you hassling the ME for?" he said. Summers still blocked my path. The sidewalk traffic was light enough so people moved around us easily.

"I wasn't hassling anyone."

"What'd you get in there?"

"The runaround," I said. "You guys don't have the monopoly on it anymore."

"I wonder if you have something under your jacket," he said. Summers put his hands on my chest. I pushed them away.

"Keep wondering."

He narrowed his eyes. "Are you refusing a lawful search?"

"If you want to conduct a lawful search, get a warrant," I said. "While you wait for it, you can use the time to read up on exactly what a lawful search is."

"You're an asshole," Summers said.

"Yeah. The guy who knows his rights is the asshole. Are we done here?"

"For now. You should stop working the Harrison case, though."

"Do I hear a threat?"

Summers shrugged and smiled. "Just a friendly piece of advice."

"I'll keep it in mind," I said.

"You do that."

CHAPTER 13

I MADE IT HOME WITHOUT FURTHER HARASSMENT. BEFORE agreeing to assist Liz Fleming, I figured this case would strain my already tenuous popularity with the BPD. The degree to which it stretched past all limits and snapped, I did not foresee. In hindsight, I should have. One of their own got gunned down, and they arrested a perfectly good suspect. Then I came onto the scene, the arrogant outsider, and threatened to throw a wrench into the wheels of justice. I could see no problem with those wheels grinding exceeding small, as the poem goes; I only wanted to make sure they did so correctly. We were on the same side. I clung to the hope I could make someone of consequence in the BPD realize this fact.

With Gloria out, I had the house to myself. I wanted the case file. It slipped through my fingers at the ME's office when Dr. Hunt got cold feet. At this point, I wondered how much it would help me. Jack Bennett fell into the BPD's lap like blood-soaked manna from Heaven. How much followup investigation did anyone do? I wanted to know.

I called Liz and managed to catch her in the office. "How's your investigation going, C.T.?" she said. "I know we haven't talked in a couple days."

"Regular reporting isn't my specialty," I said.

"So I've noticed. Maybe we could meet tomorrow morning in my office? I'll supply breakfast."

"A meal on the taxpayers' dime? How could I say no?"

"Do you have anything?" she said

"Between threats from the BPD, I've yet to get my hands on the case file," I said.

"They're threatening you?"

"A couple times. My taillight broken by a nightstick, and the department implied people of sufficient means could replace those things themselves."

"That's terrible. Is there anything I can do?"

"I think some level of harassment is unavoidable in a case like this."

"You let me know if it gets worse," Liz said. Her voice rose and gained intensity. "I know they're looking after their own, but they don't need to be harassing you to do it."

"I'll loop you in," I said, knowing I wouldn't. "In the meantime, can you get me the case file?"

"They'll be loath to share it, but we have a right to it. Are you going to your office today?"

"I can."

"Good. I'll have someone deliver a copy within an hour."

"You certainly get results."

"I can be aggressive in going after things."

The first time we worked together, I would have liked seeing if Liz's aggression extended outside the office. Now, I compared her to Gloria, and it didn't go well for the public defender. Instead of making a lascivious comment, I said, "I'll let you know if I get the file."

"Great," she said and hung up.

* * *

Fifteen minutes later, I lounged with my feet up on my desk at my office. I checked the voicemail—the landline came with my lease—heard no potential cases to interest me, and erased the messages. I got a lot of them. When word of a free detective service gets around, people with all manners of problems call. I get at least three missing pet calls a week and many more even stranger. The signal-to-noise ratio on my business line was in the toilet.

A half-hour later, the elevator dinged, and a uniformed BPD officer opened my door. Around my age, his physique suggested he peaked with high school football. Shaggy brown hair didn't do his policeman's hat any favors, though they weren't exactly stylish. He looked at me, tossed a bag onto my desk, and walked out. The bag hitting the desk didn't resound with the satisfying thud I expected. I opened it and saw what remained of many sheets of paper after being run through a cross-cut shredder. "This isn't what I was promised!" I said as the elevator dinged again. He shrugged, smiled, stepped inside, and the doors closed behind him.

I called Liz's office and the phone went to voicemail. I tried her cell and got the same result. This time, I left a message, explaining the condition of the report I received courtesy of the BPD. If need be, I could find a program to reconstruct it, but Liz could probably get a new one delivered faster.

A half-hour later, she called back and said her boss requested a new, non-shredded copy of the report be delivered to my office posthaste. Within another thirty minutes, the elevator dinged again, and a different officer stepped off. This second fellow was older, skinnier, and looked like he ran forty miles a week. He carried a nondescript manila folder. He threw the folder onto my desk and stood there as if waiting for me to thank him.

"At least this one looks intact," I said as I leafed through it.

"Always glad to be of service," the officer said. So much

sarcasm dripped from his words I needed to check the floor for a puddle.

"Thanks," I said.

He turned and left without saying anything.

I opened the report.

* * *

AFTER READING IT, I called Rich. It surprised me when he answered. "I heard you got the report," he said.

"Finally, yes," I said. "As your people intended, I wasted time going through the Public Defender's Office to get it."

"Find anything interesting?"

"Not really. I think I already knew most of what was in there. Not much detective work to show since you caught Jack Bennett."

"Did you expect us to keep looking into it?" he said. "We have our man. I keep telling you."

"And I keep telling you there's a good chance you don't have the right man," I said. "What's the harm in looking into other suspects?"

Rich sighed. "Do we really need to go over this again?"

"We're on the same side, Rich. We—"

"No, we're not," Rich said. "You're on your own side. You talk to a guy once, see puppy-dog eyes, and think he's not guilty. You think I don't know who the public defender on his case is?"

"What does that have to do with anything?" I said.

"Last time she batted her eyelashes, you ended up with the idiot blogger. You do these things for pretty girls."

"She asked me to check into the case for her. It's exactly what I'm doing." I refrained from pointing out the blogger, while solidly an idiot, turned out to be innocent. Rich wouldn't receive the reminder well.

"And her looks had no bearing on your decision?"

"They might have opened the door," I said. "But if I didn't believe in the case, I wouldn't still be working on it no matter how good the lawyer looks."

Rich didn't say anything for a moment. "You keep saying there's a chance our guy didn't do it," he said. "Get some proof he didn't. No one will listen to you without it. *I'm* not going to listen to you anymore without it."

"Can I get updates on what's going on with the case?" I said.

"What's going on is the man who killed Ben Harrison is in jail!" I pulled the phone away from my ear. When I put it back, Rich released a deep breath. "Look, I'm done talking to you about this case. Don't call me until you either give up or pull a horseshoe out of your ass."

My witty reply was all ready to go, but Rich hung up on me.

I hated it when he did.

* * *

I CLEARED ALL the accoutrements off my desk and covered it with Ben Harrison's personnel file and the police report on his murder. I banked on an overlooked clue hiding somewhere. Rich said I needed hard proof that Jack Bennett didn't kill Harrison. Poring over these documents surely held the answer. If it didn't, I would be back where I started, and Jack Bennett would be getting railroaded by a legal process eager to move on from him.

Nothing in either file mentioned Ben Harrison's belief in drug activity near his house. He wouldn't have mentioned it to his brother, and his brother wouldn't have told me unless he felt it significant. I couldn't talk to anyone in the BPD without getting stonewalled. However, if anyone Harrison worked with left the force or retired, the ex-officer might be willing to have a conversation. I combed through the personnel file for names of officers

Harrison trained or partnered with since he moved into his house eight years ago.

I came up with over twenty names. Harrison frequently served as a training officer. Despite the BPD's lack of cooperation, my PC still accessed their network as if it were one of their own. I took great care with my electronic fingerprints on this one. The BPD could be paying attention now I'd become *persona non grata*. I dug into HR records for the twenty-plus names I found. Almost all of them remained active. One retired last year, and another left on injury disability.

I tried calling both. I expected them to tow the thin blue line and stonewall me. To my surprise, they both agreed to meet me.

People wished me good luck enough during this damn case. Maybe some of it finally came my way.

CHAPTER 14

My stomach anticipated a dinner it would not soon receive. I met Tim Farmer at his home in Hamilton. He lived about four blocks from Rich. Traffic going through the city made me about ten minutes late. Taking the highway would have been fraught with even more delays. Rush hour traffic out of Baltimore backed up on I-95 from the tunnels all the way to White Marsh. I didn't need to sit in such a slow-moving minefield.

Tim Farmer let me into his house with no objection to my late arrival. His heavily-worn tan carpet meshed well with the white walls, which needed a fresh coat of paint. All his furniture looked like it fell off the back of a discount truck, complete with dings and dents. I saw no TV mounted on a wall, sitting on a stand, or anywhere. A powerful Dell XPS laptop sat closed on the coffee table.

"This is about Ben Harrison?" Farmer said. We each sat in shopworn recliners. Farmer must have retired fairly young; he didn't look much over fifty. Even a year out of the uniform, I still liked his odds to chase down the average ne'er-do-well.

"Yes," I said. "I'm working with the public defender to look into his murder."

"Independently of the police?"

"Yes," I said.

"Wow, you must be popular," he said.

"Let's say I'm not expecting many Christmas cards."

"No doubt."

"You worked with Ben for a while. I was hoping you could tell me something not in his personnel file and the police report."

"You got the police report?"

"Only via persistent pressure from the public defender."

"What are you hoping I can tell you?" he said.

"I don't think the BPD has the right man in jail," I said. "He's a convenient suspect, but I don't think he did it. I'm trying to figure out who did. To do it, I have to pull Ben Harrison's life apart."

"I worked with him. I was a cop. What makes you think I would help you?"

"Because you're not a cop anymore, and you agreed to talk to me." I paused while Farmer frowned and leaned back in his ugly red recliner. "If you liked him you should want to help me. I want to find who killed him."

"And you think you can?" he said.

"I have a pretty good track record," I said.

"I read up on you." Farmer pointed to his laptop. "I Googled you while you were on your way."

I fought the cringe I felt at the thought. "What did you find?" I said in what I hoped to be an innocuous tone.

"You get results," he said. "I like it."

"You'll help me?"

"If I can. What do you want to know?"

"I heard Ben Harrison found evidence of drug activity in his neighborhood. He mentioned it to at least one person close to him. Did he ever hint at it to you?"

Farmer took in and let out a deep breath, then another. "In a backhanded sort of way. Every now and then, we'd bust some low-level dealers or some guy growing his own pot. When we would, he'd talk about some asshole in his community he knew was doing the same thing."

"Did he ever name the asshole?"

"Not to me," Farmer said in a tone bordering on resentful.

"What about any proof he might have had?"

"Never said anything to me about it."

Now it was my turn to stew over a couple deep breaths. "So Ben Harrison was sure someone in his neighborhood was involved in drugs," I said.

"I think so, yes," he said.

"You were his partner for a few months. Why wouldn't he have gone into more detail with you?"

Farmer shook his head. "I don't know. Partners don't always share everything."

TV shows told me they did, but I believed Farmer. Why would Harrison mention the drug angle and then withhold any further information? "Was he happy?" I said after a moment of thought.

"As far as I know," he said. "Why?"

"Everyone says he was a cop's cop," I said. "He trained a lot of people and a lot of them became detectives. He never did. Maybe he thought he could collect evidence against a drug dealer in his neighborhood, make the bust, and get a new shield."

We were silent while Farmer pondered that possibility. "I don't know," he said. "The brass liked using Harrison to train."

"You said they liked using him." I shrugged. "Maybe he felt used."

"Maybe." Farmer lapsed into silence again. "If he was unhappy and wanted something more, he never said it to me."

"I wonder if he said it to anyone."

"Possibly his wife," Farmer suggested

I needed to talk to her again. "Maybe."

Farmer managed to nod without being sympathetic to my plight. Once a cop, I guess. "Good luck," he said.

"I'd love some," I said.

* * *

I LEFT Tim Farmer's house and drove to Kevin Gabrish's in Parkville. He was about my height, slightly heavier, and supported himself with a cane in his right hand. Brown hair contained streaks of gray, and his beard suggested he gave up on keeping it neat months ago.

The conversation went about the same as the prior one. Gabrish didn't know anything specific about the rumored drug activity in the Harrisons' neighborhood. He couldn't even offer me any half-decent speculation. The only nugget I got was the recent viewing at a local funeral home. Gabrish said everyone who knew Ben turned out.

I hoped this included potential enemies living nearby.

When I got home, I went right to work. Funeral homes have been big on protecting client information. They got a lot of it right. Someone like me could still gain access to the records, but they've done a good job of not being the low-hanging fruit. Their video systems, however, told a different story. Someone always forgot to secure a little piece of the puzzle.

I used a powerful search tool for Internet-connected devices to determine what cameras the Nash funeral home used. Determining the system controlling them and storing the video proved simple from there. One of the many things budding—and far more established—hackers can Google is default credentials. Companies buy solutions and don't bother to change the login which comes out of the box. I found the built-in username and password for Nash's setup and tried them.

Bingo.

Often, hacking works because people don't take the time to do basic things like change preloaded credentials. I hunted around the well-organized files until I came to the feed for the largest room in the funeral home. Despite its size, it strained to hold the many people who popped in to pay their respects to Ben Harrison.

I saw a few familiar faces. Rich. Paul King. Leon Sharpe. The police commissioner. Harrison's widow gracefully received all visitors. I flashed back to my sister's viewing thirteen years ago. Shaking hands while numb was the memory which stayed with me to this day. I took a deep breath and pushed the unpleasant recollection aside.

About halfway through the viewing, a man I'd never seen before entered. The camera showed him from the rear as he walked in. He moved like he was uncertain of the path. After avoiding someone on his right, the newcomer bumped into a person on his left. He exchanged a few quick words and a handshake with the family before walking back down the center aisle.

I paused the video. The stranger held his head down, which made his face difficult to see. Zooming didn't help. Despite what TV tells us, it rarely does. The man also kept his head cocked to the side like he was on constant alert for someone to approach from the left. I wondered if he was drunk as I resumed playback. His gait was steadier on the way out.

Jack Bennett's words played in my mind. *He walked faster on the way out.* I presumed anyone who opened fire on a police officer would move faster leaving the scene. Who was this guy? It could have been a coincidence. Maybe he was a few whiskeys into the day and needed to traverse the aisle once to get the lay of the land.

Or maybe not.

* * *

I MADE a couple of small flatbread pizzas when I got home. They quelled the rumbling in my stomach. I heard Gloria puttering around upstairs but stayed downstairs to call Julie Harrison. She picked up right at the point I expected the call to click over to voicemail.

"I recognize this number," she said.

"Mrs. Harrison, I have three very important questions," I said.

She was silent for a moment and when she came back on the line, she barely spoke above a whisper. "You're that private detective. Ferguson, right?"

"I am."

"I shouldn't be talking to you," she said.

"If we all avoided things we shouldn't do, we'd be a nation of boring skinny people."

A light chuckle fluttered into my ear. "I suppose that's true. Are you still working this case?"

"I still believe what I believed before," I said.

"I'm not sure you're right." She sighed. "But at this point, I'm not sure you're wrong, either. No one is telling me anything. It's like the whole thing is being hurried along and swept under the rug." Her voice cracked. "My husband deserves more than that."

"I agree. Did your husband mention anything about drug activity in the neighborhood?"

Julie Harrison cleared her throat and sniffed. Her voice no longer cracked when she spoke. "A few times, yes."

"Did he have anyone in mind?" I said.

"You think he got killed over drugs?" she said.

"People get killed over drugs every day, Mrs. Harrison."

"I guess they do. I asked Ben who was involved in drugs. He never came out and told me."

"Do you have a good idea?"

"I would guess the guy three doors to our right."

Hers was his second nomination. "Any particular reason?" I said.

"I noticed some late-night visitors," she said. "That doesn't make him a drug dealer, but I know people like Ben look for things like that. If that's who Ben suspected, I'm sure he had other reasons."

"All right. This might be something of an indelicate question, but I need to ask it anyway. Was your husband . . . happy at work?"

"As far as I know. Why?"

"I've talked to some people who implied that he got frustrated seeing people he trained promoted above him. They further implied he sat on his drug suspicions so he could bust someone and use it as proof he should be a detective."

Julie Harrison didn't answer right away. I figured she needed a few seconds to process it. The silence dragged on, and I became concerned. "Mrs. Harrison?" I said as the silence lingered.

"I'm here," she said. "Just need to avoid the people checking up on me."

"Did you hear my question?"

"Yes." She sighed. "Ben was happy as far as I know. Every job has politics. If those wore on him, he didn't tell me."

"You knew him better than anyone. Is it at least a plausible theory?"

"I suppose. If it helps you figure out who killed him, I'll really love it."

"So will I," I said. "One more thing. Do you remember anyone unusual coming to the viewing?"

"You were there?" she asked.

"No. Let's just say I have access to the video."

She fell silent for a second. "No. I think I knew everyone there. No one stands out."

Maybe the mystery man who walked like a drunk was a coincidence after all. "Thanks for your time, Mrs. Harrison. Stay safe."

"You, too, Mr. Ferguson," she said. "You, too."

While I appreciated her concern for my safety, she hung up before I could ask her anything about it.

* * *

A few minutes later, my cell phone rang. I didn't recognize the number—an occupational hazard in my line of work. "Hello?" I said.

"You're still on the case," said a mystery voice. It sounded distorted, like someone talked through a screen or sock. To the consternation of my inner Alex Trebek, the mystery caller did not phrase his statement in the form of a question.

"So I am. Who's this?"

"You've been warned to leave it alone."

"I'm stubborn."

"Last warning. Stay away from the case."

"Just so I'm clear, what case are we talking about?" I said.

"You know which one."

Of course I did, but I persisted. "Enlighten me anyway."

"No more chances," the mystery caller said. "Leave it alone."

"I'm afraid I can't."

A pause. "Then you leave us no choice."

"No choice but what?" I said, but the line was already dead.

I let out a slow breath and set my phone down atop the desk.

CHAPTER 15

Despite the threat from my secret admirer, I drove
the Caprice back to Ben Harrison's neighborhood. I wanted to
know more about the fellow three doors away and his possible
drug business. The area was quiet and lit by the moon and a few
flickering streetlights. I parked across from the neighbor's house
and jotted his address into a note on my phone. A police cruiser
sat in front of Harrison's house. I didn't see anyone in the black
and blue car—this hideous color scheme appeared shortly after I
left for Hong Kong—but I slumped in my seat anyway.

One by one, lights in upstairs windows winked out. I sipped
coffee long grown tepid, watching the potential drug dealer's residence for signs of possible drug activity. It was just as exciting as
it sounds. Occasionally I broke the monotony with a phone game
but I didn't play for long lest I missed something of importance.
Just after eleven, a car made a loop at the end of the cul-de-sac,
driving right past the BPD cruiser, and stopped in front of the
house in question. I couldn't see inside past the darkened
windows. A minute later, a Hispanic woman dressed to enter a
tight jeans competition got out of the car. The taut denim
injected some discomfort into her strides, but she made it to the
door, knocked, and got let inside by someone I couldn't see.

I waited a while for her to come out, but she didn't. If she and the male occupant were getting down to business, it probably took this long to pry her jeans off. At quarter to midnight, I gave up on her coming out and on this mini-stakeout in general. I fired up the Caprice and drove out of the neighborhood. The BPD cruiser sat dark and unoccupied in front of Ben Harrison's house. The light inside remained on.

* * *

THE DRUG ANGLE still bothered me. I sat in the office at my house, mulling a few notes. Ben Harrison knew someone in his community was involved in the drug business. The knowledge didn't seem to be in dispute. Depending on whose story I believed, this mystery person could have been a small-time user and maybe dealer, or he might have the cruise control set to go speeding down Tony Montana Way. Or there was the possibility no one in the Harrisons' neighborhood had any significant drug involvement.

This line of thought didn't get me anywhere. I'd found no dots to connect to anything. Ben Harrison had been shot for a reason. I wondered for the first time if Jack Bennett had been spared for a reason. The killer certainly saw him. Why not shoot him? Even if the killer knew Jack, why would he leave a witness behind? I remained convinced Jack didn't kill Ben Harrison, but the killer just ignoring him after shooting a cop in cold blood proved a difficult pill to swallow.

After a few minutes of unproductive pondering, the hairs on my neck stood up. I felt like someone watched me. I hate having people look over my shoulder, and I've developed a sixth sense about it over the years. Peter Parker has his spider-sense; I have reading-over-the-shoulder-sense. I half-turned in my chair. Gloria stood inside the doorway looking at me. She wore a tank top and a tiny pair of shorts. She smiled, and so did I—both at seeing her and at the outfit she wore.

"Long day?" she said. It didn't need to be a question.

"Another in a case full of them," I said.

"You ready for bed?" She walked into the room and plopped herself onto my lap.

I put my arms around her. "I think I am. As sleepy as you look, I don't think I'm the only one."

"Well, I'm not *too* sleepy," she said, leaning down to kiss me. "I think I can stay up for a little while."

"Just a little while?" I said.

She smiled. "Or longer. But first, you need to take the trash out. It stinks."

"It's after midnight."

"It's not like you don't normally take it out late," Gloria said.

"I don't normally have a gorgeous woman in scanty clothing in my lap, though."

"Well, if you take the trash out now, by the time you get upstairs, those small clothes will be on the floor."

"Works for me," I said.

I TIED THE TRASH BAG, lifted it out of the can, and set it on the floor. Gloria was right: it did stink. Whatever I cooked recently decided to compost in my garbage bag, and the whole kitchen area suffered for it. I put my jacket on again before going outside. I wore a 9MM pistol holstered on my hip. I never kept it on for simple things like trips to the bins, but after the phone call I got earlier, I refused to take chances. Threats are a part of the job, but never before did I receive such a convincing one. I patted the gun to double-check it was still there before I hefted the bag and carried it outside.

What passes for my backyard is a small concrete plot and parking pad. In olden days, clotheslines hung from one end of Federal Hill to another, and the posts they hung on remained in my yard. I added a nice grill to give the yard a more modern and useful feel. My trash cans were in the alley behind the house. I opened my gate and saw my containers on their sides farther down the narrow backstreet, about four houses away. This happened occasionally, sometimes because people were jerks and other times from a wayward car going too fast in a confined space. We all used plastic bins for a reason.

I walked toward my cans, passing my neighbors' parking pads. Adding mine proved the second-best thing I'd done to the house after the secret closet. With Gloria staying more often, having two guaranteed spots was huge. As I walked, I thought I heard a faint, muted bang as I neared the trash cans. It made me stop. I felt the heft of the pistol at my side.

The next thing I knew, something covered my head, and I saw only darkness. It felt coarse, whatever it was. I tried to throw it off me, but something whacked me hard in the back of the leg, forcing it to crumple and driving me to the ground. I covered my head out of instinct. Something hard like a nightstick smashed into my back. Another caught me in the ribs. Still another hammered into my hip. I felt a fourth batter the arms covering my head.

Blows rained down on me. I felt and heard one of my ribs crack. My forearms got pummeled by a series of blows intended to knock me out—or worse—if I didn't cover my head. All four batons slammed into my upper back area. I couldn't get out from under whatever covered me. I tried to crawl forward but only got hammered more. I heard unfamiliar voices cursing at me as my unknown assailants continued battering me.

A hard jab to the ribs reminded me of my gun. I risked of moving my right arm off my head. My forearm and elbow throbbed as I reached for the nine. My right hand closed around the grip as my left took a nasty shot that made me shout in pain. I heard laughter from around me. I braced the gun under my left arm, pointed it in the vague direction of one of my assailants, and pulled the trigger. The shot thundered in my ears and made me wince. The voices fell silent. I angled the gun differently and fired again. This time, someone cried out, "Fuck!" and crashed to the ground.

"Holy shit . . . he shot him," another voice said.

The assault stopped. I heard footsteps going away from me. I wanted to throw whatever covered me off and gun down every son of a bitch who beat me, but all I could do was sag to the concrete as three sets of footsteps beat a retreat.

CHAPTER 16

I DIDN'T REMEMBER LOSING CONSCIOUSNESS, BUT I MUST have at some point. I went from lying in the alley to having two paramedics standing over me. One shined a light in my eyes while the other checked the pulse at my wrist. My sides and back burned with pain. My head ached but felt mostly OK, because my arms protected it from all but a glancing blow or two. They hurt a lot worse. As a paramedic pulled the light away from my face, I saw Gloria standing off to the side. Her hands covered her mouth, and even in the irregular light, I could tell her eyes were red and puffy.

"How do you feel?" the vitals-checking paramedic said.

"Like I was on the wrong end of a blanket party," I said.

He didn't answer. Maybe he didn't know what it meant. His partner, a burlier fellow, fetched a gurney from the ambulance. I noticed a few of my neighbors watching from within the confines of their yards. How many of them saw what happened? "We're going to take you to Mercy," the paramedic said as he lowered the gurney beside me. "I don't think you have a concussion, but you've obviously been battered. Better to get you checked out." I nodded.

"I want to ride with him," Gloria said. I hoped the pain on my face masked my surprise.

"You his wife?" the paramedic said.

"No."

"Then you can follow us. We'll be ready to leave in a few minutes."

Gloria put her hand on my face, stroked my cheek, and offered me a small smile. I did my best to return it. She went into my yard and then into the house.

With a good amount of difficulty, I rose to a crouch, stood enough to clear the gurney, and fell onto it. The paramedics got me situated and wheeled me into the back of the ambulance. Once I was there, the more slender of the two hooked up vitals monitors to my torso while his partner went around and got behind the wheel. Morton, the one in back with me, put an oxygen mask on me. Nominal relief of the pain in my body flowed in and out of my lungs.

A couple minutes later, the ambulance took off. I lifted my head and saw Gloria's Mercedes behind us.

* * *

THE ER ADMITTED me to Mercy. I didn't really want to stay, but the first doctor I saw insisted and so did Gloria. Then my parents showed up and insisted even more. Being thoroughly out-insisted, I decided an overnight stay for observation sounded fantastic.

They gave me my own room. Gloria sat in a chair to the right of the bed. She would have held my hand except for the IV tube. Instead, she patted it here and there. A few months ago, I would have minded. Not now. My parents sat in identical chairs near the foot of the bed. "What happened, son?" said my father.

"I was treated to a blanket party," I said.

"A what?"

"It's where a few people throw something over your head, usually a blanket, and then beat the shit out of you."

"Coningsby!" my mother said.

"It's an accurate description," I said.

"You don't need to express it in quite that way."

"Considering what happened to me . . . yes, in fact, I do. And if you don't like it, Mom, the door is on your right."

My mother sniffed. "That sounds awful," she said after a moment.

"It was."

"Do you know who did it?" my father said.

"Knowing and proving are two different things," I said. Gloria's mouth opened like she wanted to say something, but she stayed quiet. I looked at her; she shook her head, so I continued. "I'm pretty sure it was a few of my biggest fans in the BPD. I got an ominous phone call a couple hours before it happened, with threats to leave 'the case' alone or they would have 'no choice.'"

"The police!" said my mother. "That's terrible. I know they don't like the case you're working, but to do this . . ." She trailed off and shook her head.

"Like I said, I can't prove it, but I suspect it quite strongly."

"No one else you can think of would want to do it?"

"Wow, Dad, thanks for the endorsement of my popularity."

"You know what I mean," he said.

My nod was careful, but whatever they gave me for the pain was working wonders. I felt all the soreness and throbbing fade, washed away in a sea of superior drugs. It made me close my eyes and release a long, slow sigh. Then I remembered my father said something. "Sorry, what were we talking about?" I said.

"Who else could have done it?" he said.

"Right. No one I can think of. If I've managed to stumble upon the killer without knowing it, I guess he could have. But if he'd shoot a cop in his own garage, he'd shoot me in an alley." I paused, then shrugged. "It's all I have." I felt like I knew more, but medication dulled my thoughts as it eased the pain. For now,

I would take the trade-off. "I fired a couple shots. One hit somebody."

"Where?" my father said.

"I don't know," I said. "I couldn't raise the gun very high. Probably a leg."

"Treatment of gunshots has to be reported. You might find out who did it after all."

I shrugged. "The BPD could sweep it all under the rug."

"Should we call Richard?" my mother said. "He might know something."

"No," I said, "I don't want him involved. The less he knows, the better."

"Coningsby, he's your cousin."

"He also made it pretty clear he didn't think we were on the same side on this one, Mom. I'd rather not even bring him in."

My mother shook her head again. "He wouldn't be involved in something like this."

"You heard what he said behind Tio Pepe," I said. "No, I don't think he'd be involved, but I also don't think he'd tell me who was."

"You look sleepy," Gloria said. She smiled down at me.

"I am," I said. "It's been a rough night. Mom, Dad, you can go home. Thanks for coming. I'll let you know if I need anything . . . or if the BPD marches in here and throws me out the window." My room was on the fourth floor. A trip over the pane would hurt.

"All right, dear," my mother said. "We'll come back later and check on you."

"OK."

They left. Gloria leaned down and kissed me. "Did I really look sleepy?" I said.

"Some, but I could tell you wanted them gone."

I smiled. "Definitely. Whatever medicine is in my IV bag is working wonders, and I'd love to take a nap."

"I'll see if I can keep the nurses from poking and prodding you every hour."

"You should get some rest, too," I told her. "I'll be fine."

Gloria frowned but gave a nod. "All right," she said. "This chair doesn't look too comfortable, anyway. I'll see you later."

"Sounds good. Thanks for coming." We kissed again. She lingered over me, her mouth slightly open. Whatever she wanted to say, she pursed her lips and left it unspoken.

It didn't take me long to fall asleep.

* * *

I REMEMBERED BEING VAGUELY aware of nurses checking on me every so often, but I didn't really wake up until about eight hours passed. A few minutes after my eyes fluttered open, a cute redheaded nurse walked in. She looked at the machines connected to me and smiled. "Feeling better?"

"As long as you have me hooked up to the bag of wonder," I said.

"You'll be OK without it." I didn't relish the proposition. "Breakfast is being served," she continued. "I'll make sure you get a tray."

"Thanks."

Soon after the nurse left, a heavyset lady wheeled in a large metal cart. She took a tray of food from a rack and plopped it onto my table, then gave me a lidded cup of indeterminate liquid. A smile must have cost extra. "Can I get some coffee?" I said.

"From the cafeteria, if your doctor says it's OK," she said. Her tone indicated she fielded the question frequently. She left and wheeled the cart along to the next lucky breakfast recipient. I slid the table in position over the bed and sat up to eat. Something dull ached in my side, but the narcotics blunted most of it. I took the lid off the breakfast tray. It held scrambled eggs needing another minute in the skillet to firm up, well-crisped hash browns, two depressing sausage links, and a biscuit looking like a four-hundred-pound man used it for a whoopee cushion last night. I was tempted to put the lid back on, but I needed to eat. My stomach grumbled in protest of my trepidation.

I picked up the plasticware and dug in to a mediocre breakfast. Despite being a little undercooked, the eggs tasted good, and the hash brown beat many served in restaurants. The sausage, however, was tepid and the biscuit looked too flat and too hard for me to try. The mystery liquid in the cup turned out to be apple juice. I would need to ask the doctor about coffee. If he said no, I would have someone bring me one. A pox on what the doctor wanted.

I finished my breakfast, put everything on the table, and returned it to its original position. Soon after, two men in cheap suits—one navy and one medium gray—walked in. They were both of similar height and build, and both sported haircuts to identify them as cops wherever they went. Matching white shirts and red ties made them look silly standing beside each other. Even good suits wouldn't have dragged them any closer to fashion respectability. If not for the morphine, I might have winced.

"I'm Detective Marshall," the one in the blue suit said. He nodded toward the other man. "This is Detective Maine."

Maine looked familiar. I'd seen him in a precinct before but couldn't remember which one. The drugs still toyed with my memory even as they allowed me to relax.

"Are you here to take my complaint?" I said.

"What are you complaining about?" said Maine.

"We can start with those suits."

"We're here because of what happened last night," Marshall said.

"I got treated to a blanket party."

"Can you elaborate?"

"You don't know what a blanket party is?" I said.

"Pretend I don't," he managed to say with a straight face.

I rolled my eyes but played along. "I was taking out my trash. It was after midnight. Someone moved my cans farther down the alley. When I walked to get them, somebody threw old bedding over my head. Then I got hit in the back of the leg and went down. It had to be three or four guys beating me with something . . . nightsticks, I would guess."

Both men took notes. "You didn't have any warning?" Maine said.

"You mean, did someone yell, 'Hey, hold still. We're about to throw you a quilting bee?' No. I didn't know anyone was in the alley until the cover blacked out everything. Someone called a couple hours before and threatened me, however. I don't mean to do your jobs for you, but the call and the ass-kicking are probably related."

Marshall scowled and shook his head. "What happened after you were on the ground?" Maine said.

"I got the shit beaten out of me by a few guys with sticks," I said.

"There were reports of a gunshot."

"Yes. I grabbed my gun at one point and fired blindly twice. The second shot hit someone."

"Do you know where?"

"I was too busy lying in the alley in agony to check."

"And you have no idea who did this?" Marshall said.

"You might have heard how I'm unpopular because of the Ben Harrison case," I said.

"There's a rumor," he said.

"I've been warned to back off, stay away, the usual shit a

couple times. Then I get a real threatening call last night. Then I get a blanket party." I shrugged. "You do the math."

"Nightsticks? You're saying people in the police department did this to you?" Marshall frowned. Maine looked out the door.

"It's my theory," I said. "I know I'll never be able to prove it, though."

Both men flipped their notebooks closed. "I think that's all we need for now."

"I'm sure it is."

Marshall left his card on the small table under the TV. "If you remember anything else, call me," he said

"Because my assault is at the top of the docket," I said. They left without looking at me or saying anything else. I turned the TV on. The hospital didn't offer many channels, and most of them weren't worth watching. Some war movie played in the background as I drifted off to sleep again.

* * *

I AWOKE SOMETIME LATER. The war movie battling and booming me to sleep got replaced by something tamer in black and white. Joey and Gloria sat in chairs near the foot of my bed. Gloria smiled and stood next to me when she saw I was awake. She grabbed my hand. I squeezed hers. "How are you feeling?" she said.

The blissful nothingness of the narcotics faded. My ribs hurt every time I breathed. I winced. Gloria frowned. "I feel like I'm out of morphine," I said.

"The nurse said your bag was running out. They don't want to give you another one because you're being discharged soon."

"I hope I'm getting a sweet prescription."

"I can hook you up if you don't," Joey said. "I know people."

"No doubt," I said, "but I'm in enough hot water with the BPD already."

Joey shrugged. "They wouldn't be aware."

"I'll let you know," I said. "Right now, I want to make sure I'm getting out of here soon." I pushed the call button. Gloria squeezed my hand.

A nurse I hadn't seen before came in a moment later. She was short and built like a linebacker, the type of woman who wouldn't have any trouble lifting people out of chairs. Her eyes held a softness belying her build. "Yes?" she said.

"Am I being discharged?" I said.

"As soon as the doctor signs your papers."

"Am I getting a prescription?"

"He's writing you one for Percocet. There's not much else we can do for you."

"You could give me more morphine." I flashed her a winning smile.

She didn't go for it. "You're leaving this afternoon," she said. "The doctor will be by shortly." She turned and left.

"At least I'm getting the good stuff," I said.

"I could get you better stuff," said Joey.

"I'll stick with the official scrip," I said.

A few minutes later, an Indian doctor came into the room. He smiled briefly at Gloria and me and checked my chart. "You are very lucky, Mr. Ferguson," he said with a faint accent.

"I don't feel very lucky," I said.

"You have many bruises, but the worst of your injuries are three cracked ribs. There's nothing we can do for them other than help you manage the pain. I'm writing a prescription for Percocet. You can pick it up in the pharmacy on your way out."

"How long should I take them?"

"I've given you a three-week supply," he said.

"Should be enough," I said.

"You need to take it easy, too." He put the chart down and looked at me over his small glasses. "I don't know what you do," he said. "I don't know how you came to the hospital in the condition you were in. What I do know is you can injure yourself worse if you don't take it easy for a while."

"How long?" I said.

"As long as you're taking your prescription, at least."

I had no intentions of taking it easy for even a fraction of the time, but I also had no intention of getting into a protracted argument with the doctor. "All right," I said.

"Good." He smiled again and brushed a strand of black hair from atop his glasses. "I'm signing your discharge papers. You can leave when you have some real clothes on."

"Thanks."

The doctor left. Joey tossed me a bag with my clothes from yesterday in them. I didn't see any blood on them. "I'll wait in the hallway," Joey said. "There are some things in this world I don't need to see."

"Your loss," I said.

"There went my appetite," said Joey. He closed the door behind him as he left.

* * *

SHEDDING the crummy hospital gown hurt when I needed to lift my arms but still felt liberating, like untying myself from bonds. My forearms, knee, hip, and ribs all flared with pain as I put regular clothes back on, the ribs worst of all. Everything else was only bruises which would go away in a few days. The empty holster under my arm yawned at me. "I guess the police took my gun?"

"Yes," Gloria said. "I wonder if they'll give it back?"

"They have to, but I think they'll make me wait for it."

"I guess you're on light duty for a while?" she said with a mischievous grin on her face.

"I'm afraid so," I said.

"I'm sure I'll think of something."

"I'm sure I will, too."

I opened the door to see Detectives Marshall and Maine waiting for me. "Am I getting an escort home?" I said.

"Not exactly," Marshall said. "You're under arrest for assault with a deadly weapon."

"For defending myself?"

"No one can find evidence of an assault against you," Maine said.

"Have you seen my medical chart?" I said.

"We can do this the easy way or the hard way," said Marshall. The look on his face told me which way he preferred.

"If some of your friends hadn't ambushed me, I'd go for the hard way," I said. I turned around and put my hands behind me. One of them clamped the handcuffs on me. It made my wrists hurt about three hundred percent more. Gloria watched with wide eyes. "Call James," I said. "Tell him what happened and have him meet me at Central Booking."

She nodded. "I will," she said.

Marshall and Maine led me away. Doctors, nurses, and patients gaped as they walked me through the hall. I saw Joey in a waiting area, peeking out from behind a magazine. "Take care of Gloria," I mouthed to him. He nodded.

The pain in my ribs mounted as the detectives led me outside. My Percocet felt miles away. It soon would be.

CHAPTER 17

THE BUMPY RIDE TO CENTRAL BOOKING JOSTLED MY RIBS with every pothole. A hard turn sent me into the door without my arms free to brace myself. The seatbelt barely made a difference. I couldn't take a deep breath because it hurt too much. The only positive thing about the ride was its brevity, even though it didn't feel brief as I bounced around the back of the Crown Victoria. Maine led me out of the car and to the booking counter.

The desk sergeant—Carnes according to his name tag—gave me a smug smile as Marshall and Maine brought me up for processing. The look hardly left his face the entire time. My two asshole escorts left, and the sergeant led me toward the cells. I took a quick mental inventory of potential roommates. Two small groups glared daggers at each other from separate accommodations. It was far from encouraging. "You had to go and do something stupid," he said.

"There's a lot of stupid with this case," I said, "but little of it is mine."

"Who's the one going to a cell?"

"You have curious standards for stupidity."

Carnes unlocked the door of an intake cell and undid my handcuffs. He shoved me in the back, and a new wave of pain cascaded up and down my spine as I stumbled inside. I collected myself as Carnes slid the cell door shut and locked it. "You might be here a while," he said.

I turned around and glared at him. "I spent nineteen days in a Chinese prison, Sergeant. You people are amateurs."

He frowned. "Enjoy your stay," he grumbled to save face, then walked away.

Two other men, one white and one black, shared the cell with me. They both sat on a bench appraising me. They wore jeans of different hues, though they coordinated their white shirts, black shoes, and brown bomber jackets. The white one's jeans showed a large wet spot covering most of his left thigh. I smelled beer from across the cell as I sat.

"You were in a Chinese prison?" the white one said.

"Yes," I said from an uncomfortable bench across the cell from them. I hoped they didn't decide to see how tough the Chinese prison made me. In my current condition, I doubted I could oblige.

"What for?"

"More than a bar fight." They looked at each other, then back at me. "Oh, come on. You're both dressed like hipsters, you have a beer spill on your leg, your eyes are bloodshot, and they're obviously keeping you apart from the idiots two cells down. I can do the math."

"We won the fight," the black hipster said. They looked at each other before returning their stares to me.

I eased my head back onto the concrete wall and took as deep a breath as my ribs would allow. All I needed right now was for these two morons to get riled up. "Good for you," I said. "Let's just sit here and wait to be released."

They shrugged and went back to ignoring me. Crisis averted. I closed my eyes. The two hipsters didn't say anything else. A few minutes later, I heard a familiar voice. "You will release him *now*." James Snyder had arrived.

Sergeant Carnes groused the whole way down the corridor, but he unlocked the door and beckoned me with a wave. "My client just got released from the hospital," James said, keeping on Carnes. "He has a painkiller prescription for injuries your friends inflicted on him."

"I'm releasing him," Carnes said, turning to stare down my lawyer. It would be a mistake.

Instead of backing down, James Snyder took a step forward. Carnes had about four inches, forty pounds, and twenty-five years on him, but none of it mattered. "Only because I'm here," James said. "Otherwise you'd let him rot in there without the medicine he needs." James looked at me. "Come on, C.T. Let's get you out of here."

"Not a moment too soon," I said. "What about my prescription?"

"One of my paralegals is picking it up. She'll deliver it to you as quickly as possible."

"Sergeant, I think I need my personal effects."

"Yeah, yeah," Carnes said.

* * *

"How DID you get into this mess?" James Snyder said after we settled into his Lexus. It was the nicest and cleanest car in the lot, and its gray paint matched his hair color. He'd been my parents' attorney for ages, so I knew him for much of my life. The best part was he would probably do something like this *pro bono*.

As we drove, I told him the story about Ben Harrison, how Liz Fleming roped me into working with her, the complications the BPD threw in front of me to deter me, and the blanket party. My tale of woe took us to Light Street. "I can't prove the cops gave me the blanket party," I said. "I don't know who else would have done it."

"You shot one of them?" he said.

"Yes."

"Unless he has a doctor in the family, he went to a hospital somewhere."

I thought I'd considered it but couldn't remember now. The pain in my ribs clouded my thoughts. I really needed a Percocet. "Something to look into," I said.

"Are you going to stay on this case?" James said.

"I'm invested in it now. After all I've been through, I can't simply fold up my tent and crawl home." We stopped abruptly at a red light. Rocking forward and then backward in the seat made me wince. Even Lexus' finest leather couldn't cushion the blow.

"So it's pride?" James said. If he noticed my discomfort, he didn't say anything.

"Some," I said. "Mostly, I know I can solve this."

"I've known your family for years, C.T. Your parents had to bury one child already." He looked at me. I saw sadness rim his studious blue eyes. "Make sure it stops there."

"They're not going to kill me, James," I said.

He shook his head. "Be careful," he said. "It's easy to get you out of a holding cell when they trump up charges against you." We neared my house. James pulled into the closest spot he could find. "We both know you take extra liberties with the law. Watch yourself. If they bring real charges against you, you could be in trouble."

I summoned a smile. "With a legal eagle like you in my corner?"

"I'd do my best."

"Your best is pretty damn good," I said.

"So is yours," he said. "Go in and wait for your painkillers, and promise me you won't do something stupid."

I opened the door. "Thanks, James. I promise not to do anything more reckless and ill-advised than normal."

"I guess it's something," James said.

* * *

GLORIA GAVE me a gentle hug after I walked in the door. "I was so worried," she said. "I can't believe they just hauled you away like that."

"Part of their plan to get me to back off," I said.

"Is it working?"

"I'm stubborn." I ambled slowly into my living room and sagged into my recliner.

"Do you need anything?" Gloria said.

"James is having someone drop off my prescription shortly," I said. "I'll need a Percocet."

Gloria frowned and sat on the arm of the recliner. It wobbled but she wasn't heavy enough to tip it over. "I'm glad he could straighten things out."

I shrugged. "He got me released. The BPD may still charge me with . . . whatever they're trying to hang on me."

"What if they do?" she said.

"Then I might need to pay James for his time," I said.

"Doesn't he owe you a favor?"

"He does, and he's a family friend, but getting me out of jail on dubious charges and getting my neck out of the noose the BPD makes for me are two different things."

Gloria squeezed my hand. "Solve this quickly," she said. "Get yourself out of this mess and maybe those charges will disappear."

My ribs barked at me, but I smiled anyway. "I'm surprised you're not trying to convince me to pack it in," I said.

"I know you won't."

I nodded. "You know me pretty well."

She poked me in the shoulder. "Besides, in your current condition, I couldn't be as . . . persuasive as I would normally be."

I chuckled, then grimaced when a new flare of pain coursed through my rib cage. "I don't doubt you'd find a way," I said.

"I probably would," Gloria said with a grin I would have found very inviting under normal circumstances.

Someone rapped at the door. Gloria scurried off to answer it before I could even move. I hoped it would be James' paralegal with my painkillers. What if it wasn't? What if someone in the BPD or otherwise decided to take a more direct approach to dissuading me from the Harrison case? My heart quickened. I sat up and my ribs burned. My guns were either down the hall, upstairs, or impounded. As I struggled to stand, Gloria came back into the living room. She shook a bottle of pills. My pulse eased.

"I'll get you some water," she said.

I sank back onto the recliner and took a deep breath. I didn't care if it hurt.

* * *

Percocet put me out almost right away. Every now and then, a sound fluttered near the surface of my haze and threatened to wake me. I heard voices somewhere; they sounded fuzzy and far away. At some point, I became more aware and the voices became clearer. Gloria and Rich were conversing. I opened my eyes. The two of them sat on opposite ends of the sofa, looking at me. Rich's arms were crossed under his chest.

"Talking about me?" I said. My voice sounded like it did when I'd been up for two days.

"This time, it actually is about you," Rich said.

"Oh, goody." I eased the recliner into a seated position. My ribs didn't protest overmuch. Percocet was a hell of a drug.

"You got charged with assault with a deadly weapon." Rich sounded more exasperated than surprised. He adopted the tone often when we talked.

"It was self-defense."

"I've heard your story."

"Did you hear about the blanket party?" I said.

"You know about blanket parties?" said Rich.

"Firsthand. If you mean the term, do you think I never watched *The Shield*?"

Rich frowned. "Do you really think the BPD did this?" he said.

"Nothing I can prove in court," I said, "but I think a few assholes got together and decided to discourage me from the case. I got a threatening phone call a couple hours before it happened."

"And it couldn't possibly be someone else."

"Who?" I sat up and leaned forward. My ribs throbbed past the Percocet but I ignored it. "Tell me, who else could it be? Who else doesn't want me to figure this out?"

"The killer?"

"But you have the killer in custody . . . so you say."

Rich started to reply, but his mouth clicked shut. His frown deepened. I pressed on. "Either your brethren decided to give me a blanket party, or the real killer is on to me and brought a few friends. Either way, it looks like you have the wrong man. How far down this rabbit hole do you want to go?"

"Cops didn't do this." Rich shook his head. I heard no conviction in his words.

"*Eppur si muove,*" I said.

"What?"

"Galileo." Comprehension did not come to Rich's face. "And yet it moves." Nothing. "Never mind," I said. "I'm going to find out who did it. Someone got shot, which means he needed to be treated, and the hospital is supposed to report it. Someone drove him there. Maybe the guy I shot is the one who organized it all. Maybe not. I'm going to find out who put it together, Rich, and when I do, I'm going to even the score."

"You're going to assault a cop?" he said.

"I'll assault two cops if you get in my way."

"You're unbelievable." Rich looked at Gloria. "Can you talk some sense into him?"

"I think he's right," Gloria said. "As much as I hate to say it, Rich, I think cops were involved."

"Incredible."

"I think we'll be able to prove it," Gloria said.

"Good luck," Rich said.

Gloria shrugged and looked away. She knew something. I would need to ask her about it later. Rich stewed on the couch. He stared at the hardwood floors, then looked at me with a sour expression. "What if you're right?" he finally said.

"There's no 'what if' about it," I said.

"Work with me here, dammit. What if you're right? It means someone in the BPD knows we have the wrong man in jail."

"Do you think they know who the right man is?"

"Or maybe one of them is the right man?" Gloria said.

Rich recoiled as if she struck him. "I'm not willing to go there yet," he said. "I don't even know their level of knowledge."

"You sure it's not just territorial pissings?" I said.

"No. Whoever did it might simply resent having you mucking up the investigation." Normally, I would have corrected Rich about the quality of my input, but now was not the time. He needed to work all this out on his own. Rich alternated between looking at the floor and at me. "I'm not convinced yet." He shook his head as if trying to persuade—or dissuade—himself.

"Think about it," I said.

"I am. I will." Rich looked at me. "I'm sorry this happened to you, whoever did it."

"Thanks."

"I need to go," he said. "I need to think."

"All right," I said.

Rich stood and let himself out without saying goodbye.

"I don't think I've ever seen him so out of sorts," Gloria said.

"Me, neither. Rich is usually very sure of himself and what he does. He knows he plays for the right side. This is tossing a wrench into what he believes." I pulled the lever at chairside and reclined again.

"Sleepy?" Gloria said. She walked over to me and squeezed my hand.

"Percocet always does it to me," I said. My eyelids grew heavy.

"Why don't you get some rest?"

"I feel like I'm resting a lot lately." I looked at Gloria through narrowing eyes.

"You've been through a lot. You're entitled."

I started to answer her, but sleep cut me off.

* * *

SOMEONE SHOOK MY SHOULDER. My heavy eyelids remained closed as if possessing wills of their own. It took me a minute, but I mustered enough power to open them. Gloria smiled down at me. James Snyder stood near the foot of the recliner. "Glad to see you're resting, C.T.," he said.

"Blame the Percocet," I said, sitting up with a moderate flare in my ribs. "What's up?"

"There's a hearing for your license tomorrow morning."

I rolled my eyes. "Of course there is. I thought you took care of it."

James shook his head. "I got you out of jail. The BPD wants

to pursue the charge against you. Part of the process is this hearing."

"Whatever," I said. "It won't stop me from working this case." Once the Percocet wore off, and I felt I could stand up again, I meant to get back to my investigation. Such as it was.

"I didn't think it would," he said. "Regardless, your license could be suspended."

"Are you going to be there with me?"

"Yes. I rearranged my calendar for the morning. I'll do my best, but we need to prepare for the possibility of suspension. It will mean your concealed carry permits will also be voided for the duration."

I frowned. "Could be a problem."

"Be at the Mitchell Courthouse at nine o'clock," James said. "I have a plan, but we're going to have to hope for the best."

"I'm guessing the judge will be more sympathetic to the BPD than to me."

"Most likely. Without a witness for the shooting, it's your word against the police report."

"My injuries don't paint a good enough picture for them?" I said.

"They can say you got beaten up after shooting someone," James said. "It's less likely but not implausible."

I frowned. "Maybe my best suit will impress the judge enough to rule in my favor."

"Better wear a tux, then," said James.

* * *

AFTER JAMES LEFT, I walked down the hall to what remained of my office. Ever since I rented a real one, I've minimized the equipment I keep in the house. The computers in both offices were on the same network. I sat at the laptop and looked over my last few searches while also perusing Ben Harrison's personnel file. The drug angle still bothered me. His coworkers speculated Ben may have been unhappy at work and wanted to bust some dealers to advance in the BPD. I could think of no reason to disbelieve them. Julie Harrison hadn't suspected it about her husband, and I found no reason to disbelieve her, either.

Someone was wrong. Hell, maybe all of them were.

I wondered if Paul King lied to me. Like most of his brethren, he probably didn't want me nosing around the case. We'd worked together, though. I didn't expect King to invite me to his backyard for a barbecue and general chumming around, but I also didn't expect him to condone a blanket party. At some point, if this drug angle turned into anything, I would need to talk to him again.

On my desk, my cell phone vibrated. Liz Fleming called. "Hi, Liz."

"Oh, my God, I hope you're OK," she said.

"I see word travels quickly."

"C.T., I had no idea this case would turn into such a cluster-fuck," she said. "I'm so sorry for getting you involved."

"I allowed myself to be persuaded," I said. "I'm as much to blame as you."

"Maybe, but I'm still the one who persuaded you. I apologize things went out of control."

"Shit happens, Liz. What's going on?"

"Jack Bennett got his ass beaten at Supermax."

"Shit," I said. "Is he OK?"

"More or less," Liz said. "It was pretty bad."

"I sympathize. Does this make things harder for us?"

Liz sighed into the phone. "Yeah," she said. "He's in the prison hospital. I think he avoided surgery, but he's going to be doped up for a while."

"They can't deny him the right to see his lawyer," I said.

"Visitors in jail aren't a right. Besides, in his current state, I don't think he'd have much useful to say."

"I never got much out of talking to him, anyway," I said. "I'll keep working and see what I can turn up. Is there a trial date?"

"Not yet," Liz said. "We have a hearing to determine that next week. This is a red ball. I'm sure the prosecution will want an early calendar placement."

"Here's one case where the right to a speedy trial is overrated."

She didn't answer immediately. "You sure you're all right?"

I smiled. "I'm kinda banged up, but I'll manage."

"Keep me posted, C.T.," Liz said. "And be careful. I don't want to hear that something even worse has happened to you."

"Me, either," I said.

* * *

SOMETIME LATER, I paused from a boring round of report reading to rub the bridge of my nose. A headache crept up on me to go along with the mounting pain in my ribs. I needed a Percocet soon. What I didn't need was to fall asleep on the job. Medication could wait. I picked the report up again when I noticed Gloria standing in the doorway. She gave a small smile and walked in.

"I thought you were taking it easy," she said.

"Light duty," I said. "All these reports are under five pounds."

Gloria sat on the corner of my desk. "Are you worried about tomorrow?"

"There's not much point to worrying." I shrugged. "James is damn good at what he does. He'll do his best."

"And if that's not good enough?" she said.

"Then I guess I won't be able to shoot anyone the next time I get a blanket party," I said.

Gloria frowned. "I hope there isn't a next time."

"So do I."

She leaned down and put her hand on my face. Her fingers caressed my cheek. Gloria's eyes glistened more than normal in the light of my office. "I worry about you. I don't want to see something so terrible happen to you again." A tear slid down her cheek. "I . . . I love you, C.T. Ferguson."

I felt my eyes go wide. My mouth opened and nothing came out. I should have seen the signs. She'd doted on me ever since I got hurt and had been around more than normal before. She stared at me, expecting me to say something, expecting me to say that I loved her too.

So I did.

"I love you, too, Gloria Reading."

She squeaked in delight and wrapped me in a gentle hug. I felt her body shudder lightly against me. I didn't say anything. We just sat in our loose embrace for a few minutes.

CHAPTER 18

I took a Percocet to help me fall asleep. A round of vigorous report-reading and brainstorming kept my brain firing away as I lay in bed. Percocet quieted everything down and let me relax. I didn't know if Gloria would stay, but she did. She kissed me goodnight and reminded me she loved me before I fell asleep. I confirmed the converse. It felt like being in high school in a very charming way.

In the morning, my alarm pried me from my drug-aided sleep. My waking moments lasted all of a few seconds. I fell back asleep long enough to be hazy again when I awakened to Gloria shaking my shoulder. She persisted until I grumbled and sat up in bed. "How long was I out?" I said.

"Maybe five minutes," Gloria said. "I don't want you to be late for your hearing."

"Probably wouldn't look good," I said. I climbed out of bed and took a quick shower. The water helped me shake off the opioid haze. By the time I stepped out of the hot water, I felt invigorated. I briefly considered skipping my morning coffee but didn't need to think such crazy thoughts with a hearing looming. Once more in my bedroom, I pondered my suit options in the closet.

Almost an hour remained before I was due at the courthouse. It left time for a quick breakfast. Gloria was already in the kitchen. She poured us each a mug of coffee and a glass of orange juice. I whipped up two plates of scrambled eggs and paired them with pumpernickel toast. Gloria and I ate with only sparse conversation before we both adjourned upstairs. If she wanted to come with me to the hearing, I wouldn't stop her.

Gloria wore a sharp gray business suit I didn't know she owned. I opted for a blue pinstriped Armani after considering similar ensembles from Tommy Hilfiger and Calvin Klein. They were both fine suits, but when one's future is riding on the outcome, one should trust Giorgio over Tommy or Calvin. I polished my dark brown Ferragamo shoes and headed downstairs.

"Do you need a Percocet?" Gloria said.

"Probably," I said, "but I want to be lucid for the hearing." My ribs barked after all my rushing around.

"I'll drive in case you need to take one."

"Sounds good."

"Are you nervous?" she said.

I shrugged. "I'm not sure what to expect. Maybe some trepidation of the unknown more than anything. Even if some idiot judge takes my license, I'm going to continue to try and untangle this whole mess."

Gloria smiled a wan smile. "I had a feeling you might," she said.

* * *

THE MITCHELL COURTHOUSE bustled with activity. Corrections officers led handcuffed and shackled men and women from courtrooms to waiting vans. Lawyers in cheap suits mingled with other attorneys in better threads. None of them wore Armani.

Maybe it was reserved for judges and dashing private investigators. Bailiffs led witnesses into courtrooms before shutting the doors; people sat on benches outside other rooms, each awaiting their chance to tell a story.

We met James Snyder on the third floor. "You're actually on time," James said, looking at his Rolex.

"Every now and then, the stars align," I said.

"We're down the hall in a small courtroom. I saw the docket. We're up second."

"Do you know the judge?"

"I know all the judges," James said, giving me a look.

"Fair enough," I said. "Is he an asshole?"

"*She* is something of a hardass, yes. I like our chances, though." James smiled at Gloria. "Good morning, Gloria."

She returned his smile and inclined her head. "Good morning, James." I caught a whiff of a conspiratorial vibe between them. What did James know about my chances, and how did Gloria play into them?

"Want to get some coffee?" James said. "I know a good place nearby."

"A second cup can never hurt," I said.

* * *

WE RETURNED after coffee and conversation. The first hearing was still going on, so we took our seats on the padded bench outside the courtroom. It looked like a thin couch cushion covering a stiff wooden bench and felt about the same. About ten minutes later, another lawyer showed up and sat near the other end. His off-the-rack suit got totally outclassed by James' and mine. For his part, he seemed not to notice as he busied himself looking at a notebook.

After another fifteen minutes, the courtroom door opened. A

thin man dressed for a casual day in the office muttered and cursed as he walked out. Two lawyers followed him, then the bailiff summoned us in a gravelly voice. He looked too young for the sound, as if he spent his free time chain-smoking and gargling with broken glass.

The courtroom looked like many others, only more compact. The judge's bench and surrounding area dominated the back of the room. A long table replaced the traditionally separate ones for each team of lawyers. Two rows of seats were walled off from the lone table by a three-foot wall. A flat-panel TV sat on a cart to the left of the bench. The central aisle ran from the doors to the judge's bench, about twenty feet. Gloria sat in the first row of seats directly behind James and me.

A middle-aged woman, her black hair streaked with silver, sat on the judge's bench. Once everyone assembled themselves, she called the hearing to order. "Mr. Ferguson," she said, "this is to determine the status of your private investigator's license after a shooting. Do you understand?"

"I do, your honor," I said.

"Good." She looked at the other lawyer. "Mr. Mills, the floor is yours."

"Thank you, judge." Mills stood and buttoned his suit over his ample paunch. It forced his shirt and pants to do work for which they were ill-equipped. Beady blues stared out from behind his thick glasses. I rolled my eyes. James caught me and smirked. "We're here because C.T. Ferguson shot a man. He's licensed to carry several guns in this state but with that privilege comes responsibility. Mr. Ferguson did not act responsibly when he shot an innocent man in an alley." I rolled my eyes again and this time, the judge caught me.

"Mr. Ferguson, the eye gymnastics are unnecessary," she said.

"Objection," I said.

"To what?" the judge said, looking perplexed.

"Quite a few things, but we'll start with the 'innocent man' part."

"You'll have your chance to speak, Mr. Ferguson. Mr. Snyder, please advise your client that he's not helping his case by speaking out of turn."

"I will, your honor," James said, glaring at me. He didn't say anything and didn't need to. I nodded and folded my hands in my lap. My ribs throbbed. I hoped this hearing would end soon so I could pop a pill.

The judge said, "Mr. Mills, continue."

"Thank you, Judge. As I said, Mr. Ferguson shot an innocent man in an alley. He claimed this to be in self-defense, but no one saw him get assaulted. The police looked for witnesses and couldn't find any. Mr. Ferguson abused the privilege of carrying a gun, and the state believes he should lose his license for it."

"Mr. Mills, has your office initiated any proceedings against Mr. Ferguson in the past?" the judge said

"None, Judge," said Mills.

"Is there anything else?"

"Not at this time, your honor."

"Very well." She turned to James. "Mr. Snyder?"

James did not stand and did not button any buttons on his suit jacket. "Good morning, Judge Calhoun," he said. He leaned back in the chair and cracked a smile. "We're not disputing Mr. Ferguson fired his gun. We're not even disputing he shot someone when he did. We're asserting he fired his gun in self-defense, and we're going to prove it."

"Let's hear what you have," said Judge Calhoun.

"You will be able to hear and see it, your honor. Mr. Ferguson was taking out his trash on the night in question when he was surprised in the alley behind his home. A group of people threw a blanket over his head and beat him. Mr. Ferguson feared for his life, so he fired his gun to dissuade the attackers. One of them happened to get hit."

"That's a compelling story, Mr. Snyder. Do you have any proof?"

James flashed the kind of smile a veteran lawyer displays when he knows the case is in the bag—or the kind a shark might flash when he sees a wounded catfish. "I was hoping you'd ask." He stood, took a CD from his briefcase, and now buttoned the top button of his coat. "If I may, your honor, we have some very enlightening evidence on this disc."

The bailiff put it into a DVD player. He turned the TV on. A minute later, the disc showed an alley filmed through a window, white-painted crossbars at the outside of the shot. I made out Gloria's faint reflection in the glass and turned to look at her. She gave me a shrug. In the video, Gloria banged the glass as I walked into an ambush. A group of four men rushed out from hiding. A blanket went over my head. A nightstick took out my leg, driving me to my knees, and then the beating began in earnest. They got some good shots in. I squinted but couldn't discern any faces. Blows rained down on me under the blanket, and then a loud bang caused Judge Calhoun to jump in her chair. Another loud bang rang out from the video, and a man screamed and fell. The other three rushed off with him.

After my attackers ran away, the video stopped. James looked at Judge Calhoun, his hands spread out. "I think this video clearly shows my client only fired his gun in self-defense," he said.

"Your honor, Mr. Snyder did not share this with me or anyone in my office," Mills said from his seat.

"This isn't a trial, Ken," James said. "Your office knew better than to make it into one, especially without naming a victim."

"Mr. Ferguson," the judge said, "it's clear to me that you were the victim of an unexpected beating. I am not going to suspend your license." She turned to Mills. "Mr. Mills, I suggest you tell whoever sent you here that this court does not appreciate your office wasting its time. Grind your axes elsewhere."

"But your honor—"

"That will be all," Judge Calhoun said. "Good day, gentlemen." She banged the gavel.

We walked out of the courtroom. Gloria fell in step beside me. "What made you start filming with your cell?" I said.

"I saw people in the shadows you didn't see," she said, "I tried to warn you, but I couldn't get your crappy old window open and didn't have time to get outside. You really need new windows upstairs."

I grinned at her. "I'll call someone when this case is over," I said.

* * *

AT HOME, I played and replayed Gloria's cell phone video of the blanket party. No matter how many times I watched it, I couldn't identify any of the people involved. Gloria shot it at night through a window with a phone camera; I understood the limiting factors in the resolution. I applied several digital fixes to try and clean up the video. They helped but not much. As far as I could tell, the cowards who gave me the blanket party wore masks. Trying to zoom in on them only made things more pixelated.

A thought interrupted me. In some form, this constituted a surveillance video. I wondered how the police would react to the judicial drubbing James and I laid on them. Would they surveil me? Try to bug my phones? Intercept my communications? I wasn't worried about my technology—they'd never peel back all the layers of security in time for anything meaningful—but other aspects concerned me. Would a patrol car follow me everywhere?

Maybe the BPD would get a bullshit warrant and kick down my front door. The thoughts were enough to spike my pulse. A few China flashbacks danced in my head. I took a series of breaths as deep as my ribs would allow to calm myself.

I just started watching the footage again when Gloria interrupted me. "I know you're going to watch the hell out of that," she said, "but you do still have a case to solve."

I nodded, not taking my eyes off the video in the hope I somehow overlooked some important detail in my previous twenty viewings. "I know."

Gloria's footsteps came closer. I saw her reflection in the monitor. She leaned down and rubbed my shoulders. "I realize you want justice for yourself, but there's a man in jail right now."

"There need to be four more," I said.

The shoulder rubbing stopped. "You can worry about them later," Gloria said.

The video ended. Gloria was right. Jack Bennett lay in the infirmary in Supermax for a crime he didn't commit while I sat in my house watching a video and nursing cracked ribs. He definitely suffered worse. "You're right." I smiled. She saw it in the monitor and grinned as well. "I'll get back to work."

Gloria leaned down and kissed my cheek. "I knew you would." She padded out of the office. I watched her reflection walk away in the monitor.

How could I not love her?

CHAPTER 19

THE CORE OF THE CASE STILL CONFOUNDED ME: HOW DID the shooter not even notice Jack Bennett standing in the garage? No one is so focused on their work at such a time. Anyone nearby is a potential witness. Yet this shooter completely ignored the potential witness standing mere feet away. It didn't make sense. I read the case file and my notes until my eyes hurt more than my ribs, and it still didn't make sense.

I needed to see the crime scene again. The circumstances of my last visit compelled me to sneaking around under cover of darkness, looking for anything I could use to highlight Jack Bennett's innocence. I guessed I would be returning under the same circumstances. Staging the shooting would be best. If I walked in as the shooter I might gain an idea for how he could have overlooked an obvious witness.

I called Rich. "Tell your friends I've given up on the case," I said.

"Have you?" he asked.

"What do you think?"

"What do you hope this will do?"

"Get your friends to leave me alone, mostly."

"While you continue to do what you've been doing," Rich said.

"Only with less harassment," I said.

Rich sighed into the receiver. "All right," he said, "I'll talk it up in the squadroom."

"Given my recent surge in popularity, I'm sure word will spread quickly," I said.

"No doubt."

"Thanks, Rich." I hung up and resumed contemplating my next move. If I were going to stage a shooting, I needed a couple of volunteers. My parents were usually willing to help. I called my mother and ran the situation by her.

"Absolutely not," she said.

"Why not?" I said.

"Coningsby, you're going to break into that man's house."

"Just his garage, most likely."

"You should be resting and not focusing on this case so much," my mother said. "What if you get assaulted again?

"I think the chances are slim," I said. "Rich is spreading the word I've given up on the case."

"But you haven't, and now you want us to help you break and enter."

"Mom, I can do the breaking and entering all by myself. You'll simply be helping me visualize what happened."

"You know your father and I want you to solve this case, Coningsby," she said. "We always want you to succeed and help the people who come to you. However, we can't take part in something like this."

I shouldn't have been surprised. My mother couldn't show her face at the weekly Snooty Wives Club meeting if she got arrested for breaking and entering. My father would go along with me but not through the filter of my mother. "All right,

Mom," I said. "I'll find people who are actually willing to help me when I need it." I hung up before she could answer.

Gloria walked back into the office, sipping a freshly-made coffee. I could smell the strong brew from where she stood near the door. "How's it going?" she said.

"Would you be willing to help me do something for the case?" I said.

"What is it?" I told her what I had in mind. "Isn't that illegal?" she said.

"Doubly so if we get caught," I said.

"You think it'll really help, though?"

"I don't see any other way to puzzle out what happened in the garage."

"You don't have to use that specific one, do you?" she said.

"Is there a better choice?" I said.

"Any would work. Your parents have a garage."

"It's a four-car."

"So use half of it," Gloria suggested. "Use half of my parents'."

Her offer reminded me I'd never formally met Gloria's parents. I didn't think she offered her suggestion to wrangle me into it. Still, staging a crime scene struck me as a poor introduction. "My parents are committed to helping as long as it doesn't involve anything illegal," I said.

"Using their garage isn't illegal," Gloria said.

"It also isn't as helpful." I paused and frowned. "I'll think about it." I rubbed my eyes. "Right now, I need to stop looking at these files."

"You're also a few hours overdue for a Percocet."

"I'll take one, but I need to keep working," I said.

"What are you going to do next?" Gloria said.

I shook my head. "I have no idea."

* * *

I DROVE into Little Italy and parked a couple blocks from *Il Buon Cibo*. Like other good restaurant owners, Tony Rizzo closed his place for a few hours between lunch and dinner. Friends of the man, however, could still come in. Tony ran most organized crime in Baltimore. I didn't know the width and breadth of his operation, but he possessed a lot of reach and influence, and even though I'd known him for ages, I remained mindful of both. I walked through the uncrowded dining hall to find Tony sitting in his usual table near the fireplace. He smiled as I approached.

"Come for a late lunch?" he said. Tony neared seventy. Before I left for my thirty-nine months in Hong Kong, he'd been overweight but looked ten years younger. Upon my return, I noticed Tony lost weight and gained years. He was probably a little too slender now, and his thinner face made him look his age.

"I was thinking more of an early dinner," I said.

"Either way." Tony glanced around and found a waiter nearby. "Jerry! Take my friend's order."

Jerry hustled to the table like someone chased him with a cattle prod. "Yessir, Mr. Rizzo," he said, looking over at me. "What can I get you, sir?"

"Chicken parmesan and an unsweetened iced tea will be fine," I said.

"That's it?" said Tony. "Jerry, bring him some bruschetta too. You'll like it, C.T. We added fresh mozzarella as a topping."

"Sounds good," I said.

Jerry sped toward the kitchen. "What brings you by?" Tony said.

"You heard about a cop getting shot in his garage?"

Tony nodded. "Everyone has," he said. "I hear the wife is still in hiding."

"Lucky me, I agreed to work with the public defender and

figure out who really did it. So far, all it's gotten me is a pile of frustration and a blanket party."

"A blanket party?" Tony frowned. "I thought you sat down a little gently. You find out who did it yet?"

"I'm working on it," I said.

"You're wondering if I know anything about who killed that cop," said Tony.

"I am."

"And here I thought you were simply using me for my free Italian food."

"It's a nice perk."

Tony laughed and slapped the table. The goon sitting nearby turned and looked but saw nothing requiring his narrow skillset. Jerry appeared from the kitchen as if he took the table slap as a clue to hustle along. "Your tea and bruschetta, sir," he said, setting both down on the table. "The chicken parm will be out soon."

"Chicken parmesan," Tony said. "Let the customers do the abbreviations, Jerry."

"Yes, sir," Jerry said and scurried off.

"Chicken parm," Tony said, shaking his head. "What an asshole."

"Not Italian?" I said.

"On his mother's side. But the kid was raised by his father. Some dumb Mick."

I bit into the bruschetta and realized Tony dropped an ethnic slur most times I talked to him. He represented the old guard of Little Italy. As other restaurants met changing tastes by offering lighter, more upscale fare, Tony stuck with what made him famous. An occasional bit of innovation like my appetizer was inevitable. I even liked the olives on it; they served their purpose diced with garlic and tomatoes and mixed with fresh mozzarella atop the sliver of crispy bread. "*Congratulazioni*," I said.

"I'll forgive your pronunciation because you like the bruschetta," said Tony.

Jerry returned with my chicken parmesan and made sure to call it by its full name this time. Tony snacked on the occasional piece of bruschetta while I enjoyed the main course. Every time I lunched with Tony, the portions could feed me for three days. At least the meals kept me on my running schedule. When I finished a normal portion of chicken parmesan—or less than half the contents of my plate—Tony struck up the conversation again.

"I haven't heard anything about who killed the cop," he said.

I wiped my mouth and shrugged. "I doubted you did, but I figured I should check."

Tony nodded, then frowned. "I haven't heard anything."

"You mentioned that already," I said.

"I know, but I just realized what it means. Killing a cop is serious shit. Some people will love you for it, but the cops will have a major hard-on to catch you. The only people who would say they killed a cop are serious players."

"So the fact you haven't heard anything means whoever killed him was small time."

"I think so," Tony said with a slight nod.

It jibed with a drug dealer from the neighborhood. Paul King hadn't heard of whoever it was, and it definitely made the killer a minor player. "Thanks, Tony," I said. "Your info gets me over one hurdle."

"But you still have others," he said.

"I certainly do."

"Want to tell me about them?"

I really didn't, but I knew Tony would invoke the fact he knew me since my childhood. "The whole shooting just doesn't make a lot of sense," I said. There's a detail I can't work out. I want to stage the shooting in the victim's garage."

"So why don't you?" he said.

"I asked my parents to help, and they said no. My mother doesn't want to be a part of anything which might get her bounced from the rotary club."

Tony showed a smile his eyes tinged with sadness. "Why do you think your folks don't come by here anymore?" I thought of a good reason. "Your father knew what I did, but he didn't care. Once your mother found out, they stopped coming by. It's a shame. Your parents are good people, C.T. I've known them a long time."

"I know," I said.

"You can find other people to help you out," Tony said.

"I'm sure I can. It's interesting, you know? My parents will get me out of China, where I did a lot worse things than break into someone's garage to find a killer, but they won't help me here." Tony stared down and sipped his wine. He didn't look back up at me. The wine couldn't have been so fascinating. "What's going on, Tony?" I said.

"Nothing, nothing," he said a little too quickly.

"Either you've found a holy image on the surface of your wine or you're trying to avoid saying something about my parents."

Tony waved his hand. "Forget it."

"No, I won't," I said. "What is it?"

He looked up at me. "They never told you?" he said.

"Told me what?"

"Of course not. It would probably give your mother a spasm of some sort."

"Tony, what are you talking about?"

Tony regarded me for a few seconds. I noted again the increasing thinness of his face. "Your parents didn't get you out of Hong Kong, C.T," he said after a long moment.

I dropped my fork and heard it rattle off the plate. Tony looked straight at me. Despite his thinner face, his serious expression was the same as always. "Who did?" I finally said. I had a feeling I knew the answer.

Tony said, "Your parents have money, but what they lack is influence, at least past the city limits. Your father called me one night, told me his son was in a Chinese jail for computer hacking, and could I help? I said I'd see what I could do. Turns out I knew someone who owed me a favor . . . his brother happened to work for the state department. You probably know the rest."

I didn't know what to say. My parents lied about getting me out of jail overseas. Or did they? They never took direct credit for it, only telling me how hard it was to pull off. The difficult part was my mother seeking help from a gangster. My father wouldn't do something like ask Tony for help if my mother hadn't been on board. Or would he?

"Don't be mad at your parents," Tony said, filling in the silence. "They did what they needed to do to get you home."

"And now they owe you?" I said.

Tony shook his head. "No. Your parents loaned me money I needed to open this place. I paid them back, but that was just the money. It was a hell of a gesture on their part. I'd say we're even."

Jerry wandered back to the table. Tony shooed him away, and he hurried off to be anywhere else. "Wow," I said. "Why are you telling me this now?"

"To let you know your parents will do what's right for you," Tony said. "They don't want you to get caught breaking into a dead cop's garage. Hell, I don't want you to get caught for it, either. You think the blanket party was bad?"

"It was, but I think I've taken care of the cops snooping around everything I do."

"You better hope so."

"I guess I'll find out," I said. I drank tea to cover not knowing what to say about the bombshell Tony dropped into my lap.

"Thanks, Tony," I said after a few more seconds of awkward silence.

"For what?" he said.

"Getting me out of jail in Hong Kong, for one. For telling me the truth about the whole thing."

"I don't want you to go yell at your parents, C.T. They're only trying to do right by you, even if you think they're not helping."

I nodded. "I think I got caught up in the fact everyone in this case is throwing obstacles at me."

"Maybe you should come by for lunch more often," Tony said.

"I don't know if my waistline could handle more visits."

"Mine's doing OK." Tony smiled again but I saw the same sadness as before. This time, I would keep my mouth shut and not ask any questions. I doubted Tony would be so forthcoming with the answers.

"We all can't thrive on pasta and bruschetta, Tony. Not all of us are Italian."

"Fucking shame," said Tony.

CHAPTER 20

"I need your help," I said to Joey over the phone once I had returned home.

"What's going on?" he said.

"This is a venture of dubious legality."

"I pretty much assume it with everything you do."

I might have tried to act wounded, but it wouldn't do any good with Joey. "Pot, kettle, black," I said.

"What is this dubious venture?" said Joey.

I filled Joey in on anything new in the Ben Harrison case. "I think I'm missing something big," I said. I want to set the scene in the victim's garage."

"You want to break in and stage a shooting." I heard nary a trace of surprise in Joey's voice.

"Yep."

"Can I play the shooter?" Joey said.

"I'm still working on the cast list," I said. "Can you be at my house at eleven tonight?"

"You know I don't have much else going on." Joey hung up.

I needed one more participant, and I knew who to ask.

* * *

"I'll do it," Gloria said.

I hadn't even gotten to my protracted explanation yet. "You're agreeing to do something patently illegal," I said.

"I know," she said, "but you need the help, and I want to help you."

"If only everyone saw things so clearly."

"What do you mean?"

"My parents. I guess their interest in my cases goes only so far."

Gloria walked up to my chair and sat in my lap, wrapping her arms around my neck. She minded my ribs and didn't crowd me. I held her around her waist. "Well, I guess I'm just more helpful than your parents," she said.

"It means a lot to me," I said.

"Good," Gloria said with a smile and a kiss. "When do we leave?"

"Joey is meeting us here at eleven."

"You're going to do it at night?"

"We can't very well skulk around in the daylight," I said.

"Won't lights in the garage attract attention?" Gloria said.

I should have considered it. Did the Percocet I took a few hours ago make me hazy enough to overlook something so obvious? "We'll figure something out. I have a few hours to brainstorm."

"You'd better come up with something good," she said.

"I'll do my best," I said.

I had until eleven. With nothing else to do on the main case, I turned my attention back to the blanket party and who assaulted me. I popped a Percocet and settled in behind my monitor. Despite its high resolution and my suite of photo and video software, I could never get a clear look at anyone in the video. If I didn't know I was the victim, I may not have been able to identify myself.

There had to be another way. I cranked up the audio track and isolated Gloria's desperate pleas. I smiled as I listened to them. She loved me, and the proof was on tape. Regardless how it made me feel, I deleted the track. After some cleanup, I heard fuzzy voices. Every now and again, something came through clearly. The gunshots I got off pierced the silence of my office and startled me. I heard curses after the first bang and more after the second. Then I heard what sounded like a name.

I rewound the video and tweaked my audio settings. If someone's name made it into the video, I damned sure wanted to hear it. I donned headphones to try and hear better. The first report rang out. Swearing ensued. The second shot came next, followed by a scream, then by a name.

"Taylor, shit!"

Taylor. I didn't know if it was a first or last name, but at least I had something. A minute later, I brought up the BPD's employment database. The sensitive nature of HR information necessitated better security, but because the BPD's network believed my computer to be one of its own, I bypassed whatever measures blocked casual eyes. I searched for any officers or detectives with a surname of Taylor.

While it ran, I pondered what would have happened after I shot Taylor in the leg. My assailants fled with Taylor needing swift medical attention. If I happened to hit him in the femoral artery—I couldn't tell from the video—he could bleed out before he made it five minutes down the road. Necessity meant his friends would take him somewhere nearby. Even if I didn't hit the artery, a gunshot wound needs immediate attention. If my assailants were cops, they would know it, and they wouldn't risk the life of a brother to drive farther away.

The law required hospitals to report gunshot wounds to the police. Compliance would muddy the waters for my assailants. Even though they were cops, they couldn't have the incident on the record. No self-respecting doctor—and in my experience, doctors did not lack self-respect—would fail to report something like three cops coming in to get their wounded friend treated. *Oh, by the way . . . don't tell anyone about this. We're the police and we'll handle it.* I couldn't see it happening.

The two closest emergency rooms to my street were University of Maryland Medical Center and Mercy Hospital. I needed to know if either reported a shooting the night of my assault. I called UM first and asked for media relations. A moment later, a woman whose voice sounded infected with perkiness came on the line. "Thank you for calling University of Maryland Medicine," she said. "How can I help you?"

"Hi, my name is Trent, with the *City Paper*," I said. "We're doing a story on recent shootings. I was wondering if your hospital reported any two nights ago."

"Let me check for you, sir. One moment, please." She put me on hold. A pop song I hadn't heard in years and didn't need to hear now whiled away the wait. When I had stomached all I could of it, my lively helper came back on the line. "We did report one in the last thirty-six hours, sir."

I started to say the info was great but caught myself. "I see. Can you tell me anything else about it?"

"The victim came to our hospital around midnight," she said. "He was a middle-aged African-American male."

"Thank you," I said. "I'll probably need to follow up in person before I publish."

"You're welcome. Have a nice evening."

I assured her I would and hung up. A similar call to Mercy got me a much less perky voice and no results. Taylor went to one of those hospitals, and it stayed off the books. This meant they knew someone who would keep everything hush-hush, and this someone possessed a certain degree of pull. Someone's cousin in the cafeteria couldn't swing it.

I checked into UM and Mercy. Database administrators use a language called SQL to do much of their work, and it's vulnerable to specific attacks. Mercy's network succumbed quickly to an injection attack, so I started with them. I assumed Taylor to be a surname again and searched for employees with the same name. A couple minutes later, UM's electronic defenses yielded, and I ran the same search there.

All my results hit at the same time. I started with the BPD. Three people popped up on my screen. Taylor was a last name for all three. The video and voices confirmed all my assailants were men, so I removed Debra Taylor from consideration. It left Philip and Ambrose Taylor. I hoped it was Ambrose because I didn't like that name. Then I remembered I had no room to talk when it came to lousy first names. I scanned their personnel files and found their listed relatives. Ambrose's parents were both still living, and there was a younger brother. Philip's parents were deceased, but two sisters and a brother remained.

Cross-checking the lists of Taylors from the hospitals was easy. Philip Taylor's sister Ashley worked as a nursing supervisor at UM. A nursing supervisor could bully enough junior nurses into not reporting her brother's injury and would know enough doctors to get one of them to treat him on the sly. I checked her schedule. She worked tonight, five PM until two the following morning. I didn't have to be anywhere until eleven.

It left plenty of time to pay her a visit.

* * *

A VOLUNTEER GREETER directed me to the cardiac care unit where Ashley Taylor worked. I found her at the nurses' station staring at her computer screen. She wore her blond hair pulled back into a tight ponytail. In a nice touch, her light purple scrubs matched her nail polish. I wondered how many different colors she wore and how often she pulled off the synchronization. "Miss Taylor?" I said.

She looked up at me. If I didn't dislike her for helping one of the men who beat me, I might have called her pretty. "Can I help you?" she said.

"I have a sensitive matter to discuss with you."

"Is it about a patient?"

"Unofficially," I said.

My qualification drew a frown. The other nurse at the station who had been processing paperwork also looked up then. Ashley rose from her chair and walked over to me. "What do you mean by 'unofficially?'" she said in a lowered voice.

"I think you know what I mean," I said. I matched her tone not out of courtesy but because I didn't want her coworker eavesdropping. "Is there someplace we can talk?"

"Yes." She pursed her lips and thought about it. "There's a staff office around the corner to the left." Ashley gestured in that direction. "It's room number 418. Give me a half-hour, and I'll meet you there."

"All right," I said.

A half-hour gave her ample time to summon reinforcements. I resolved to be ready.

CHAPTER 21

A HALF-HOUR LATER, AFTER ENJOYING A SURPRISINGLY tasty latte in the cafeteria, I knocked on the door to 418 after waiting for the hallway to clear. "Come in," Ashley said from within the room.

I turned the knob, put my shoulder against the door, and pushed into the room. The door didn't hit anyone. This made my entrance awkward, but I ignored it. Ashley sat behind the desk. A burly hospital security guard stood beside her and gave me a cocksure smile. I guessed him to be about six-five. A spare tire hung over his belt, but muscles on his arms and the curve of his shoulders meant he kept in shape. I closed and locked the door. "Does he moonlight in the legal department?" I said.

"He's here to dissuade you," said Ashley, "by force, if necessary."

"Uh-oh."

"Walk away, pal," the guard said.

"I don't take orders well," I said.

"Vince, show him out," Ashley said. She leaned back in the chair and smiled.

"Yes, ma'am." Vince pounded his fist into his palm. He needed three steps to close the distance to me. After he took the second one, I kicked him in the knee, which took his leg out. My ribs complained. I needed to end this quickly. Vince tried to regain his feet, and I planted a side kick flush in his face. He bent backwards over his right leg and ended up on his back. He shook his head to clear the cobwebs. I didn't give him the chance. A snap kick to his head sent him to dreamland.

I turned to Ashley. She sat wide-eyed behind the desk. I took a seat in a guest chair while she gaped at me. The fear in her eyes made me smile. "You would have done better with a lawyer," I said. I pasted on another grin to hide a wince as my ribs barked from my sudden exertion. It's amazing how much they're involved in most everything we do. "Why are you here?" she said in a small voice. I watched to make sure she didn't reach for the phone.

"I told you; I'm here to talk about an unofficial patient."

"Who's that?"

"Your brother," I said.

Ashley tried to hide her look of surprise with a frown, but it didn't work. "I don't know what you're talking about."

"Sure you do. See, I didn't know for sure you were involved when I came here. It was a good guess but no more. Then when you arranged this welcoming committee for me, I knew I was right."

She sighed and shook her head. "What do you want?"

"Did your brother come here with a gunshot wound to the leg a few nights ago?" I said.

"I think you already know the answer."

"I want to hear you say it."

"Yes," Ashley said. "He came here. Three other cops brought him in."

"What did they say?"

"They called me while they were on the way and said he got

hurt in some kind of unofficial operation. They wanted to know if I could have him treated and keep it off the books."

"And you could," I said.

"Yes. Dr. McDowell agreed to treat him."

"In exchange for what?" She frowned and cast her eyes down at the desk. "Never mind; you gave me enough of an answer."

"He's my brother," she said, looking back up at me. "I had to help him."

"I'm going to show you a video," I queued Gloria's video on my phone and showed it to Ashley. She watched it like a horror movie: a mix of wide eyes, gasps, and winces. The only thing missing was a scream, and I didn't need her screaming while we were in this small office together.

"What *is* that?" she said after I finished playing the video a second time.

"It's called a blanket party," I said. "The man being beaten under said blanket is me."

"You?"

"Yes. The police and I disagree on the identity of a cop killer. This was their attempt to get me off the case."

"My brother did that to you?" She shook her head as if she expected denial to undo what happened.

"Him and three of his friends, yes," I said. "I want you to tell me who they are."

My demand got her to lean back in the chair again, this time with her head bowed. "He's my brother," she said. "Right or wrong, I don't know if I can sell him out."

"You're not. I already know who he is, or I wouldn't be here talking to you. You're selling out the other three assholes who assaulted me."

Ashley pondered the situation for close to a minute. "What are you going to do if I don't help you?" she said.

"Inform your bosses about your little bedroom deal with Dr.

McDowell and how the two of you broke the law by not reporting a gunshot victim."

"You can't!"

"I can," I said, 'and I will if you don't tell me what I want to know."

"That's blackmail," she said.

"Now look who's all law-and-order." I shrugged. "Sometimes, people need incentives to do the right thing. You're a felon, Miss Taylor, but I'll give you until this time tomorrow."

"Not a lot of time."

"Use it well. Remember what happened to Vince when you wasted time setting up an ambush," I said. "If you rat me out to your brother, you both can update your résumés. I'll make sure the press goes straight to the hospital board and police commissioner."

"You're a dick," Ashley said through a glower.

"I'm an assault victim, Miss Taylor," I said. "I'm entitled to be."

* * *

A few minutes after eleven, I herded Gloria and Joey into the Audi. I debated driving the Caprice but chose the Audi because of its speed advantage. If the police caught us, they were unlikely to shoot us as we fled, even with their hatred of yours truly, negating the Caprice's resistance to common bullets.

We made it to the Harrisons' house without even seeing a police car on patrol. The street was dark save for the scattered lights on poles as we approached. Only two homes showed any illumination at all. No cruisers sat in front of the Harrisons'. Maybe Rich spreading the false scuttlebutt worked.

I parked the Audi a couple houses away. The three of us walked around to the back, ducking behind fences as we moved.

We went through the gate—easily opened—to the Harrisons' backyard and padded up to the rear stoop. Gloria held the storm door open and Joey played lookout while I worked on the lock. A minute later, we went inside. I felt surprised a cop would have such a poor lock on his house, but then, who breaks into a cop's house?

This time, my illegal entry into the Harrisons' house felt like an invasion of privacy. No one had been here for days, but I still felt like we intruded on something. We clicked on our small LED flashlights and walked through the dining room. Nothing looked different from my last illicit visit. Mail lay scattered on the table, and the plaid tablecloth hung unevenly. We moved on through the kitchen and into the garage.

Gloria and I turned our flashlights off. Joey kept his on to give me light as I taped trash bags over garage door windows. With our privacy guaranteed, we got to work. "I'm the shooter," I said, keeping my voice only loud enough to be heard within the garage. "Joey, you're Ben Harrison. Gloria, you're Jack Bennett."

"Why am I the dead guy?" Joey said.

"It's right in your acting wheelhouse," I said.

"You're hilarious."

"At least you get to show off your range and act surprised before you die."

"I'll try not to lose myself in the part," Joey grumbled.

"Good. You start out behind the car there."

Joey inspected the bullet hole in the hood and frowned. "Ominous," he said.

"Gloria, you stand there . . . to your left," I said. She inched sideways, and I held up my hand to stop her where Jack Bennett said he'd been standing. "The garage door was open, so I walked in." I took a few steps forward. Between the Honda's hood and body, I could see Joey's ample midsection. "Joey, lean down like you're working on the engine." He did; now his face and head peeked out in the gap.

"I see you working on the car," I said. I looked at Gloria. "Somehow, I don't see you. If I do, I don't care. I fire a shot into the hood, over your head, Joey." I made a gun of my thumb and forefinger.

"You can see me," said Joey, "so you could have shot me."

"Maybe. I'd have to step around the body of the car, though, and that gives you more time to spot me."

"What if I'm engrossed in my work?" Joey said.

He made a good point. The hood wouldn't stop a bullet. "I could have easily shot you," I said. "I didn't. Why didn't I?"

"You wanted to see his face," said Gloria.

"Maybe."

"You wanted to talk to me," Joey said. He stepped out into the open and spared a frown for the bloodstains on the garage floor. They already turned brown and looked like they'd been painted on the concrete.

"I could talk to you while you were under the hood," I said.

"Now you can see his hands," Gloria offered.

"Very true," I said with a nod. "I may not have seen him going for a gun from under the hood. OK, Joey, I tell you to come out into the open and you do."

"I'm hoping you won't shoot me," Joey said, "and my family is inside. If I cooperate, you'll leave them alone."

"Julie is a cop's wife," I said. "She must've heard the report. She's going to get the kids to safety and then call nine-one-one. They'll respond quickly. Doesn't leave me much time to talk to you."

"Maybe you ask me one or two questions," Joey said.

"I guess I don't like your answers, then, because I shoot you twice."

"And I stay quiet over here the whole time?" Gloria said. "Even while I'm watching someone I know get shot?"

"Your survival depends on it," I said. "You're freaking out, but you manage to be silent."

"You shoot him, and now you want to leave," Gloria said. "You need a car."

"I take one from the driveway," I said. "There's no time to rummage for a key."

"Did I give you one?" Joey said.

"Not according to our witness. I turn"—I pivoted toward Gloria and saw her even by flashlight—"and toss the gun down before I exit the garage."

"You don't care about prints," Joey said. "Maybe you wore gloves."

"I must have," I said. "I drop the pistol, go to the driveway, and get into a car."

"Then I pick up the gun," Gloria said, moving away from the wall shelving, "and fire at the car."

"It's how you got GSR on your hands."

"Then I realize everything that's happened, and I get the hell out of here," she said. "I don't have a car, so I have to run."

"Sounds like the way things went down," Joey said.

"Except I somehow don't react to the witness against the wall," I said. "It still doesn't make sense."

"What if it's a frame job?"

"You think someone set Jack up?"

"It's a possibility," Joey said. He was right. I considered it once or twice when nothing else made sense. But the frame angle invited more questions than it answered.

"Who would try to make him the fall guy? And why?"

"Maybe the cop was the target," said Joey. "Jack was just a convenient patsy."

"It fits on some level." I frowned. "The problem is the gun. If someone's setting Jack up, why leave him a gun? If he's a good shot, this master criminal is dead before the end of the driveway."

Joey fell silent a moment. "New idea, then. Maybe you don't care about leaving someone at the scene."

I shook my head. "I have to care. I'm shooting a cop. If I'm a pro or an amateur, I'm not going to want to leave a witness."

"Do you know I'm a cop?" said Joey

Good question. "I don't know," I said. "I think I must. Why would I shoot you if you were just some random guy?"

"Maybe you had a beef with me."

"Even so, I think I know you're a cop."

"That means you don't see me," Gloria said. She went back to standing on the side of the garage. "You came here to kill a cop. You're not leaving a witness."

"But I look right at you when I turn." I spun toward Gloria to demonstrate this.

"Then maybe you pivoted the other way."

"All right." I went around a hundred eighty degrees. "Now you're behind me if I'm leaving but how did I not notice you before?" I twisted around toward the Honda and Joey. "The garage was well-lit if you're working on a car. Gloria, I should see you in my peripheral vision, and I do."

"Did I stand here the whole time?" Gloria said.

"Jack said he didn't move until the shooter left," I said. "He didn't want to do anything that would reveal his position."

"Then you should have seen me."

"Definitely. We need to think outside the box."

"Maybe the garage wasn't fully lit," Gloria offered.

I shook my head. "He was working on a car. It would have to be."

"What if he only used a light over his head?" Gloria nodded toward an additional light hanging from the garage ceiling. "The rest of the garage might be shadowy enough that I could hide."

"I doubt it," I said. "You were here talking to him. Why would he leave the rest of the garage dark?"

"Maybe you're blind in one eye," Joey said.

I rolled my eyes. "Seriously?"

"Think about it," he said. "Gloria's on your left. You never see her. After you shoot me, you turn to the right because you lead with your good eye. You never see her until she shoots at your car, and you're not stopping then."

I was forced to admit the idea had merit. "'When you eliminate the impossible,'" I said, "'whatever remains, however improbable, must be the truth.'"

"Now you're just quoting Spock," Joey said.

"Sherlock Holmes," I said. "Conan Doyle wrote it long before Leonard Nimoy said it."

"Whatever."

I remembered the man from the funeral home video. When I watched it, I thought he'd been drunk. His movements fit our current theory, however. "Blind in one eye is a possibility. Proving it will be hard."

"At least you know more than you did when you came here," said Joey.

I replayed the scene in my head. Joey's hypothesis made sense. Now I simply needed to red team it as a squad of one. "I do," I said. "But I have more questions to answer, too."

CHAPTER 22

The Internet has democratized information. Some data is easy to obtain, and some is learned through more surreptitious means. The number of good eyes someone possesses, however, is not easily found. I looked through Ben Harrison's paper records to see if he kept any notes on his clients. He did—any good cop would have—but speculation about someone being blind in one eye was not among his scribblings.

The next day, my parents were out congratulating themselves for being patrons of the arts, but Rich and I still used their house to meet for lunch. He brought a pepperoni pie from Pizza John's and a six-pack of Heavy Seas. The pizza's heat succumbed to the drive from Dundalk, so we warmed it in the oven before diving in. We each finished two wonderfully greasy slices and a beer before we said more than hello to each other.

"I need Ben Harrison's client files," I said.

Rich looked askance at me. "Why are you telling me?"

"Because the eager beavers who got to his house took his computer, which means you guys have his hard drive somewhere."

"It's evidence."

"It's important to my case," I said.

"I suppose you have a theory now," Rich said, leaning back as much as the chair would allow. He looked amused, and I hadn't even told him the idea yet.

"I do." I shared the idea with Rich.

He laughed.

"Not exactly the validation I hoped for," I admitted as Rich finished chuckling and shook his head. His reaction wasn't unexpected. I was, after all, tilting at a one-eyed windmill.

"The guy on *The Fugitive* searched for a one-armed man," he said. "Now you think you should be looking for a one-eyed man." This set off a new round of chortling. The goodwill Rich engendered by bringing Pizza John's and my favorite beer faded.

"It's a valid theory," I said, trying not to sound defensive. I knew how foolish it sounded; the problem was it fit the facts. Besides, I didn't have a bunch of spare theories burning a hole in my finely-tailored back pocket. "If you think about the way it went down, there's no other good explanation for why the shooter doesn't see Jack Bennett."

Rich concluded his guffawing and took a swig from a fresh beer. "Unless he didn't care," he said.

"Because people who shoot cops never care about witnesses."

"Good point. I just can't get past the idea. It's so. . . ."

"Foolish?" I offered.

"Something along those lines," Rich said with a nod.

"I didn't like it at first, either. The more I thought about things and played them in my head, though, the more it made sense."

Rich looked off into the distance. I could almost see the wheels turning as he ran through the scenario. "OK, so it's a better theory than it sounds at first listen," he said. "Now what?"

"I need Ben Harrison's complete files," I said. "He might have notes about one of his clients being blind in one eye or something to point us in the right direction."

"I doubt he'd take such notes."

I grabbed another slice of pizza from the box. The bottom of the box darkened with grease. Before Rich set it on the table, I put a layer of paper towels down. The decision looked prescient now. My mother would not want her tablecloth besmirched by pizza drippings. "He was a cop," I said. "He was probably observant." I couldn't mention the handwritten notes. "I'm sure he would have noted anything weird or suspicious."

"Maybe," Rich said with a shrug. He helped himself to another slice and bit off a large chunk.

"Does that mean you'll snag his hard drive for me?"

"Are you serious?" he said. "Not a chance."

"I'm sure your tech people made some copies for forensics," I said. "It can be one of them."

"I'm not taking a hard drive out of evidence and giving it to you, C.T. Not happening." Rich accentuated his point by tearing off another large chunk of pizza with his teeth.

I thought for a moment. "All right . . . don't take it out of evidence and give it to me," I said. "Take it out and hook it up in your own computer."

"What?" Rich said.

"I'm sure you have a spare SATA cable in your PC. Hook it up to a cable and power connector. I can get to it as long as it's plugged in."

"You could?"

I rolled my eyes at Rich. "How can you be a detective and know so little about how computers work?" I said.

"You're asking me to compromise evidence," he shot back. "How can *you* be a detective and know so little about how the law works?"

"I know plenty about it. Let's start with 'slowly' and 'inefficiently.' I'm sure I could come up with a bunch more uncharitable adverbs."

Rich grimaced. "You're asking an awful lot."

"All you have to do is tell someone you need to see the files," I said.

"They'll wonder why. They'll think I'm working with you, and I made sure to spread the word that you were off the case."

I frowned. Something so trivial could prove insurmountable. "There's no other way you could get a copy of the drive out of evidence?" I said.

Rich paused to think while he ate some more pizza. "I'll see what I can do. Maybe inspiration will strike."

"I'll hope for the best," I said. "Thanks, Rich."

"Don't mention it," said Rich. "Really."

WHILE I WAITED for my cousin, I kept rummaging through Ben Harrison's hard-copy files. Incomplete though they were, they still could contain a vital clue. Most of the notes dealt with a car's make and model, positives or deficiencies of same, parts used, parts needed for general stock, and similar boring things. Client notes contained little helpful information, and none broached the possibility of a problem with one eye.

As it often does, my ringing cell phone interrupted me. Caller ID pegged it as BPD Headquarters. Had Ashley Taylor ratted me out to her brother's bosses? I kept copies of the video in case something untoward happened. The phone kept ringing. Paranoia wouldn't get me anywhere. I picked it up.

"Mr. Ferguson?"

"Yes."

"This is Sheila with Captain Sharpe's office. The captain would like to know if you could come in sometime today."

"What for?" I said.

"He said it would be to have a conversation," Sheila said.

"Did he mention the subject of this conversation?"

"He did not."

This could be good or bad. "I'm free for the next few hours," I said.

"Very good," she said. "Can you be at the captain's office in thirty-five minutes?"

"I wouldn't miss it."

We hung up. I wondered why Sharpe wanted to talk now. The last time we conversed, he wasn't at all receptive to my ideas or the harassment I'd experienced. Thirty-five minutes. It gave me time to keep looking through Ben Harrison's files.

* * *

THIRTY-NINE MINUTES LATER, I stood before Sheila's desk in Leon Sharpe's office. She gave me a perfunctory smile. "The captain said to send you in when you get here," she said.

"Who am I to keep him waiting, then?" I said, walking into Sharpe's office and closed the door behind me. Sharpe worked on a paper atop his desk and didn't look up when I entered. His bald black head with nary a hair nor whisker reflected the light from his banker's lamp. Not everyone can look good with a shaved head. Leon Sharpe managed to excel at it. I strode to the desk and eased onto one of the guest chairs. Sharpe focused on his paperwork for a minute or two longer, then shoved the documents inside a manila folder and looked up at me.

"I hear you dropped the case," he said.

"I'm OK, Leon," I said. "Thanks for asking. How are you?"

Sharpe smirked. I'd never seen him laugh, and he rarely smiled. Smirking, however, was a regular part of his arsenal. "I guess I should ask how you're doing, considering."

"Seeing as a few of your boys threw me a party under a blanket?"

"Like I said, considering."

"I'm taking painkillers for my ribs," I said. "They're not as strong as my personality."

"I'm sorry it happened to you," he said. It sounded sincere.

"You didn't know about it in advance?"

"If you mean, did I direct anyone to do it? No." Sharpe fixed me with one of his patented thousand-yard stares. I'm sure it shook the knees of plenty of cadets.

"Not what I meant," I said, "but it's good to know."

"Word is you're off the case," Sharpe said.

"Obviously, word travels fast."

"We both know it's bullshit," he said. "What's really going on?"

"Are you going to stop me from investigating?"

"If a blanket party can't keep you away, I don't know what I could do."

"You could tell people my backing off was bullshit," I said.

Sharpe shook his head. "Not getting involved. I figured you spread the word to keep people off your back. I know you've had a hard time of this. We cops can be . . . provincial when one of our own is dead, and an outsider is sniffing around. I can't say I like someone else looking into it, but I know you, C.T., and I know the kind of work you do. If we have the wrong man, I think you can find the right one."

"Wow," I said. "Those words sound dangerously close to an endorsement."

"Feel free to transcribe it for your Yellow Pages ad. Just attribute it to someone else."

"I will."

"I found out about your hearing," Sharpe said, leaning back in his chair. "There's a video of the assault?"

"There is," I said.

"And you're not filing charges?"

"Would anyone take my report right now?"

"Of course."

"Do I need to point out the BPD's spotty history of taking reports?"

Sharpe took in and released a slow, deep breath. It was my usual effect on him. "My point is I wouldn't want to see that video released to the public," he said.

I smiled. "And now we come to the real reason for my visit—damage control."

"Something like your video gives people the wrong idea," Sharpe said, continuing a planned message as if I hadn't said anything.

"Yeah, it sends the message the BPD might assault you if you disagree with them. It's good such a thing doesn't happen. Oh, wait, it does." Sharpe shook his head. I continued. "It might also send the message the police haven't learned anything from the Freddie Gray fallout."

"Look," Sharpe said, breaking in, "I know you got a raw deal with this one, and I'm sorry you went through it." He leaned forward again. "However, I don't want to see your video end up on the local news."

"It'd be worse for you if it ended up on the Internet," I said. "How fast do you think it would go viral? How willing do you think people are to believe the worst about your department?"

"You want something."

"We all want something, Leon. Not all of us have the ammunition to get it."

"What is it?" he said.

"I'm working on discovering who the men in the video are," I said. "When I know, I'm going to find them and kick the shit out of them. I want you to look the other way while it happens."

"You want me to ignore you assaulting four police officers?" Sharpe said with a prominent frown.

"The alternative is worse," I said. "The video goes out into the world, I figure out who they are anyway, and then you have to deal with the outcry." I offered a mock wince. "It sure wouldn't jibe with the positive press the BPD has managed to get recently."

Sharpe glared at me. I'd been on the receiving end of it before—and worse in China—but I could see how it would unnerve spine-deficient criminals. "You came here to blackmail me?" he said.

"No," I said. "It never crossed my mind as a possibility. When you started hammering me about the footage, I needed to make sure I could protect myself."

"And your need for revenge."

I shrugged. "Sure."

"It won't make you feel better," said Sharpe.

"I'm willing to find out."

Sharpe leaned back again and stared at me. I did the same. "What about the ringleader?" he said.

"What about him?"

"You want revenge; I get that. I'm not going to look the other way while you beat on four of my men, and I don't give a shit what you threaten me with." He paused for a breath. "However, if you were to go after the ringleader and let me deal with the others, I might consider it a reasonable compromise."

I thought about it for a few seconds. "Fine," I said.

"Listen to me." Sharpe pointed at me. "If you do anything worse to him than what happened to you, I'll go after you with both barrels. Your fancy lawyer and a cell phone video won't get you off the hook. We clear?"

This couldn't have been easy for Sharpe. He needed to sign off on the beating of one of his cops to keep the department's image clean. The BPD carried missteps of earlier administrations, Freddie Gray, and a damning DOJ report in their rearview, and they still managed to make some recent favorable strides. Sharpe couldn't afford to undo all of those gains with one video, and he couldn't condone me going after four men. I didn't envy his dilemma. "We're clear," I said.

* * *

RICH CALLED after I got back from my *tête-a-tête* with Leon Sharpe. "I have the drive," he said in a hushed tone.

"Is it hooked up?" I said.

"Yes. Someone else helped me get it setup inside my PC."

I chuckled at Rich's lack of computer aptitude. "OK, thanks, Rich. I'll drop you a line when I have what I need."

Rich hung up, and I got to work. I knew his IP address from my first case, when he left his PC unattended and me in a guest chair. The BPD never changed it, which was a poor security practice. I didn't understand organizations that used static public addresses. The alternatives were easier and at least a little more secure. I browsed to Rich's computer, found the additional drive, and mounted it on my PC. I poked around for a while in Ben Harrison's filing system. It amazed me how some people organized their hard drives. I found the client files three subfolders deep under the "Temp" folder. Once I had scoured the drive for anything else useful, I copied all the client files to my PC. When I finished, I called Rich.

"The eagle has flown," I said when he picked up.

"What?" said Rich.

"I think you were supposed to say, 'but the dove came in for a nice landing.' Haven't you ever watched a spy movie?"

"Are you trying to tell me you're finished?" he said.

"I am. Thanks for the assist."

"Don't mention it."

"I won't," I said.

We hung up. I started combing the files.

* * *

THE ELECTRONIC DATA filled in the gaps of its paper counterpart, but I still didn't have anything to work with. I hoped this wouldn't be the end of Joey's theory because I didn't have another one. I dumped all the names from Ben Harrison's records into a text file. Even if Harrison didn't have much information on these people, I knew I could find some. It would take a while to access the kinds of records to tell me a person was blind in one eye. Health information privacy laws—namely HIPAA—presented an annoying speed bump.

I went after the names in batches. My targets were local hospitals and insurance companies who operated in the area. If I didn't get what I wanted there, I would break into the MVA and see what their data could tell me. Cultivating my targets took a while. Health information is very sensitive and places storing it do a good job of guarding content. Once I got into the last insurance company, I wrote a script to extract the information.

While the data crunched, I tried to get some exercise. Running had been impossible since the blanket party. I worked up to the point where I could walk briskly. Jogging still shot pain throughout my torso. I couldn't keep up the pace for more than a half-hour without the intrusion of pain, but I kept going out there to stay in shape. The warming weather also meant I would see more walkers and joggers, some of them attractive women, in my jaunts around Federal Hill Park.

Today, only a couple of dog walkers provided company. The dogs darted to and fro, dragging their owners off the sidewalks to investigate all manners of things they found interesting. I walked until breathing became a challenge, then slowed my pace and started for home. As I did, I wondered what kind of information my searches would uncover. Medical records can be spotty, especially if someone has moved around and changed doctors, or just hasn't been ill or injured much. A general practitioner might not even make a note that a patient is blind in one eye. What could he or she do about it, after all? I resolved to add MVA records regardless of what my medical searches found. One-eyed men could be considered a liability while driving; the MVA conducts vision tests for all potential drivers and would retain those records.

As I walked down my block, a girl I encountered before ran the opposite direction toward the park. Normally, if I saw her doing her laps, I would fall in stride behind her. The small jogging shorts she favored gave me plenty of motivation to keep up my pace. When she saw my languid steps, she smiled and said, "Slacker" as she sprinted past.

Considering my current limitations, I accepted my status as I neared my house.

By the time I got out of the shower and came back downstairs, all my scripts finished their various illicit operations. As an added precaution, I would destroy the virtual machine I used later. I stared at a pile of mixed results. Medical records were only as reliable as the information entered. I established liberal search parameters, hoping the cast of a wider net would ensnare the person I sought, even if I needed to weed through some chaff to get there.

I took the results plus the rest of the names I started with and broke into the MVA database. I hoped its record of drivers and their vision tests would provide me better answers. A lot of this case revolved around wishful thinking. Working as a detective sapped the hope out of me over the last year and a half. It was hard to summon it again when I stumbled into roadblocks.

For a bureaucratic mess of an agency nearly everyone hated dealing with, the Motor Vehicle Administration operated with a clean and efficient database. This time, I emerged with five possible names: the same three as before plus two new ones. Maybe my first search hadn't been as bad as I thought. Armed with a much shorter list of suspects, I now went back to the BPD and looked up arrest records. Three of the five had been arrested before, none by Ben Harrison. That eliminated a vendetta as the motive.

I printed out records for the three and looked them over. One was a white-collar criminal, busted for trying to pull a fast one on the state treasury. The other two owned records involving minor drug offenses and assaults. It didn't mean they were likely to gun someone down, but it made them better suspects than someone who tried to gyp the state taxman.

According to his medical records, Frank Manning lost the vision in his left eye in an accident eight years ago. In the time before and since, he had been busted for possession of marijuana and for assaulting a stranger. Kyle Snell lost his left eye to the blade of a knife. His photo showed he wore a convincing prosthetic. Kyle dabbled in marijuana possession and distribution, got popped for cocaine once, and enjoyed assaulting former girlfriends. Both were assholes, drove silver cars, and lived reasonably close to Ben Harrison.

I couldn't narrow it down by myself.

"TALK FAST," PAUL KING SAID OVER AN ICED TEA AT Magerks, "I have the streets of Baltimore to keep safe."

""It's a big city," I said. "You must be very busy."

"I usually am. What's up?"

I slid two folded pieces of paper across the table. "Two people who might be good for the Harrison shooting," I said.

King eyed me over his glass. "No shit?" he said.

"They're maybes. I don't know if they did it. They both have drug arrests, and drugs are a possible motive for Ben Harrison getting shot."

"If you believe his brother."

I sipped my beer. It tasted bitter, even as India pale ales went, but it helped pay fair rental for a table in this pub. Despite his disheveled appearance, something in King's eyes screamed he was a cop. Because of it, he always procured tables away from the crowd, and tonight was no exception. "Right now, I don't know what to believe," I said. "All I've tried to do is find who really killed a cop, and I've gotten nothing but hassled for it every step of the way. So . . . if you don't mind . . . can you look over the fucking files and tell me what you think?"

"Aren't we touchy?" King said. He put his tea down and

looked at me for a few seconds. "I know you've caught a lot of shit for this. It's fucked up. Some cops don't like people like you snooping around things we prefer to take care of ourselves."

"As far as I can tell, you have the wrong man in jail," I said. "How's taking care of it yourself working out?"

"Hey, I'm giving you a hand here. Dial it back."

It was true I gave King a lot of grief. The obstacles thrown in front of me hadn't been his fault. "Sorry," I said. "This is a frustrating case."

King shrugged. "I get it." He read the first file, then the second. "You want to know which one is a better suspect?"

"I want to know if either of them could be good for it. They're not killers, but they do have histories of assault."

"Big leap from punching a broad to killing a cop," King said, campaigning for the BPD's Sensitivity Award. His eyes scanned the files again. "I don't know much about either of them. From our perspective, they're small time." He shook his head. "I don't have much to offer you here, sorry."

"It's all good," I said. King refolded the papers and slid them back to me. And so another complication sprang up before me. "OK. I guess I'll have to look into both of them."

"If I hear anything or get an idea, I'll let you know."

"Thanks."

"I gotta go," King said, and downed the rest of his iced tea in one protracted gulp. "Keeping the city safe and all."

"Good luck," I said.

"I need it," said King.

* * *

WHEN ALL ELSE FAILS, go alphabetically. This is a tried and true investigative technique, ranking barely above flipping a coin. It also made things faster than deciding which man would be heads and which tails. I drove by Frank Manning's house. His silver car sat in front. The dwelling was small with a brick front and a nice wraparound patio. A light burned inside, and I noticed the irregular flashes of a TV. Frank Manning spent an exciting evening on his couch. When the light downstairs went out and was soon replaced by one on the second level, I packed it in to try again tomorrow.

The next morning, I dragged myself out of bed at the beastly hour of 7:30. Gloria snored while I showered and only stirred when I kissed her and bade her farewell. I sat across the street and two doors down from Manning's house a half-hour later with a thermos full of coffee, a breakfast sandwich and snacks from Starbucks, and a Kindle to help pass the time. To get into the proper sleuthing spirit, I perused a classic mystery. How many boring stakeouts did Spenser suffer through?

About forty minutes later, I got my wish. He limped out of the house toward his car. Manning was tall, looked about forty, and took on a stocky look with the onset of age. His left foot turned in toward his body as he limped. He never grimaced, instead appearing resigned to the fact he couldn't walk properly. This was the limp of a man who had been forced to get around this way for a while. It didn't disqualify him as the killer, but it made the scenario more difficult. Jack Bennett would have noticed the unusual gait.

Manning got in his silver car, and I followed him about fifteen minutes to a Target. I gave him room as I tailed him into the store. He went toward the back and doffed his jacket, revealing a red polo beneath it. The jacket seemed to hang on his right arm before he slid the sleeve off and disappeared into an employees-only area. I lingered and looked at a bunch of tzotchkes I didn't want to buy until Manning came out again, pushing a dolly filled with boxes and totes.

I puttered around nearby and circled back a couple minutes

later. Manning opened a tote and stocked the shelf with plastic bathroom cups. His right arm never straightened, and he leaned to and fro to accommodate it. The arm also never moved far from his body. I saw him unload a few more totes, all containing non-fragile items. He had lost vision in one eye, had a limp, and had a serious problem using his right arm. Even if Jack Bennett hadn't noticed the limp, the right arm would have given Manning away. He couldn't be the killer. His file mentioned "other complications" from the accident taking the sight in his left eye. More specificity would have saved me hours of time.

I left Target without buying anything.

* * *

I SCOURED Kyle Snell's records. After finding incomplete information in Frank Manning's, I wanted to be sure I unearthed every snippet. Unlike Manning, Kyle Snell's blindness was not a part of a much larger issue: Kyle got stabbed in the eye. No doubt he deserved it. I didn't really care if he used drugs, but he sold them, and a level of violence often goes hand-in-hand with being a dealer. Toss in Kyle's fondness for hitting women, and I wondered why the person with the knife stopped after the first eye.

Police arrested Snell twice for simple possession of marijuana, and he got popped once with a large enough quantity to add intent to distribute. The narcotics unit also suspected him of dabbling in the much more dangerous cocaine trade, but they'd compiled no solid proof. Snell hung with a few known associates whose pasts were as checkered as his own. He had the makings of a small drug enterprise if he wanted one. None of the other guys seemed smart or industrious enough to take on something along those lines. In the land of the blind and lazy, Snell was the one-eyed man with just enough motivation to be king.

I researched the officers who arrested Snell, none of whom were Ben Harrison. One of the names looked familiar, and I cross-referenced it: Brian Carnes once trained under Ben Harrison and built a promising career before a few disciplinary incidents relegated him to working Central Booking. He was the desk sergeant I met there. Now I understood why he had been such an ass during my brief stay as a guest of the BPD. I wondered if his close ties to Ben Harrison compelled him to be part of my blanket party.

Armed with new information, I called Paul King and asked him to meet me again. He didn't sound happy I woke him. I told him to suck it up and enjoy a free lunch. He grunted.

I took it as a yes.

* * *

KING CHOSE The Greene Turtle in Fells Point. I didn't eat there often, but the food was perfectly good for a casual sports bar (and grille, the sign informed patrons). I liked some of the sauces they served with appetizers. Whatever could be used to justify the pretentious extra E at the end of *grille*. When I arrived, King already sat in a secluded booth munching on fried pickle chips. Once again, he scored a remote table.

I slid onto the opposite booth and snagged a pickled delicacy right away. Years of lunching with Joey Trovato taught me to grab food at the first opportunity. King shrugged and gestured to the bowl as he took a sip of his amber beer. "Off duty today?" I said.

"Maybe I need a drink to get through another meeting with you," said King.

"Says the man whoring himself out for a free lunch."

"If I were a whore, I'd pick a classier place," he said. King popped another chip into his mouth.

I sampled the appetizer along with its chipotle-flavored

dipping sauce. The sauce was spicy enough to make me pay attention. I requested an unsweetened tea from the waiter who came by. He zoomed off before I could order my food. I resigned myself to eating more pickle chips. There were worse fates.

"What does my lunch at the establishment buy me?" I said.

"The pleasure of my company," King said.

"McDonald's would be too much, then."

The waiter came back with my tea and a straw. I ordered a turkey burger. After the server keyed in our order, he dashed to a table of four college girls. If I were his age, I would have done the same. The girls were a hell of a lot prettier than King and me.

"You brought me something to look over, I presume?" King said.

"I did." I slid Snell's file across the table.

"This is one of the names you showed me already."

"I have more information this time," I said. "Check it out."

King scanned the file. While he did, our waiter pried himself away from the sorority sisters long enough to set King's cheeseburger down. Before he could scamper away again, I stopped him. "You're trying to hit on the redhead, right?" I said.

He glanced at their table. The young woman I mentioned enjoyed a light-hearted conversation with two brunettes and a blonde. I would have fancied one of the brunettes, but to each his own. "Yeah, how'd you know?" he said.

"Because you're filling her water glass more than the other girls."

He showed a conspiratorial smile. "You think it's working?"

"Not at all," I said. "You should pay attention to the other women at the table."

"But why—?"

"Trust me. I've never been a waiter, but I've talked to a lot of pretty girls over the years."

The waiter pursed his lips but nodded after a few seconds of thought. "OK, I'll see how it goes," he said, and off he went. King chuckled around bites of his burger.

"You think he has a chance with her?" he said.

"Not really," I said. "This might give him a little help for the future, though."

"And you love to help people."

"I'm in a service industry."

King interspersed scanning the file with eating his cheeseburger. While he perused, the waiter returned with my turkey burger. I ate my lunch while King continued his review. "Could be the guy," he said. "If drugs were involved, I guess he fits."

"You don't know much about him?"

"We could never pin any coke charges on him," King said. "Just a lot of suspicion. We got a warrant once and didn't find anything. The brass was gun-shy toward him afterward."

"But you think he's doing more than selling joints," I said.

"I do," King said with a nod. "Only we can't prove it."

"I like Snell for this. Maybe we can pin Ben Harrison and some cocaine trade on him at the same time." I left the Carnes connection out. King had enough to turn over in his head.

"More conjecture isn't going to get the brass moving," King said.

"I wouldn't dream of rousing them from their torpor," I said. "This would be smaller. You, me, Rich—that's probably about it. The more people there are sniffing around, the more suspicious he's going to get."

"Just three of us?" King said. "He might have a lot of men."

"He'll need them," I said.

King smiled. "He will, won't he?"

* * *

AN HOUR LATER, Rich and I sat in the Audi, watching Kyle Snell's house for any sign of suspicious silver cars, shady associates, and shenanigans. I hoped to find all three. So far, we'd seen enough of the house to draw it from memory but nothing else. "I've worked a full shift today already," said Rich. "They need to do something soon."

"I'll let them know to coordinate their activities around your work schedule," I said.

"Mighty nice of you."

"I have my moments."

Rich was on his second cup of coffee when we saw someone. A woman came out of the house. Her blond hair was the best shade a five-dollar bottle could buy. She wore a sweatshirt a size too big and paired it with shorts small enough to give some Instagram models pause. Baltimore's brief spring hadn't passed yet, so the shorts were impractical unless she wore them for someone's benefit. Rich observed her through a pair of binoculars as she checked the mailbox and went back inside.

"Looks like she has a black eye," he said, shaking his head.

"Snell has a history of abusing women," I said."

"He's beating her. We can use that against him."

"Not so fast." Rich glared over at me. "If we were to ask her how she got her shiner, what do you think she's going to say? She's going to stick up for Snell unless we can convince her he's not worth the effort."

"You think she'll turn on him?" Rich said.

I shrugged. "Have to talk to her to find out. We'll need to get her alone and out of the house. She needs to be free of anything reminding her of him."

"I guess. She might turn easier than someone who works for Snell."

"How are we going to isolate her, though?" I said. "If he hits her, he probably doesn't let her out of his sight for long."

"Let's see what happens with everyone else," said Rich.

About a half-hour later, three men walked out of the house. Rich and I glanced at a picture of Kyle Snell. He was one of them. The other two looked like they were on loan from Gold's Gym. Rich's hands flexed into white-knuckled fists. "Let them go," I said.

"We can take them," Rich said.

"I don't doubt it." Honestly, I did. With me at much less than a hundred percent, we wouldn't have an easy time of the fight, and I could turn out to be a liability,

"What if they're going to buy drugs?" Rich said. "Or sell drugs?"

"What if they're going to eat lunch?" I said. "Why overplay our hand?"

Rich let out a long, slow breath. His fists unclenched. "All right," he said. "We'll let them go." The three men got into a black SUV, which backed out of the driveway, revealing a silver Honda Accord.

"Look at the car," I said.

"The son of a bitch killed him," Rich said. "He's the guy. We had the wrong guy all along."

"While I'm inclined to agree I've been right this whole time, let's do some more digging." I took a tablet out of a small laptop bag.

"What are you doing?"

"Looking up the girlfriend's number." I used a tool called InSSIDer to find a wireless network whose owner hadn't received the memo about good security. Several popped up. I chose one running Wired Equivalent Privacy—which offered nothing of the sort—and then set about breaking it with a nifty program I wrote in Hong Kong and updated a few times since returning.

"Should I be looking the other way?" Rich said.

"As a detective, I'm sure you're duty-bound to act on any crimes you see being committed," I said.

"I'll make sure no one else leaves the house."

"Good idea." A few seconds later, my script cracked WEP, and I was on the network. My tablet would anonymize my traffic, protecting both me and whoever I stole the signal from. Don't believe hackers can't be polite. I used the police file on Kyle Snell to find his girlfriend's name: Tracie Potter. The file didn't have her phone number, so I went online and found it after a few seconds. I took out my cell phone and sent her a text.

Kyle is going down. Help me & help yourself. Not a cop. Text back if interested.

"You think she'll answer?" Rich said.

"We'll see," I said.

"Can they trace your phone?"

"Have we met?"

Rich chuckled. "How silly of me."

My phone vibrated. I had a text.

Who r u?

"She's nibbling the bait." I sent a reply.

Someone who can help. Meet me & we can talk. Needs to be very soon.

"Have you ever been fishing?" Rich said.

"No," I said, "but I've read about it enough to know I used the metaphor correctly." Rich's father—my uncle—offered to take me a few times, but I had never gone.

"You did."

I got another reply.

Café 3 blocks away 5 minutes.

"Should I use another fishing metaphor, or would it offend your inner sportsman?" I said.

"She's going to meet you?" said Rich.

"Apparently, there's a café three blocks from here. We're meeting in five minutes."

"What am I going to do?"

"Stay here," I said. "Keep the car warm. If you have to sit in the driver's seat, try to look handsome."

"What are you going to do?" Rich said.

Tracie came around the back of the house, pushing a shop-worn bike down the driveway. She got onto the seat when she hit the sidewalk and turned left, pedaling slowly. I got out of the S4. "I'm going to follow the girl on the bike," I said.

CHAPTER 24

Tracie set a relaxed pedal pace, allowing me to keep up with her at a brisk walk. It didn't do wonders for my ribs, but I could maintain it for a while. Three blocks later, she pulled into the parking lot of a small corner café. Her bike was new enough not to have a kickstand, so she propped it up against a pole. Securing the chain proved a challenge, and the delay allowed me to slip into Corey's Corner Café ahead of her.

A cute barista smiled and greeted me as I walked in. The café walls reinforced my idea paneling should be confined to the basements of people who lacked the funds or good sense to use something better. Pictures of Italian villas and landscapes hung on the walls. The counter dominated the right side of the café, leaving at least two-thirds of the floor space for tables.

The barista gave me another smile. "How can I help you today?" she said.

"Do I need to order alliteratively?" I said.

She maintained her smile, but it morphed into a hollow one, like she kept it up to make me think she knew what I meant. What were they teaching kids in high school and college these days? And when did I become old enough to think of them as kids? I fought down my disappointment in both the education system and my own age and looked at the menu board. "A vanilla latte and two blueberry scones, please," I said. "Also put whatever the blonde lady outside gets on my tab."

The barista got me two scones and went about making my latte. Of the dozen tables in Corey's Corner Café, only three were occupied, and all by people engrossed in whatever they viewed on their laptops. I picked a spot away from them in case their infatuation ended and they decided to pay attention. A minute later, Tracie walked in, ordered something, and looked around. I waved at her, and she swayed her hips between tables to mine.

Her hair looked more natural up close. She wore a large, gaudy pair of sunglasses doing a good job to hide the black eye. Tracie drummed her fingers on the tabletop as her left leg bounced on raw nerves. She'd replaced the shorts with a more sensible pair of jean capris. "You're the one who texted me," she said, demonstrating a firm grasp of the obvious.

"I am," I said. The barista brought our drinks. Tracie got something smelling vaguely of caramel and coming with enough whipped cream to make a vegan sob. The barista set a receipt in front of me, smiled, and walked away.

"You said you could help me," she said after a moment.

"I can," I replied.

"Who says I need help?"

"You do."

"I do?"

"The sunglasses are a pretty big giveaway," I said.

She shrugged. "Maybe I drank too much last night," Tracie said.

"Maybe you did." I nudged a scone toward her. Pushing her wouldn't accomplish anything. I needed to show Tracie her boyfriend was an asshole, which meant I needed to be a nice and patient person by comparison. I hoped I had it in me.

"What's this?" she said.

"A blueberry scone." The pastry was an appealing beige color with bright blueberries bursting through the surface. I broke off a piece of mine and tasted it. The dough had a subtle sweetness balanced by the tartness of the blueberries. Were I to rate the scones I'd sampled in my life, this one would come in near the top of the brief list.

Tracie frowned at the baked good. I hoped she didn't eat it; I would gladly scarf down a second. She ignored it for the nonce and sipped her decadent beverage. "So how can you help me?"

"Your boyfriend is going down," I said. "I can rescue you from the sinking ship."

"In exchange for what?" she said.

I sipped my latte. It tasted stronger of vanilla than the ones I got from Starbucks. "Information."

"You want the goods on Kyle."

"It would help me a lot." She stared at me like she didn't believe me. Maybe she thought Kyle Snell would never be teetering on the edge like this. Maybe she thought I wasn't up to the task of pushing him off. "Do you know what he did?" I said while she pondered my powers and virtues.

"Sold drugs?" Tracie said.

"Worse."

"I don't know, then. That's usually the worst he does."

I didn't bring up her sunglasses again, even with such a perfect lead-in. "The silver car in the driveway," I said. "Tell me what's happened to it over the last week or so."

"The Accord?" Tracie took a larger sip and a bit of whipped cream hung on the edge of her lip. It distracted me as she talked. "I took it to a guy I know to have some work done on it," she said. "Kyle wondered where it was when he got back. He was all frantic and shit. I told him where I took it. He said he needed to get it back."

"Why was he so desperate?" I said.

"He didn't say, but I'm sure he had drugs in the trunk. No way he'd freak out so much about anything else."

"So he went and got the car back."

"Yeah," she said, "the same day. It was back after a couple hours."

"The man you took it to was Ben Harrison," I said.

"Yeah, Ben. Good guy. You know he's a cop?"

"I do. How do you know him?"

Color flooded Tracie's cheeks. "He busted me a few years ago," she said. "Took interest in me afterwards, though, and tried to help me keep on the straight and narrow, you know? Just a real good guy." She smiled, then frowned and all happiness vanished from her face. "Wait, you think Kyle did something to Ben?"

"My theory is Kyle killed him," I said.

"No." Tracie shook her head vigorously as if her denial possessed the power to change the past. "No, no, no."

"No, he couldn't do it or no, you wish it weren't true?"

Tracie said something, but I couldn't understand it past her tears. She put her face—sunglasses and all—in her hands and cried. I let her sob and glared at any patrons who took interest in the events of our table. After a couple minutes, she stopped crying and dabbed at her eyes with a napkin without taking her gaudy sunglasses off. "I wish it weren't true," she said. "I kept telling myself it wasn't."

"What happened the night Ben died, Tracie?"

"Kyle got home and wondered where the Accord was," she said. "I told him I drove it to Ben's to get the brakes replaced. He freaked out. Didn't tell me why, of course, but it dawned on me soon enough. He . . . he hit me a couple times, then stormed out. Soon, he was back with the Accord. Said he had taken care of the situation." Tracie shook her head again. A couple tears emerged from behind her sunglasses and slid down her cheeks. "I hoped he hadn't done anything to Ben. He wouldn't tell me. I should have known.

I patted Tracie's hand. She didn't pull it away. "Don't go back there today," I said. "You're done with Kyle Snell."

"Where am I gonna go?"

"Is there anyone you can stay with?"

"I have a few friends," Tracie said.

"Good," I said. "Stay with them . . . at least for tonight."

"You're going to take down Kyle?"

"Not alone. I'm working with a few cops on this one. They're not going to let Kyle get away with what he did."

"It'll feel weird, not being with him. Him and me, we been together for two years." Tracie showed a wistful smile. "Longest relationship of my life."

"He's an abuser," I said. "It's not a relationship."

Tracie nodded. "Part of me can see that," she said.

I changed the subject before I lost her to introspection. "Can you tell me where Kyle and his friends went?" I said.

"A movie and lunch." She rolled her eyes. "Every month, he and his asshole buddies go and see some lame movie, then eat food and get shit-faced."

"So he'll be gone for a while."

"A few hours," she said.

I smiled. "Good."

* * *

"I THINK WE CAN USE HER," I said to Rich when I rejoined him.

"You have a nice little chat in the coffee shop?" Rich said, punctuating his question with an annoyed tone I'd grown used to hearing.

"As a matter of fact, I did."

"That's nice. While you were sipping your espresso, I—"

"Latte," I said.

"What?"

"Vanilla, to be exact."

"I don't care," said Rich.

"And a scone."

Rich rolled his eyes. "While you and the queen mum were having tea and crumpets, I called in a couple of narcs. They're en route with a drug-sniffing dog."

"You know the more people we involve in this, the greater the chance it goes all to hell, right?"

"I didn't tell these guys much about what they were coming here for," Rich said. "They're doing me a solid."

"A solid?" I said.

"Yeah."

"And you mocked me for having a latte and a scone."

A couple minutes later, an unmarked van pulled to the curb. Two cops, one white and one Hispanic, got out. The white one opened the back of the van and led a German shepherd toward Rich and me. The dog tugged at his leash but heeled and walked beside his escort as they drew closer. Both cops stared at me for a few seconds before their expressions softened. The dog, for his part, held no enmity toward me.

"Burns, Gomez, this is my cousin, C.T." said Rich.

"We know who he is," Burns said. He was a couple inches shorter than I with hard gray eyes and a haircut that suggested a military background.

"Always good to be recognized," I said. To offer an olive branch, I extended my hand to the two cops. Both shook it.

"Not always good," Gomez said.

"True, but it's improving."

"This is Zeus," Burns said, nodding to his side as if any of us held any doubts who the dog was.

I held out my left hand toward Zeus. He sniffed it a few times but did not give my hand a friendly lick. He also didn't give it an unfriendly bite. I counted it as a win. "Is he going to let loose the kraken?" I said. They all gave me vacant looks. "*Clash of the Titans?*" Nothing. "It's Zeus' most famous line in the movie. They even kept it in the shitty remake."

Burns recovered from being a cinematic philistine and shook his head. "He'll find drugs."

"That's the car?" Gomez said, pointing at the silver Accord. All business, these narcs.

"It's the one," Rich said.

Burns led the shepherd toward the Accord. "Zeus is trained to detect popular drugs like marijuana and cocaine," Gomez said. "If he smells any residue, we'll know soon enough."

The drug dog sniffed the back of the Accord with an eagerness I wished most people displayed in their jobs. It didn't take long before he barked. Burns patted his side and led him to the other side of the trunk. Sure enough, Zeus quickly smelled drugs or drug residue there, as well. "Good boy," Burns said as he led the dog back toward us. Zeus wagged his tail in appreciation.

Rich thanked Burns and Gomez (and Zeus), and they drove off in the van. "Now we know drugs were involved," Rich said.

"We had a pretty good idea before," I said.

"It's always better to have confirmation."

"Ben Harrison suspected drug activity in the area. This is more like three blocks away rather than three doors, but I guess he was right."

"Ben was a good cop," Rich said.

"What do you think we should do next?" I said.

"We wait for this asshole to get back. Did his girl give you an idea how long he'd be gone?"

"She said he was taking his crew out for food and a movie."

"So we have some time to wait," Rich said. "I'll call King and ask him to join us."

"Sounds like a party," I said.

* * *

WE WAITED FOR AN HOUR. Paul King joined us about twenty minutes in. Our conversation about the Orioles' upcoming season filled some time. I hoped their down year after a run of success would be the springboard to something better. King served as a wet blanket and harped on the World Series drought. After a while, Rich fidgeted in his seat. I grew tired of looking in my rearview mirror and seeing King. I offered to head back to the café and get more coffee but got no takers. "Did she say where he was going?" Rich said after we endured a few more minutes of uncomfortable silence.

"The movies and lunch," I said. "Apparently, he treats his crew to this every so often."

"Nice guy for a drug dealer," King said.

"I think we need to know where he is," said Rich. "What theater? What restaurant? How do we know he really went there?"

"I don't think she lied to me," I said.

"He could have lied to her," Rich said.

"Good point." I called Tracie and asked her to call Snell. She didn't want to at first, but I reminded her how a simple phone call could help us put Snell away for good. It ramped up her eagerness. "She'll get back to us," I said to Rich and King as I hung up.

"Can't wait," King said. He ran his hand through his scraggly dark blond hair. I couldn't fathom living with so many tangles and knots. I would grab a razor in a fit of pique and desperation first. The hair let King fit in with the kinds of people he often went after, though. I would have needed to request a transfer to a more white collar unit rather than scuzz it up like he did.

My phone rang a few minutes later. "It took me a couple tries to reach him," Tracie said.

"If he answered the phone, he's probably not at the movies," I said. Rich and King both frowned.

"No, they're at some pub. I don't think they're going to the movies."

"Why? Did Snell say anything?"

"That asshole don't tell me shit. I heard one of his crew yelling about going to whack some bitch."

"Did you hear anything else?"

"Something about White Marsh. I don't know if that's where they were or where they were going."

"OK. Thanks, Tracie." I hung up.

"What did she say?" Rich said.

"They're not going to the movies," I said. "She overheard one of Snell's crew say something about going to whack a bitch."

"Where?"

"They mentioned White Marsh, but she didn't know if they were already there or going there."

In my rearview mirror, I saw King's eyes go wide. He sat forward in the seat. "Julie Harrison is staying in White Marsh," he said.

I fired up the Audi. "Why there?" I said. "It's in the county."

"We hope the bad guys overlook it, too. We tell BCPD just enough about what's going on."

"She didn't say anything else about the location?" Rich said.

"No." I zoomed through an intersection as the light turned red. "Don't write me a ticket."

"I'll call BCPD and let them know," King said.

"You do your part and drive fast," Rich said to me.

I stepped harder on the gas. The engine roared in a satisfying supercharged growl, the tachometer surged, and I blew through the gearbox like a street racer bearing down on the finish line. "I'm on it."

CHAPTER 25

WE MADE IT IN RECORD TIME. PAUL KING GUIDED ME FROM the backseat. In the last few years, a lot of new houses sprang up within a two-mile radius of White Marsh Mall. It looked like the BPD and BCPD spared no expense on their collaborative safe-house. Maybe the bad guys were used to looking for their witnesses at dingy townhouses and ranchers. These muscular single-family homes, each with a two-car garage and available in one of several cookie-cutter designs, would certainly throw them off.

"We beat the BCPD here," King said, flipping his cell phone shut and shaking his head. "Let's hope we beat the crew of assholes, too. Make the next right. Then it's the first one on the left."

I swung the Audi hard into the right, pulled off a sudden U-turn, and stopped at the curb in front of the safehouse. We all teetered in our seats a couple times, but the car came to rest directly in front, a couple inches from the curb. An unmarked car sat in the driveway. The closest car on the street was two addresses down. "What's our weapon situation?" said King.

"I have my nine and one spare clip," I said.

"Nine with two spare clips," Rich said.

"And I have two spares also," King said. "Should be enough to hold off a few assholes."

"We going in?" I said.

"Let's go." King got out; Rich and I followed him to the door. "I know one of the cops inside," King said as we walked up three steps to the porch. The beige siding made this house look like every other one I could see on the street. Did no one aspire to the individuality of a brick or stone front anymore? King rapped on the door in a particular sequence. We waited. King tapped his foot. Rich checked up and down the street. We waited some more.

No one answered.

King knocked again, harder this time. Again, no one answered. I didn't hear anyone stirring inside. I took out my phone and called Julie Harrison. It rang five times and went to voicemail. "Something's wrong," King said, showing a true mastery of the obvious.

"Move aside," I said. One of these times, I would need to remember the snap gun. My regular tools would have to suffice.

"We could try to kick it in."

"Wouldn't be much of a safehouse if we succeeded." I crouched at the doorknob. My eyes fell on the car in the driveway. I spied something on the ground, just past the front of the car. It looked like an arm. "Um . . . guys," I said, pointing at the car. "Tell me that's not a body in the grass over there."

Rich and King dashed off the porch. Both possessed skills in emergency medicine, so I went to work on the doorknob. As I massaged the tumblers, Rich walked back up to the porch.

"Cecil Franklin," he said. "We call him Frankie. Knocked out." Rich shook his head. "King is calling for a bus."

"If he's knocked out . . ." I said, trailing off.

"I know," Rich said. "How's the door?"

"Almost got it." A few seconds later, I heard a satisfying click.

I had expected more of the front door lock on a safehouse. Rich took out his pistol and moved around me to open the door. I stood and drew my gun. He looked at me. I nodded. We went in.

In the living room, an overhead light remained on, showing the ugly brown carpeting in all its glory. From the outside, this place looked way too nice to be a BPD safehouse. That illusion shattered when you opened the door. It was like learning the magician never really sawed his lovely assistant in half. Interior walls were white with crown molding somewhere in between the shade of the walls and the vomit brown of the carpet. The furniture came straight from a discount store and showed the wear one would expect from second-rate goods. My parents would have called this a sitting room and insisted it be for sipping wine and swapping pretentious stories. They also would have decorated and furnished it a million times better.

Rich pressed on into the dining room. We had enough light to see no one was in it, either. The table was dark brown and rectangular with six chairs set around it. One leg showed evidence a dog chewed on it. I wondered if the BPD bought damaged goods to save a few bucks. Budget cuts were hell on local governments.

Our light petered out. Rich drew his flashlight and held it under his gun. I did the same with my LED model. It didn't have the candlepower of the larger police flashlights, but it was smaller, easier to carry, and still bright enough to be disorienting when shined in someone's face. Rich led us into the kitchen. We walked around the island, looked all around the breakfast nook, and came up empty again. The room held a nice linoleum floor, granite countertops, and an island with both style and function. If required to stay here, I would insist on spending all my time in the kitchen. There was space for a small futon. Other than using the bathroom, I'd never leave it and inflict the rest of the house on myself.

The laundry area sat off the kitchen and led to the garage. We checked out both and found nothing. Rich walked back toward the front. He made sure no one hid somewhere we'd already been before going to the second floor. I knew Rich would rather be clearing the house with King rather than with me, but he didn't complain about it. The stairs were carpeted in the same ugly brown as the first floor. The carpet changed to a more sensible and neutral beige color on the second floor. The first area we came to was a spare room repurposed as a den. Two men lay slumped on the couch, each having flopped to a different side. Rich and I ran to them.

"They're alive," I said, noting the breathing of the unconscious man I checked. "I don't see any signs of injury." The cop I looked at had some acne scarring from his teen years but looked no worse for the wear otherwise.

"Same here," Rich said.

I stood and looked around. Both of them had apparently passed out. Containers of food sat on the coffee table, still open and already cool. A fork lay on the floor in front of the cop closer to me. "They were eating," I said. "I wonder if someone drugged their food."

Rich shook his head. "I hope they'd know better than to keep ordering from the same place," he said.

"Maybe they didn't."

"The basement," Rich said, and he bolted out of the room. I ran after him. He devoured the stairs two and three at a time on the way down. I blitzed through them one a time and managed to keep up. Adrenaline took the edge off the pain in my ribs. We found the door in the hallway across from a powder room. Rich and I stood on opposite sides, guns at the ready. Rich banged on the door. "Julie! Are you down there? Are you OK?"

No answer.

We looked at each other. I made a circular motion with my free hand.

"Julie, it's Rich Ferguson!"

"Rich!" a woman's voice shouted from the basement. "We're down here. We're OK."

"I'm opening the door," Rich said, and he did. At the bottom of the stairs, Julie Harrison held a shotgun at her side. Her short hair had gone about half gray from its natural brown. I wondered how much color faded since her husband's death. Worry lines creased her face and the dark rings encircling her eyes spoke of the toll this ordeal claimed.

"Are you the private investigator I've talked to?" she said.

"Yes," I said, "I am. What happened here?"

"Hell if I know. The guys got dinner delivered from Casa Mia. They love the place. The kids and I ate what was in the fridge. The guys were all eating and suddenly sacked out. If one of them fell asleep, I might not have thought anything of it, but with all of them out, I figured something was up. I got the kids and came down here." I heard some shuffling in the basement, but both children remained out of sight.

"What about Frankie?" Rich said.

"He wolfed his down and went outside for a smoke. He didn't come back in before we headed down."

"He's outside. He's OK."

"Rich, if someone drugged the food, they must've cased the house," I said.

"Which means they may not be far away," Rich said. "Julie, stay down there. We're going to see what's happening outside. Backup should be here soon."

Rich's phone rang. He answered it. "OK," he said after a few seconds, then hung up. "King said a car approached from the other end of the street and stopped two houses down."

"Let's go," I said.

"You go. I'll stay here and protect this place."

I ran to the laundry room and entered the garage. The BPD left the door open, which struck me as a bad idea. Maybe Franklin came out this way and never got to close the door because he succumbed to the tainted food. I kept low and moved over to King, who crouched behind the car in the driveway. "Rich is holding down the fort," I said. My ribs barked. I was glad to be still. "It's you and me out here."

"Let's hope they don't have a fucking truckload of guys a minute out, then," said King.

"I don't think one more of us would matter much if they did."

"Can you shoot?"

"I hope it doesn't come to it . . . but yes." I thought of the times I fired a gun before. I'd shot three people in my career, all to save either myself or someone else. While I could live with it, I didn't like to dwell on it. The Glock felt heavy in my hand. "Any word on the BCPD?"

"Any minute now."

Three car doors opened across the street. Kyle Snell emerged from the back of the sedan, trailing his two flunkies. One of them pointed at the Audi. After the demise of my Lexus, I would empty my magazine at anyone who wantonly damaged the Audi. The gesture didn't turn into anything, at least. The same flunky who noticed my car now pointed at the open garage door. They gave no indication they noticed King and I crouched behind the car. The three cretins drew closer. My pulse quickened.

"Now," King said in a harsh whisper. He went to the trunk and leveled his pistol at Snell and company. I did the same at the hood. Our actions got some excitement coursing through them. Snell's cronies fumbled for their guns.

"Don't do it!" King said. "We'll shoot you."

I stared at all three. Snell stood behind the other two, rooted in place. He didn't try to advance or retreat, and he didn't make a move for a weapon. The other two already moved their hands inside their jackets. I focused on those hands. I studied the creases in the light windbreakers as the sleeves vanished inside the coat. Any movement, and I was ready to fire. It would be saving me or King or any of the people inside the house. I made sure to take steady breaths.

"I guess we have the wrong house," Snell said in a lame attempt to defuse the situation.

"Do you really think we don't know who you are?" I said.

"Or what you did?" King added.

"I don't know what you gentlemen heard, but I'm just a guy trying to make a living."

"There's only two of them," the flunky closer to King said. I watched his arm. A new crease appeared in the sleeve.

"Move your hand another inch, and you're dead," King said.

"Gentlemen, we don't need to do this," Snell said. He edged closer to his crew but still stood behind them. "We have the wrong house. We'll just go back to the car and—"

"You're not going anywhere," King said. "We're taking all of you to jail."

"Or the morgue," I said.

The one closer to King stuck his hand farther into his jacket. King and I both fired. I hit him in the collarbone, but King's shot nailed him center mass. The guy staggered back a step, looked around in great surprise at the fact his arm didn't work anymore, and pitched forward onto the grass. The other lackey put his hands up immediately. Snell glanced around like a little kid lost at the circus and backed away slowly.

"I got him," I said to King and darted around the car as Snell took off. He had a headstart. My ribs protested at the impact as I ran, but I ignored them and kept going. Snell didn't have the legs to outrun me. I gained on him as he looked over his shoulder near the car. He unlocked the driver's door with a keyfob, but I ran into him before he could get in. He spun and threw a punch. I expected it, blocked it with my forearm, then drove my elbow into his face. Snell rocked back into the car. I hit him in the stomach, and he doubled over, allowing me the room to get beside him and put him in a chokehold. Snell tried to pull my arm away, but his strength ebbed as his air diminished. If he thought to elbow me in the ribs, I would've had a problem, but he didn't. A few seconds later, Snell lapsed into unconsciousness. I tossed him against the car. His head bounced off it before he landed on the grass.

Sirens blared from down the street. Four BCPD cruisers screeched to the curb. Rich escorted the Harrisons outside a few minutes later.

* * *

Rich and I walked Kyle Snell into BPD Headquarters. As soon as we came in the front door, all gazes moved to us. Snell received enough evil eyes to curse the next ten generations of his family if his worthless genes survived the ages. I didn't like his odds. As we made our way across the floor, the assembled cops broke out in applause. I gave the crowd a wave. Rich rolled his eyes. We got into an elevator.

Rich shoved Snell into an interrogation room. I walked into the observation area. Rich left the interrogation room and joined me. "I'm sure you want to be in there," he said.

"I do, but this is one I should sit out," I said.

"Kind of you," Rich said with a smile. "Look, I know we had our disagreements over this one. I'm sorry about it all. I'm sorry about what happened to you along the way."

"Don't worry about it," I said. "Go make Snell cry like the coward he is."

"I plan to. Thanks." Rich traded his parting smile for a game face and went back to the interrogation room. Leon Sharpe joined him a moment later. The first thing Sharpe did was stand to the side and disconnect the camera recording the goings-on in the room.

The second thing he did was grab Snell by his hair and wallop him in the stomach. Snell doubled over so hard he nearly hit his head on the table. He sagged into the chair. Sharpe stood over him. He faced away from me, but I could imagine his expression. I didn't envy Snell—not as though I ever would, but I especially didn't right now. He coughed and said something I couldn't hear.

"The hell with what you want," Sharpe said, reconnecting the camera cable. "You killed a good man and a good cop."

"I had to," Snell said, his voice regaining power.

Sharpe sat down. Rich cuffed Snell to the table and then took a seat beside Sharpe. "I know my rights," said Snell.

"How nice for you," Sharpe said. "TV shows don't tell you everything."

"You can't hit me."

"Wanna bet?" Sharpe leaned forward. Snell scooted back as much as the handcuff would allow.

"Why did you do it, Snell?" Rich said, trying to steer the interrogation back toward something productive. Or at least more productive than threatening and pummeling a cop killer.

"I had to," Snell repeated. "My girl took the car to get it fixed. Said it needed a brake job." He rolled his eyes and shook his head in exasperation. "I asked her where she took it. She told me. I knew a cop lived there."

"You could have just taken the car when he wasn't there," Rich said.

"I couldn't take the chance he'd already poked around in it. Some product was still in the trunk."

"A good man had to die because you couldn't get your shit out of the trunk when you should?" Sharpe said. He must have given Snell a withering look because the prisoner recoiled.

"I couldn't take the chance," Snell said in a small voice. He looked between Rich and Sharpe. "How'd you all catch me, anyway?"

"You left a witness," Rich said. "He was standing to your left." Rich pointed at Snell's blind eye. "You never saw him."

"He must be the guy who shot at the car." Snell shook his head. "I knew I should've dealt with him then."

"We thought he was the killer for a while, but we eventually figured it out." Rich turned and glanced over his shoulder at me. I decided not to burst into the room and point out my role. I was not Chesterton's aged rioter and demagogue, and I knew not all men were brothers. The last eighteen months of my life seared the knowledge into my brain.

"We want a full confession, Snell," Sharpe said. "We want to know where you got the drugs, who your cronies are, how many times you smacked your girlfriend for taking the car to Ben Harrison—everything. If I think you've left a syllable out, I'll break your arm and write it myself."

"Can I make a deal?" Snell said.

"You killed a cop." I didn't need to see Sharpe's face to know that he spoke through clenched teeth. "The only deal I'm willing to offer you is not beating you to death before you're carried out of this room. And I'll only do it if you sign a full confession."

"Yeah, OK," Snell said after a moment of useless consideration. "I want a lawyer when I sign it, though."

"You'd better have your own," Rich said. "No one in the Public Defender's Office will touch you right now."

"I have a lawyer."

"Scumbags always do," said Sharpe.

* * *

SNELL SIGNED THE CONFESSION. His attorney produced some questions but couldn't delay the inevitable. The lawyer was thin, with a loose, jowly face indicating his thinness came upon him recently. He spoke like a high school kid accustomed to being surrounded by bullies. Every time Sharpe looked at him, the lawyer averted his eyes. He tried to get some extra concessions, like a promise of a parole opportunity, but Sharpe wouldn't budge. In the end, Snell signed the confession, and Sharpe said they could talk with someone in the state's attorney's office before the arraignment hearing.

After a couple of cops led Snell away—politely, at least while his mouthpiece lingered—Sharpe asked Rich and me to join him in his office. We rode the elevator in silence. When we got off, smiles greeted us. Word spreads fast. We walked into Sharpe's office. Rich and I sat in his guest chairs while Sharpe shut the door.

"Jack Bennett is going to be released shortly," the captain said when he sat. "None of this will appear on his record, of course."

"Good," I said.

"We got the bastard. He killed Ben Harrison." Sharpe nodded as if confirming this for himself. "He thought he could get away with it. He almost did, but we got him." I waited for a thank-you. Any minute now. "C.T., I know this was an especially tough case for you," Sharpe said. "Thanks for sticking it out."

Ordinarily, I would point out I'd been right all along, plus how the BPD had frustrated me at every turn. I would go on to mention my exemplary record when it came to being right, even at times when everyone in the BPD thought I was wrong. Rich would roll his eyes, Sharpe would mutter something, and all would be right with the world. This, however, was not an ordinary case. It hit much closer to home for the BPD than any other case I worked. Instead of my usual spiel, I simply said, "You're welcome, Leon."

"We'll be easier on you next time," Rich said.

"I hope so, but it'll have to wait. I think I need a little time off."

"Enjoy it," Sharpe said. "You've earned it."

"I do have a question, though. Not trying to be a wet blanket, but it came to me on the way up here."

"What is it?"

"How did this asshole know where Julie Harrison was staying?"

"Someone must have told him," Sharpe said after a second. His eyes narrowed.

"Right. How many people knew about the safehouse?"

"Not many."

"I don't think this is quite over yet," I said.

Maybe my pursuit of the blanket party ringleader would overlap with whomever gave up the safehouse to Kyle Snell. I called Ashley Taylor on my way home. She wasn't pleased to hear from me. "I had hoped you'd forgotten," she said.

"Never," I said. "The case got complicated, but we got the right man. Now I want to know if you thought about what I said."

Her sigh hissed in my ear. "I guess I don't have much of a choice."

I almost felt offended she hadn't offered me a bedroom deal in exchange for forgetting the whole thing. The thought passed quickly; I wouldn't have taken it anyway. "I guess you don't," I said. "What are their names?"

"My brother, obviously." She hesitated. "I'm really not comfortable doing this."

"I hope the unemployment line is more comfortable, then. Goodbye."

"No, wait!" I let her twist in the wind. "Hello?"

"I'm still here," I said after making her sweat it out a few more seconds.

Ashley let out another sigh. "Brian Carnes, Sean Brown, and Roy Maine."

I knew two of them. Maine was the one who questioned and arrested me earlier. He knew the whole time he was participating in a cruel sham but went along with it anyway. "Do you know who masterminded it?" I said.

"My brother didn't come out and say it directly," Ashley said. "He's on pain medication, though, so he has his moments. My best guess is Carnes, but I'm not sure about that."

"Thank you, Miss Taylor."

"Promise me you won't hurt my brother."

"No more than I have to," I said.

"That's not very comforting," she said.

"Why? You can get him treated for anything by slinking out of your scrubs."

"That's a cheap shot!"

"It is," I said. "I can afford more, but the cheap ones are often good enough."

She hung up on me. Score another one for the low blow.

I sat outside Philip Taylor's house. It was as exciting as it sounds. I brought the Caprice in case he recognized the Audi. While waiting for Taylor, I used my laptop and a custom-made antenna to break into his wireless network and get his calendar. It showed a physical therapy appointment starting soon. A few minutes later, Taylor came limping out on a cane and hobbled to his car, a late-model Ford sedan. He got in and drove off. I followed him.

The physical therapy appointment lasted an hour. Taylor's limp looked as painful on the way out as it did on the way in. It served him right. Taylor drove away, and I settled in a few cars behind him for the drive back down Northern Parkway. To mix things up, I got off, drove on a parallel street, and then reacquired

Northern Parkway a few blocks up. Who said you can't learn anything from the movies? Taylor's red Ford built a larger lead on me, but I caught up and kept him in sight.

I followed Taylor back home. He got out of his car and trudged toward the house. I reached for my door handle. The mailman strolled down the sidewalk in view of Taylor's house. Across the street, a neighbor trimmed some kind of evergreen tree. Either or both would be able to see me accost Taylor, and I figured both knew he was a cop. I would have to wait.

About an hour later, I considered looking into one of the other assholes who assaulted me when Taylor went online and ordered a pizza for delivery. I could have sniffed his credit card over the wi-fi but refrained. He may have been an asshole to me, but he still needed the money more than I did. When the pizza website announced the delivery time loomed, I got out of the car. No one was on the street now. I made it to the rear of Taylor's house without being seen. His wooden privacy fence concealed me in his backyard. I prowled around for an open window and found one which emptied into an extra bedroom Taylor used for an office. I cracked the wooden frame and camped out beneath it, using the fence and the skeletal azaleas in Taylor's garden for cover.

I heard the doorbell ring a minute later. No dogs barking was a relief. Taylor's cane thumped the floor as he walked to the door. I opened the window wider, climbed inside, and lowered myself to the floor. I shut the sash behind me, moved out of the office, and stood at the end of a hallway. Ahead and to the left, I saw a bathroom. To the right, another corridor led to the main rooms of the house. A TV played what sounded like a lame reality show.

Taylor closed the door. I stayed in the side corridor and peeked out. He limped into the kitchen, got a bottle of beer, and thumped back to the living room. I wondered if he still took painkillers. The thought made me realize I needed a Percocet. My ribs ached as I leaned against the wall. After I heard Taylor sink into his chair, I crept along the main hallway. Light from the TV threw irregular shadows. As I got closer, I heard Taylor smacking his lips as he ate the pizza.

"Didn't you learn better manners?" I said as I stepped into the living room.

Taylor nearly jumped out of his seat. He dropped the slice topping-side down onto the mottled carpet. It wouldn't make a difference. "How the hell did you get in?" he said.

"It doesn't matter," I said. "How's the leg, Phil?"

"Fuck you." He reached for his cane.

"Don't get up," I said. I patted the .45 at my side. "I didn't come here unprepared."

"They'll find you if you shoot me."

I laughed. "I didn't come here to shoot you, you dumb son of a bitch. At least not again." He glared at me. I continued. "I'm here to find out who masterminded your little blanket party."

"What are you going to do . . . shoot him?" he said.

"No," I said. "Unlike you assholes, I'm not completely cruel. I'll offer whoever planned it the confrontation he obviously wants, just on equal terms."

"I'm not selling anyone out to you." Taylor said. He took another slice of pizza. I stepped around the chair and grabbed his cane. "What the hell are you doing?" he roared.

I regarded the cane. It was more functional than ornate, with a solid black body and faux silver handle. I held it in my hand like I might use it to walk. "You know, Phil, I don't know which leg I shot you in. Maybe if your coward friends hadn't thrown a blanket over my head, I would." I changed my grip on the cane, wielding it like a hammer. Taylor frowned. "I have a fifty-fifty chance, I guess." I raised the cane.

"Wait!" Taylor said. "What do you think you're doing?"

"I want to know who put the ambush together. You don't want to tell me. I'm going to provide you some incentive." I looked at Taylor's legs. He wore faded jeans. His left thigh was a little thicker than his right. I looked at both of his legs to keep him guessing.

"You wouldn't!"

I brought the cane down. It whacked the arm of Taylor's chair with a crack like a small-caliber gunshot. Taylor recoiled and leaned away. "The next one won't miss," I said. I held the cane at the ready, poised to strike with it again.

"All right, all right!" he said. "It was Carnes. Brian Carnes."

"Singing like a canary wasn't so hard . . . was it, Phil?" Taylor looked at me through wide eyes for another few breaths, then relaxed. He sat more evenly in the chair. His breathing slowed.

"You're not going to kill him, are you?"

"Of course not," I said. "And you're not going to warn him I'm coming for him."

"Oh, yeah?" Taylor smirked at me. "Why not?"

I hit him hard in the right leg with the cane. Taylor cried out and grabbed his thigh. "Because if you do, I'll come back and pummel you in the one I put a bullet in," I said. "Understand?" Taylor nodded while he winced. "Good. By the way . . . who sold out Julie Harrison?"

"What?" he said through gritted teeth.

"Kyle Snell and a couple of his minions showed up at the safehouse." I cut him off before he could get a word in. "You're probably going to tell me you don't know who he is. I doubt it, but I'll play along. He's the guy who killed Ben Harrison. Julie and the kids went into hiding. Not many people knew where they were."

"You think I ratted them out?"

"Did you?"

"No," he said, practically spitting the denial at me.

I took him at his word. "Fine. I guess I'll ask your buddy Carnes." I tossed the cane to the other end of the hall. "I'll let myself out. Remember our little deal."

Taylor grunted something at me. I assumed it to be uncharitable.

CHAPTER 27

I WAS ON MY WAY BACK HOME TO PLOT MY NEXT MOVE WHEN my phone rang. Caller ID pegged it as BPD headquarters. This was becoming too frequent for my tastes.

"Please hold for Captain Leon Sharpe," a female voice said. The line went dead for a moment, then Sharpe came on.

"Hello, C.T.," he said.

"You must really be a big baller," I said. "Not only do you have people answer your phones, you have people make calls for you."

"It's not a bad gig."

"When you're commissioner, will you have people type your emails, too?"

"I'll let you know," he said. "Look, I wanted to tell you we're taking your arrest off the books."

"I would hope so," I said. "It was bullshit."

Sharpe cleared his throat before he spoke again. "In light of everything, we obviously think the arrest can't be justified."

"I'm glad you came to your senses, Leon."

"There's more," he said.

"Do tell."

"Rodgers, the officer who . . . damaged your car, is on administrative duty for two weeks. We're going to cover the cost of the repairs."

"I don't mean to sound ungrateful," I said, "but these are things you should be doing. I'm glad you are, and I think you probably pushed for them, but they should be happening."

"You're right," Sharpe said. "We can get kind of provincial when our own are involved."

"Baltimore is a provincial city," I said. "More so when it comes to sports."

"Don't I know it? I grew up a Phillies fan."

"No wonder you're not commissioner yet."

"Very funny. Now I want you to tell me something."

I suspected where this would go. "What do you want to know?" I said.

"You don't like to let things go," said Sharpe. "What are you doing about that blanket party?"

"Like you said, I don't like letting things go."

"I don't want you stalking my cops like some vigilante."

"Sure, I'll just hand over some names with no real proof anyone did anything. It'll be really productive."

"Get some proof."

"I'll send you the video," I said.

"It's not proof," Sharpe said. "We can't see anyone's face."

"I know. I've learned who organized the blanket party, but I doubt I'll get him to sign a full confession."

"You might try."

I tried to fight it, but I couldn't help laughing. "Listen to yourself, Leon. Would *you* sign a confession if you had done something like these assholes did?"

"I wouldn't have done it," he said.

"Be that as it may," I said, "I don't think someone who broke the law and got his friend shot will be eager to autograph something laying out the full details."

Sharpe sighed into the phone. "Promise me you'll remember our agreement."

"I remember, Leon. I won't do any worse than what was done to me."

"You'd better not," he said. "And I still want whatever proof you put together. You understand?"

I confirmed I did.

* * *

LATER THE SAME NIGHT, Gloria and I lay in bed. She rested her head on my shoulder and draped her arm across my chest. I listened to her breathe as I watched the ceiling fan blades spin around and around. Thoughts of Brian Carnes fluttered into my head. He had been in Central Booking after my arrest. It meant he organized the attack, participated, helped Philip Taylor to the hospital, and showed up for his shift like nothing happened. On top of it all, he harassed me from the desk, knowing he and his friends put me in the hospital the night before. This level of asshole required genes the average person did not possess.

"And then the aliens showed up and everyone died," Gloria said.

"What?" I said.

"Were you listening to me?"

"I heard something about murderous aliens."

"I was trying to tell you something important, but you were a million miles away," Gloria said.

"Thinking about the guy who organized my blanket party," I said.

"What about him?"

"You first."

Gloria sighed. She looked down for a moment, then back up at me. "I want to get involved more with charity work," she said.

"That's noble of you."

"Remember when we were out with Rich and Jeanne, and she asked what I did?" I nodded. "I didn't really have an answer."

"So you're doing this to have a better answer to a common party question?" I said.

"No. I'm doing it because I need to do something," said Gloria. "I don't need to work. It's something I want to do. I have the time. I have money, and I know other people who have money. Your parents put on a great fundraiser for House of Ruth, and that's such a good charity."

"I'm sure you'll do a great job," I said with a smile.

Gloria continued like my contributions to the conversation were superfluous. "I know you never wanted to work, but look at the job you do. Every day, I see you make a difference." I waved my hand, but Gloria wasn't having any of it. "No, don't dismiss it. It's true. You do good work for people who might not otherwise be able to get it done. You . . . you inspired me, I guess. I even took a couple online classes." It explained the times I saw Gloria squinting at a laptop or absorbed in her phone. She wasn't the type to care about games and apps. "I feel I need to do more, and it's mostly because of watching you work."

"Wow.," I said, and Gloria's eyes grew shinier. "I never thought my job would be inspiring."

"False modesty doesn't become you," she said with a small smile.

"Most modesty doesn't become me," I said and kissed Gloria's forehead. "I'm glad you're getting passionate about something. You're smart and capable. I'm sure you'll be an asset to any charity you want to work with."

Gloria smiled and nuzzled my neck. I felt a warm tear slide onto my collarbone. How could I not love this woman? It took a lot for her to lie in bed with me and admit I inspired her to do more with her life. I saw signs of Gloria coming around and becoming more interested in connecting with people and even helping them. As much as I never wanted to work the job I now do almost every day, I had to admit it's been rewarding. Gloria obviously got caught up in my unexpected altruism.

Good for her.

My thoughts returned to Brian Carnes as Gloria drifted off to sleep.

* * *

My INITIAL BREACH of the BPD's network nearly a year and a half ago proved to be the gift to keep on giving. Not only could I monitor case files and access crime scene photos—when someone bothered to upload them—but I could get into payroll and scheduling with only a couple more clicks. Payroll gave me Carnes' address (and a hearty chuckle at his salary); one more click got me his schedule.

I gained more information. Now what was I going to do with it? I could accost Carnes as he left for work, which seemed both suboptimal and incomplete. I didn't just want to cuff him around. Carnes masterminded a plot to put me in the hospital. He may also have led Kyle Snell to Julie Harrison. His sins deserved more. I pondered what to do as I sat in my real office drinking my second coffee of the morning. I washed down a Percocet with the last swallow in the cup and resumed thinking.

I needed to know more about Carnes. Where did he go in his spare time? What did he enjoy? Could I diminish him in the eyes of a significant other? Some of this stuff I could find online. For the rest, I would need to follow him and see how he passed his time, whom he hung out with, and such. For as much as I didn't like the cycle of following people, sitting around while they did something, then tailing them some more, I'd certainly honed my craft at it these last few days.

Carnes proved smart enough to organize the blanket party on short notice. It meant he knew a good bit about me. He'd spot the Audi and the Caprice. I needed a car he wouldn't recognize. Rich wouldn't lend me his Camaro for something like this. Joey's seat would be deformed by his ample backside. I was down to Gloria or my parents. My parents, my mother especially, would ask questions about why I needed the car, then tsk and sniff about my reasons. Asking Gloria minimized the odds of an inquisition. Besides, hers was a blast to drive. The ridiculous AMG V8 almost made up for the lack of a third pedal.

There I sat in Gloria's rocket-shaped and rocket-colored Mercedes coupe, parked close enough to Central Booking to see Carnes leave. Of course, he drove a pickup truck. If this were the south, he would have mounted a gun rack in the back and flown a small confederate flag on his antenna. If I didn't know better, I'd presume he lived in Cecil County.

Carnes' pickup pulled out of the lot. I let a couple of cars pass me before following the caravan into moderate traffic. In light traffic, I would have been worried about Gloria's distinctive car sticking out. Even with more vehicles on the road, it needed to be a concern. Carnes wouldn't need to be a genius at operational security to notice it. I scouted around and found another sporty red coupe hanging behind me. Maneuvering beside the other car was easy.

If Carnes noticed me following him, I never saw any sign of it. He eventually picked up Eastern Avenue and took it into Fells Point, stopping at a Tae Kwon Do studio I'd never heard of. I wondered if he learned the proper technique for kicking a prone, mostly defenseless opponent there. Carnes found a parking spot on the street nearby. I didn't enjoy that kind of luck.

In lieu of waiting for Carnes, I parked nearby and got lunch at Las Palmas on the other side of Broadway. The menu clued me in to the fact I sat in a real Mexican restaurant, not a faux "Tex-

Mex" or some random Latin American blend. It was written in Spanish (with English translations for the gringos) and boasted of authentic Mexican fare. Of course, they served chips and salsa, and I made it a point to try all the salsas. I ended up getting flautas and eating way too many tortilla chips. I would have been tempted to scarf down more if I didn't need to get back to tailing Carnes.

Required to pass the dojo on the way back to Gloria's car, I did so with my hood pulled up. Carnes' truck, which stood out like a polka-dotted couch in a furniture store, remained where he left it. I pitied anyone with a normal-sized car who possessed the temerity to try and parallel park in front of or behind his pickup. For the first time ever, I thought of a practical use for a Smart car.

I could see Carnes' truck from where I parked Gloria's car. I could also see it from International Space Station, no doubt. A few minutes later, Carnes came out of the dojo, got back into his truck, and drove off. He stopped at a McDonald's for drive-thru on his way home. I remained near his house for an hour, but he didn't go anywhere else. I passed some more time reading an ebook on my phone. Still nothing. I considered going home, when Carnes—now dressed in a cheap pair of khakis and a polo he should have tucked in—emerged from his house and got back into his truck. I let him get to the end of his street before following him again.

Carnes pulled into a bank a few blocks away. I lingered enough behind to keep him in view. He didn't get out of his obnoxious vehicle. A woman wearing a sharp professional dress came out of the bank. She stopped and smiled at Carnes. I grabbed my phone and snapped a couple of quick pictures of her before she got into the truck. Carnes leaned to her and they kissed before he drove off again.

This time, he drove to a movie theater. I broke off my pursuit here for the day. At least I learned a couple things about him today. I figured I would follow him for a couple more days and see what else I could learn.

Then I simply needed to devise the best way to use it all against him.

* * *

THE NEXT MORNING, I set about tearing Carnes' miserable life apart electronically. I needed to go way beyond what the BPD held in its files. I started with social media. Carnes, his family, and his friends all went under a microscope. I owned a program which scraped social networks and mapped relationships graphically. It proved a great help with investigations like these. I simply fed it a few people to start with, and it did the rest.

Clicking on a picture showed the associated name and highlighted the lines indicating a relationship. It made combing through contacts so much easier. I spent some time exploring the people on Carnes' friends list. Humiliating him would be great, but I wanted to find a way to tie him to Kyle Snell.

I found one.

For some reason, Carnes remained friends with his ex-wife on Facebook. There were no signs they communicated regularly, so it took me a few minutes to locate her. She maintained a small network of friends, but among them was Kyle Snell, listed as her brother.

Carnes was looking out for his ex-brother-in-law.

I presumed Carnes to be an asshole—with good reason—so I figured he didn't do it out of the kindness of his heart. Snell was a drug dealer, not a profession he discovered last week, so he probably dealt in narcotics while he and Carnes were related by marriage.

By now, the BPD would have processed Snell. I searched their network for new additions to the case file. In the wee hours of the morning, a technician posted a forensic copy of his cell phone. It would do nicely. I dove into his texts. None were from Carnes' number. Undeterred, I searched the messages themselves, looking for strings like "Julie" or "widow."

The latter gave me a hit.

The widow is in White Marsh. Watch email for the address.

The number sending the message did not belong to Carnes. It must have been a burner. The BPD could figure it out easily enough. I was curious how Carnes relayed the address. I opened a new browser tab, went to Snell's email provider, and clicked on the "Forgot Password" link. A security question popped up. "What high school did you attend?" I had plenty of information on Snell to answer this. A few seconds later, I provided a new password and scrolled through his emails.

Carnes was clever. He sent the address in the form of a real estate listing. The message came from his personal address, and there would be a record of the search in his browsing history. The BPD could pull those, too.

I snagged some screenshots, took a few notes, and typed up everything I discovered. I thought about sending it to Rich but instead chose Leon Sharpe. His opinion on the results-to-process ratio tilted a little more in my favor than Rich's. Besides, I promised him I would confine myself to going after the ringleader. In the spirit of my pursuit, I asked Leon for 48 hours to wrap things up with Carnes.

After then, the BPD could have him.

CHAPTER 28

I followed Carnes the rest of the afternoon, but his routine remained the same on working days. The next morning, Friday, he showed late to begin his time off. I tailed him to a Starbucks, then a riveting trip to the dry cleaners, succeeded by a visit to the gym. Carnes really knew how to dial up the excitement. While he worked off his lousy food choices on exercise machines, I snagged some semi-healthy lunch and snack items. After the gym, Carnes went back home. This allowed me to pass the time with a tuna sub, a Greek yogurt, and an iced tea. I read another book on my phone while I waited for him to do something. I hoped I wouldn't need to read something interminable like *War and Peace* while I waited.

At 1:45, Carnes came back outside, an exercise bag in his hand. I followed him to his dojo and waited while he failed to grasp the concept of honor. An hour and 15 minutes later, a freshly-showered Carnes emerged and stopped at the Greene Turtle. I gave him a couple minutes, then went in myself. My hat, sunglasses, and hoodie would minimize the odds of him spotting me. Besides, I had long grown sick of sitting in my car and watching Carnes live a life to cure insomnia.

Carnes occupied a small table to himself at the far end of the bar. I sidled to the opposite end. The bar-length mirror allowed me to keep an eye on him without being obvious about it. Not letting your quarry spot you was surely a lesson unto itself in PI school, and here I'd figured it out on my own.

The bartender, a pretty blonde who buttoned her shirt just high enough to cover the bottom halves of her breasts, gave me a rote smile as she slapped a cardboard coaster atop the bar. "It's not very bright in here," she said.

I touched the arm of my sunglasses. "They're for my bright future," I said.

She looked at me as if I'd answered her in Chinese—which I could have. Some people have no appreciation for the classics. "What'll you have?"

I glanced in the mirror. A drink sat before Carnes. "What do you recommend?" I said.

"Depends," she said. "Are you a cheap domestic guy or a beer snob?"

"My snobbery extends far beyond beer."

At last, an earnest smile. "I have just the thing." She leaned down, reached into a refrigerator, and set a bottle of Dogfish Head 60-Minute IPA before me.

"Excellent," I said as she opened the bottle. I didn't think it filled the snobbery quotient, but Dogfish Head made a perfectly good IPA. The bartender poured the beer into a frosty glass I would have declined if given the option. I sipped the IPA. It tasted appropriately bitter.

"What's with the hoodie?" she said.

"I'm in stealth mode."

She lowered her voice. "You a cop or something?"

I smiled. "Or something."

A few customers came to the bar, and the bartender moved to greet them. I saw the same rote smile on her face, and I watched the men stare at her chest when they thought she wasn't looking.

I didn't blame them. The mirror showed Carnes enjoying his drink. He didn't look around much. I didn't mind—his lack of situational awareness only helped me.

After a couple more minutes, a waiter delivered food to Carnes' table. I saw a burger slathered with cheese, covered in bacon, and paired with enough fries to frighten a diabetic. Why go to the gym and a dojo if you followed it up by eating garbage? I enjoyed the occasional splurge, but Carnes ate this way by habit. It was his life—such as it was for now.

While Carnes chowed down on his slow demise, the bartender broke free of the hordes and planted herself in front of me. "Need another?" she said, eyeing my empty glass.

"I'd like to switch to an iced tea," I said, "and not the Long Island variety."

"Don't want to drink too much on the job?"

"More or less."

She got me an iced tea, and I handed her my credit card. Carnes polished off his burger and fries, declining another drink in lieu of the check. I downed a few sips of my tea, left the bartender a generous tip, and signed my bill. Carnes shrugged into his light jacket and made for the door. I went out a few seconds behind him. Enough people prowled the midday side-walks of Fells Point to allow me to blend in. My city's love of pubs and greasy food had never made me prouder.

Carnes got back into his truck. I followed him to his house. Then I doffed the sunglasses and hoodie and left again.

I had places to go.

* * *

I PARKED at the bank where Carnes' paramour worked. A quick glance at the desks and nameplates told me her name was Jackie Mullins. I grabbed some papers the bank provided to help me look official, signed in on the list, and took a seat. When someone else called my name about ten minutes later, I said I had been working with Jackie. After about five more minutes, she came out to greet me. I saw a look of non-recognition flash across her face, but she masked it with a quick, winning smile. The gesture alone made her too good for a piece of shit like Carnes. In my younger days, I would have added the conquest of Jackie to my to-do list. Now I only wanted to ruin Carnes. Ah, maturity.

"Can I help you?" Jackie said. She wore a sharp dark gray business suit with a skirt that stopped just above her knee and an aggressively white blouse, which surely spent half its life on a dry cleaner's rack.

"Yes, I think we've been talking by phone," I said. "It's about my loan." I rustled the face-down papers in my hand.

"Of course, sir. Follow me." I followed Jackie Mullins to her desk. The skirt hugged her hips, and the walk to her desk was shorter than I hoped. I sat in a generic fabric guest chair with hard wooden arms. "How can I help you?"

I turned the papers over, showing her they were blank. She frowned at me. "I lied," I said. "This isn't about my loan. It's about your boyfriend."

"Who are you?" she said.

"I'd like to show you something—something to illuminate you as to the kind of man you're dealing with."

Jackie Mullins leaned back in her chair and regarded me. "Why shouldn't I call security?"

"Because you're leaning back. You're relaxed and a little curious, not tense and aggressive."

She looked at me some more, then nodded. "All right. What do you have to show me?"

"A short video." I took out my phone, queued up the video Gloria shot of the blanket party, and adjusted the sound. I set my phone on the desk before Jackie. She tapped the screen, leaned forward, and watched the clip behind frowning brows at first. When the ambush began, her brows shot up, her eyes went wide, and her mouth hung open. Her lips opened and closed like she wanted to ask something, but no question came, even when I shot Philip Taylor.

The video ended. Jackie Mullins leaned back and sighed. The frown returned to crease her brows. "What was that?" she said.

"It's called a blanket party," I said. "They're usually given to punish or discourage someone. In this case, the man being assaulted was me, and the ringleader of the whole thing was Brian Carnes."

Jackie looked at me, then at my phone, then back at me. "I don't believe you."

"I think you know it's possible he could have done it."

"How do you know it was him?" she said.

"I tracked down the man I shot in the leg," I told her. "He confessed his part in it and said Carnes organized it all."

"Of course he wouldn't finger himself as the leader."

"Maybe. Or maybe your boyfriend really did it. Either way, he willingly and gladly participated in beating a person who couldn't defend himself. Is he really the kind of man you want to spend your time with?"

Jackie looked down at my phone again. She watched the video a second time. At the end, she shook her head, closed her eyes, and sighed. "Why are you here?"

"So you can make an informed decision," I said. "If you're going to spend your time with someone, shouldn't you know him?"

"Why not just go to his lieutenant?" Jackie said.

"I will. There are a couple things I want to tie up first."

"Why . . . why did they do this?"

"I'm a private investigator who disagreed with the police on a high-profile case. I was right, I might add."

She nodded, then said, "I'm sorry that . . . he did that to you."

I shrugged. "In the end, I think he'll be sorrier," I said.

* * *

THE ONLINE SCHEDULE AT CARNES' dojo told me my antagonist would be back tomorrow afternoon for a semi-private lesson. It jibed with the time I asked Leon Sharpe to give me. I formulated a plan for how to handle the situation.

To her credit, Gloria did not try to dissuade me when I discussed this with her over dinner. My parents invited us out with them, but I declined. The less they knew about everything, the better. Instead, I made a simple dinner of baked salmon, broccoli, and mashed potatoes. Gloria wanted to help, so I let her stir the potatoes. Her kitchen ineptitude would not mar our dinner.

We'd each eaten about half our meals when Gloria posed her first question about my plan. "What if he gets physical?"

"I don't think he will," I said.

"Isn't he an asshole?"

I smiled. "Big time. The police will be there, though. I'm basically going to be a bystander."

"Could you take him if it came down to it?" she said.

"He just got his brown belt," I said. "If I can't, I'm going to burn my black one."

"You're pretty hot when you talk about fighting." A lascivious grin spread over Gloria's face.

"If I knew I could impress you with it, I would have done it sooner." She chuckled. "Should I flex my bicep for good measure?"

The grin remained. "Sure."

I did. Gloria scooted her chair closer and squeezed my arm at the muscle. "Nice and hard," she said. "What are you doing later?"

A bit of warmth came into my cheeks. "Having gentler-than-normal sex with a beautiful woman."

"Your ribs?" she said, and I bobbed my head. "We'll figure something out."

"The benefit of us both being so smart," I said.

* * *

I GOT to the dojo about fifteen minutes early. Not being late was unusual for me, but I wanted to beat Carnes there. The lack of an obnoxious truck in the area told me I succeeded. A class of beginners finished learning and practicing their first couple forms. I watched the children in the class step through them while their brows furrowed in thought about what to do next. With practice, the forms would become burned into their muscle memories.

Once the students left, I filled Master Yi in on the details. I told him the cops were coming, and Carnes would be leaving with them, voluntarily or otherwise. Master Yi told me he was a failure. I absolved him and said the problem lay with Carnes. His frown told me he remained unconvinced. "What about the others?" I said.

"They can stay in my office with you," Master Yi said. "With the door closed and the blind drawn, Brian won't see any of you." We made it our plan, and two people I didn't know joined me a couple minutes later. We sat in silence like the office were an elevator and we just had to endure a ride to the twelfth floor.

A few minutes later, Master Yi poked his head in and said, "Here he comes." I texted Rich as Carnes opened the door and walked in. He looked around and frowned. Master Yi moved behind him, locked the door, and flipped his sign to "Closed."

"What's going on?" Carnes said. "Where are the others?"

"Do you know their names?" Master Yi said.

"Is this a quiz?"

"Brian, I got some distressing news recently."

"What happened?" Carnes said.

"I learned you attacked someone," Master Yi said. I could hear the disappointment in his voice.

Carnes snorted. "He had it coming."

"Have I taught you to attack people you think have it coming?"

The rebuke made Carnes fall silent for a few seconds. I wondered if he felt any kind of shame at letting Master Yi down. "No, Master Yi."

"Then why did you do it?"

"He had it coming," Carnes said again, as if repetition alone had the power to change facts.

Master Yi shook his head. Carnes scowled. I wished I could have seen Master Yi's face, but he stood with his back to me. If Carnes felt any reaction to the disappointment I imagined was etched there, he didn't show it. "Brian, I cannot allow you to continue to study from me," he said. "You have failed my teachings. You have failed me. Maybe I have failed you. I need to think about it."

"So what now?" Carnes said.

I stepped out of the office. "Now you pay for what you did."

Carnes spiked his bag to the ground. "You! You son of a bitch. This is all your fault."

"Right. I'm the one who made you round up a posse for your sneak attack."

"You had it coming," Carnes said.

"You keep saying it," I said. "But I showed the video to a few people. They know differently. To them, you're nothing but a cowardly asshole."

His face showed the sting of words like slaps. "It's just you and me now. No friends, no blanket."

"I know. You're hopelessly overmatched."

Carnes offered a hollow laugh and shook his head. I knew a punch was coming, so when he launched it, I already moved out of the way. Before I could prepare for another assault, Master Yi stepped between us. "Enough, Brian. You must stop this at once."

"Outta my way!" Carnes moved to his left. Master Yi mirrored him.

"I will not let you attack this man again."

"You're a pussy," Carnes spat at me. "Hiding behind another man."

"Next time, I'll hide behind three and bring a blanket," I said.

The door opened, interrupting Carnes' uncharitable reply. Leon Sharpe walked in first, filling most of the doorway. After he entered, Rich and Paul King came in behind him. "The fuck is this?" Carnes said.

"The end of the line," Sharpe said.

"What are you talking about, Captain? You gonna believe him over me?"

"You gave up Ben Harrison's widow and kids to that piece of shit Snell," Sharpe said. His voice boomed across the empty space. Carnes' defiant posture evaporated, and his shoulders slumped. "And you were on the take from him. You put drug money over your brothers." Sharpe strode up to him. "You learned a bunch of fancy kicks here. Wanna try them on me?"

"Captain, I—"

"Do you. Want. To try them. On me?"

Carnes' head lowered. "No," he said in a small voice.

"Get this asshole out of my sight," Sharpe said. He didn't take his eyes from Carnes as Rich Mirandized him and King cuffed him.

Once in restraints, Carnes found his spine again. "This ain't over." He glared at me. "I'll remember you. This ain't over."

"Sure," I said. "Look me up in ten to twenty. If you survive prison."

Rich and King led Carnes outside. Sharpe gave me a nod. "Thanks."

"You guys can make the charges stick?"

"State's attorney will figure it out," he said. "The link between him and Snell is strong, though."

"Good."

"You didn't even have to beat him up."

"His girlfriend knows he's a piece of shit, an honorable man shamed him, he's out of a job, and he's going to jail." I shrugged. "It's all a lot more demoralizing than an ass-kicking."

"I guess you got your wish." Sharpe paused. "How's the ribs?"

"A little better. I'll be on light duty for a couple weeks, I think."

"I'm sorry how all this went down," Sharpe said.

"Try to hold down the fort while I convalesce, Leon," I said. "I don't think the city can take a crime spree."

Sharpe chuckled and shook his head. "I think we'll be all right."

* * *

Gloria smiled as I walked in the front door. "You came back in one piece." She wrapped me in a gentle hug. I squeezed her tight. This inequality could not be resolved until my ribs mended.

"Never a doubt," I said.

Before we could continue the conversation, my phone rang. Liz Fleming. "Jack Bennett says he's going to bring breakfast

Monday morning," she said. "You want to come? You had as much to do with him getting released as I did."

"Liz, where did you go to college?"

"University of Baltimore, why?"

"Did you take a math class?"

"All right . . . you may have played a bigger role."

"Good of you to acknowledge it," I said. "Thanks for the offer, but I'll pass. I'd really like to put this case behind me."

"I understand," she said. "I'll try not to call you for a few weeks."

After this, I didn't think I'd answer another of her calls for six months. "I appreciate it. Good luck, Liz."

"Thanks." We hung up.

"You going to take it easy for a few weeks?" said Gloria.

"I need to," I said. "Percocet is great, but I can't take it forever. I just helped Rich with a case involving opioids. Getting hooked on them would be a bad look."

"We can't have you looking bad." Gloria grinned.

"You've seen my closet. No worries there."

Gloria stepped close and placed a gentle hand on my chest. "What does light duty entail?"

"I can't exert myself too much," I said.

"Hmm." Gloria ran her hand over my torso. "I guess I'll just have to work a little harder for a couple weeks."

"Rib injuries can linger, you know." I kissed her. She pulled me backwards until she butted up against the front door, where we kissed some more.

"Is that so?" She trailed her lips over my jaw to my neck. I wrapped my hand in her chestnut hair.

"It is," I said when I could form words. "Could be a couple months."

Gloria stared up at me. "I love you," she said, "but you're full of shit."

"You can't fault a fellow for trying," I said before we went upstairs.

END of Novel #4

Hɪ ᴛʜᴇʀᴇ,

Thanks for coming along on this adventure of C.T.'s.

This was his most professionally challenging case. His next would be his most personally taxing one.

C.T. is already working an investigation when he receives personal news which shatters him in Daughters and Sons. I think you'll like it.

Thanks,

Tom

THE END

Do you like free books? You can get the prequel novella to the C.T. Ferguson mystery series for free. This is unavailable for sale and is exclusive to my readers. Visit https://bit.ly/CTprequel to get your book!

If you enjoyed this novel, I hope you'll leave a review. Even a short writeup makes a difference. Reviews help independent authors get their books discovered by more readers and qualify for promotions. To leave a review, go to the book's sales page, select a star rating, and enter your comments. If you read this book on a tablet or phone, your reading app will likely prompt you to leave a review at the end.

The C.T. Ferguson Crime Novels:

1. The Reluctant Detective
2. The Unknown Devil
3. The Workers of Iniquity
4. Already Guilty
5. Daughters and Sons
6. A March from Innocence

7. Inside Cut
8. The Next Girl
9. In the Blood

While this is the suggested reading sequence, the books can be enjoyed in whatever order you happen upon them.

Connect with me:

For the many ways of finding and reaching me online, please visit https://tomfowlerwrites.com/contact. I'm always happy to talk to readers.

This is a work of fiction. Characters and places are either fictitious or used in a fictitious manner.

"Self-publishing" is something of a misnomer. This book would not have been possible without the contributions of many people.

- The cover design team at 100 Covers.
- My editor extraordinaire, Chase Nottingham.
- My wonderful advance reader team, the Fell Street Irregulars.

www.ingramcontent.com/pod-product-compliance
Lightning Source LLC
Chambersburg PA
CBHW050338190726
48284CB00007BB/2054